Holmes, Margaret and Poe

A list of titles by James Patterson appears
at the back of this book

Holmes, Margaret and Poe

JAMES PATTERSON

& BRIAN SITTS

C

CENTURY

1 3 5 7 9 10 8 6 4 2

Century
20 Vauxhall Bridge Road
London SW1V 2SA

Century is part of the Penguin Random House group of companies
whose addresses can be found at global.penguinrandomhouse.com.

Penguin
Random House
UK

First published by Century in 2024

www.penguin.co.uk

A CIP catalogue record for this book is available from the British Library.

ISBN: 978–1–529–13649–4 (hardback)
ISBN: 978–1–529–13650–0 (trade paperback)

Printed and bound in Great Britain by Clays Ltd, Elcograf S.p.A.

The authorised representative in the EEA is Penguin Random House Ireland,
Morrison Chambers, 32 Nassau Street, Dublin D02 YH68

www.greenpenguin.co.uk

MIX
Paper | Supporting
responsible forestry
FSC
www.fsc.org
FSC® C018179

Penguin Random House is committed to a
sustainable future for our business, our readers
and our planet. This book is made from Forest
Stewardship Council® certified paper.

"Very few of us are what we seem."

—AGATHA CHRISTIE

Holmes, Margaret and Poe

CHAPTER 1

Last year

THE VACANT INDUSTRIAL space that Realtor Gretchen Wik was trying to unload was located in a recently gentrified Brooklyn neighborhood called Bushwick. The area was becoming trendier by the month, but this particular building was cold and dead—and apparently unsellable.

Gretchen had been sitting at her sales table on the first floor since noon, tapping her nails while she stared out through a grime-coated window. In five hours, she had not been visited by a single prospect.

The property consisted of nine thousand square feet on two levels. But it was run-down and needed a lot of work. At this point, Gretchen felt like the worn wood floors and flaking brick walls were mocking her. She checked her watch. In exactly two minutes, her open house would officially be a bust.

Then she heard the front door open.

"Hello?" A voice from the entry hall. Gretchen's pulse perked up. She pushed back her chair and walked briskly toward the door, her three-inch heels clicking on the hardwood. She rounded the corner to the entryway.

"It's *you!*" said a tall, light-skinned Black man in a camel over-coat. For a second, Gretchen was thrown. Then the man pointed at the folding sign in the foyer, the one with Gretchen's face plastered on it.

"Right. Yes," said Gretchen, turning on her best smile. "Positive ID." She held out her hand. "Gretchen Wik, Lexington Realty."

"Brendan," said the visitor, "Holmes." He had large brown eyes and a neatly shaved head. Gretchen did her routine two-second over-view. Coat: expensive, well tailored. Shoes: Alexander McQueen. This guy might be a lookie-loo, but at least he didn't seem like a total waste of time. And right now, he was the only game in town.

"Welcome to your future," said Gretchen. She waved her arm toward the open space. Then she heard the door opening again.

"Sorry, have I missed it?" Another male voice.

This time it was a fit, compact man with wavy, dark hair and the kind of thin moustache that can look either silly or sexy, depending on the owner. On him, Gretchen thought it worked—kind of brood-ing and rakish at the same time. Most important, he was another prospect. The day was looking up.

"You're in luck," she said. "Right under the wire."

"I'm Auguste. Auguste Poe." Soft voice, with a solemn tone. And the slightest wisp of liquor on his breath.

"I'm Gretchen," said the agent. She paused for a second as the names registered. *Wait.* First somebody named *Holmes,* and now *Poe?* What were the odds? Or was this some kind of put-on?

Before Gretchen could ask any questions, both men walked ahead of her into the main space. She caught up and launched into her spiel—the same one she'd been practicing at her lonely table all morning.

"Gentlemen, you're looking at the very best bargain in Bushwick. Late nineteenth century construction, slate roof, terra cotta details, original skylights..."

"Pardon me? Anybody home?" The door again. A female voice this time, with a charming British accent.

Gretchen switched on her greeting smile again, getting even more excited. Two minutes ago, she had zero prospects.

Now, suddenly, she had three.

CHAPTER 2

"AM I TOO late?" the woman asked.

"Not at all," said the Realtor. "I'm Gretchen."

"I'm Margaret Marple."

Hold on, thought Gretchen. *Holmes. Poe.* And now *Marple*??

She registered a quick impression of the new arrival: Attractive, but not flashy. Minimal makeup. Tweed skirt with an inexpensive top. The accent was refined. The look was practical.

"I have to ask," said Gretchen. "Your names…"

"Tell me something," said Holmes, ignoring the impending question. He was picking a piece of loose mortar from a brick wall. "Why is it still on the market?"

Gretchen cleared her throat. "I'm sorry, what?" Never mind the names. She had some selling to do.

"Your price per square foot dropped from six forty-five to five ninety in two weeks," said Holmes. "So I'm just wondering…" He stopped mid-sentence and wrinkled his nose. "What is that *smell*?"

Gretchen realized that she was now playing defense. "Well, the building used to be a bakery," she said. "Maybe it's…?"

"No," Holmes said firmly, moving toward the other side of the room. "This is recent—and quite caustic."

When he reached the large factory window on one wall of the space, he pushed the bottom half open and leaned out. "There was a tattoo parlor next door," he said. It was a statement, not a question. Poe and Marple walked over to join Holmes at the window.

Gretchen was familiar with the view, and it wasn't great. Her prospects were looking at the neighboring building, a one-story wreck with a corrugated door sealing the front. Plastic bins and trash littered a small paved area at the rear.

"I can check the property records," said Gretchen, trying to glide past the unsavory subject. "I know it's unoccupied at the moment."

"PAHs," said Holmes.

"Pardon?" said Gretchen.

"Polycyclic aromatic hydrocarbons. Used in black inks. They have a bit of a car-tire taint."

"Funny," said Gretchen. "I don't smell a thing."

"I'm hyperosmic," said Holmes. "Blessing and a curse."

Gretchen realized that she was quickly losing control of the tour. "Sorry, I don't—"

"Unnaturally acute sense of smell," said Holmes. "A genetic fluke."

"Maybe we should check out the second floor?" Gretchen hinted, pointing toward a rusted metal staircase.

Poe gestured graciously. "Ladies first." Gretchen took the lead, praying that the corroded treads would support the weight of four people. The second floor was as wide-open and empty as the first, except for a scattering of abandoned office furniture. "Take your time," said Gretchen. "Any questions, just ask."

As Marple ran a finger across a dusty bookshelf, Holmes dipped to one knee and scratched a floor plank with his fingernail. "Low-grade pine," he mumbled. He pulled a small metal ball from his pocket, placed it on the floor, and watched it roll lazily toward the wall. "Two-point-five-centimeter slope," he added with a frown.

Gretchen was trying to decide which of the three she should focus on. Holmes was clearly a fastidious nitpicker, maybe even obsessive. Marple seemed quiet and thoughtful. Poe was harder to read. Gretchen studied his face as he pulled open the top drawer of a creaking metal office filing cabinet and peeked in. He hadn't smiled once since he arrived, but there was something darkly magnetic about him.

"Just so I'm clear," Gretchen asked, realizing her three prospects might be shopping together, "are all of you . . . ?"

"My God!" Poe exclaimed. "Murder!"

Gretchen froze as Poe pulled a yellowed newspaper clipping out of a file. His expression turned even more dour. "Someone was killed here," he said.

"What?" said Holmes, suddenly energized.

"Really?" said Marple.

Poe waved the clipping. "Take a look."

He smoothed the scrap of newsprint on top of the file. Gretchen's gut was churning. The seller had warned her about this grim historical factoid. *Dammit!* She should have checked the drawers before the showing.

Marple ran her finger down the article and turned to Gretchen. "So it's true?"

Gretchen cleared her throat. "I'd heard rumors," she said carefully, "but—"

"Not a rumor," snapped Holmes. "It's right here in black and white."

Gretchen stepped closer and looked over Poe's shoulder. The paper was brittle, but the type was clear. DEATH IN A BAKERY, the headline read. And underneath, "Young Girl Slain Before Dawn." The one-column story was accompanied by a photograph of a building.

The building they were in.

"Her throat was slit," said Poe. "On the floor right below us. In 1954. She was just nineteen."

Marple winced. "That poor child."

Gretchen pictured her commission evaporating before her eyes. She did a quick mental calculation, ready to cut the price on the spot. Who the hell would pay almost six hundred dollars per square foot for a murder site?

Before she could float a new number, all three of her prospects turned and spoke at once.

"We'll take it!"

CHAPTER *3*

Present day

AUGUSTE POE WAS anxious to get moving. A teacher had once described him as having an excitable temperament, and it was showing this morning.

As he exited the newly renovated bakery building in a crisp linen suit, Poe glanced at the fresh lettering on the front door. Gold leaf in a classic font. It looked expensive and exclusive. Holmes, Marple & Poe Investigations finally felt legit, and today was the day that would put them on the map. Poe was sure of it. They had the right case. They had the right skills. They just needed to execute flawlessly—as a team.

As he waited impatiently for his two partners, Poe walked to the bakery's former loading bay and wiped a speck of dust off the hood of his newly acquired 1966 Pontiac GTO. Montero Red. Tri-Power upgrade. XS Ram Air package. He'd paid fifty thousand to a Newark collector and considered it a steal. Poe was obsessive about anything mechanical, and muscle cars were a particular weakness. Despite outrageous Brooklyn garage fees, he owned an impressive collection, rotating his rides according to his mood.

"Good God, Auguste, what is that *monstrosity*?"

Margaret Marple was standing outside the office door in a neat business jacket and skirt, staring at the Pontiac.

"It rides as smooth as a town car," Poe said, knowing she preferred more discreet transportation. "I promise you."

Marple frowned. "I'll wrinkle my outfit, folding myself into that thing."

"Margaret, you need to be more flexible," said Brendan Holmes, exiting the door right behind her. He plucked a speck of lint from his suit jacket as he walked toward the car.

"Let's go!" Poe said as he slid in behind the steering wheel.

The powerful Pontiac was no advantage on the trip to One Police Plaza. The crosstown drive through Brooklyn was torturous, with a lot of stop-and-go on the way. Poe could feel his partners' nerves too. Their plan hinged on getting in front of Police Commissioner Jock Boolin. And Boolin was a notoriously hard man to corner.

The commissioner was new to his post, recently appointed by New York City mayor Felix Rollins after a long career in Chicago. This would be their first in-person encounter. By all accounts, Boolin was a hard-nosed cop and a savvy political operator. Poe and his partners had done their due diligence. Now it was time for a critical face-to-face.

The topic they wanted to discuss was a case that was consuming the city: the mysterious disappearance of a young Black attorney named Sloane Stone.

Sloane's impressive résumé ticked through Poe's mind as he drove. Brooklyn girl made good. Harvard undergraduate. Yale Law. Junior associate at a top New York law firm. Brilliant and beautiful. The profile picture on her law-firm website showed Sloane Stone to be a young woman with bright eyes, a huge smile, and dark hair worn full and natural, with a few tight curls falling across her forehead. Missing for two weeks now without a trace. The pressure on NYPD—and the new commissioner in particular—was growing more intense by the day.

The new firm had gotten an anonymous tip, and what they'd learned was about to shake up the whole city. Poe glanced in the rearview mirror as Marple pulled up the latest reports on her iPhone.

"Any breakthroughs?" asked Poe.

"The authorities are still baffled," said Marple.

"Good," said Holmes. "We're not."

As Poe headed for the Brooklyn Bridge crossing into Manhattan, he got a fresh tingle of anticipation. This was it—their first high-profile case—and he and his partners were determined to break it wide open.

Even if nobody had actually hired them.

CHAPTER 4

WHEN THE THREE investigators arrived on the top floor of One Police Plaza, Poe led the way to the commissioner's suite, where a late-twentysomething receptionist sat behind a huge oak desk. He glanced at the assistant's nameplate as he stepped forward, then cleared his throat and adjusted his voice to a tone of warm familiarity, as if he had known her forever.

"Samantha," he said. "Good morning. How are you? We need to see the commissioner—immediately."

"*Who* does?" the receptionist shot back. In just two words, Poe detected the distinctive inflection of a Queens native. He looked closer. Samantha's wardrobe and jewelry conveyed a tone of edgy self-assurance, and her manicured nails looked as sharp as daggers. Poe immediately realized that she was no pushover.

"Holmes, Marple, and Poe Investigations," he said. He flicked a business card from his wallet with the flair of an illusionist.

Samantha took it.

"Holmes, Marple, and Poe?" she said. "Is that a joke?"

Holmes leaned over the desk. "We're private investigators. And we have important information for the commissioner. *Critical information.*"

Samantha shifted her cold stare in his direction. "Do you have an appointment?"

Marple stepped forward. "We have intelligence on the disappearance of Sloane Stone," she said softly. "It involves the mayor."

Samantha tilted her head. "Sloane Stone?" Poe noticed a sudden uptick of interest. The receptionist lowered her head and tapped her touchscreen. Poe could hear her speaking tersely into her headset.

About thirty seconds later, a blond-haired woman in a dark suit walked into the reception area. She was tall and elegant. Also, Poe gathered from her body language, stern and efficient.

"I understand you have information concerning the mayor," she said.

Poe nodded and handed her a business card. "Holmes, Marple, and Poe Investigations. Are you from the mayor's office?"

"I'm Kristin Rove, special assistant to Mayor Rollins. Anything you have for the mayor, you can tell me."

"Not this, I'm afraid," said Poe.

"For the commissioner's ears only at this point," Marple added politely.

"Well, let me tell you how it works," Kristin said, shifting her eyes from Marple to Holmes to Poe. "You don't see the commissioner without going through Samantha, and you don't see the mayor without going through me." She glanced down at the business card. "So unless you've actually found Ms. Stone, you've come all the way from Brooklyn for nothing." She handed the card back to Poe, then walked off.

Poe turned to Marple and nodded toward the reception desk. "You try." It was time for a tag-team approach. Maybe Marple's people skills would be more productive.

Poe knew that in addition to being a natural snoop, his partner was an intuitive student of human psychology. He stood back with Holmes and watched as Marple walked up to Samantha's station and rested a hand on the polished oak top. The receptionist was clearly doing her best to ignore Marple's presence, but she eventually looked up. "Can I help you?"

"About your age. Am I right?" said Marple.

"Who?" asked Samantha.

"Sloane Stone."

Samantha shifted awkwardly in her seat. "I guess." A long pause. "But I went to Queensborough Community and she went to a fancy Ivy, so I think Sloane and I are sort of on different levels."

"Were."

"What?"

"*Were*. Past tense. One of you is dead."

Samantha blinked. "You don't know that!"

"Actually, we do," said Marple. "We're very good at our job. That's why we're here." She lowered her voice to a confidential whisper. "The truth is, Samantha, we know more about the different kinds of human wickedness than anyone you've ever met."

The receptionist stared at Marple for a second. Then she pulled off her headset, got up from her chair, and walked through a thick door behind the reception area. Success! Poe and Holmes stepped forward, poised and ready. A few seconds later, Samantha was back. She sat down and picked up her headset again.

"Sorry." She shrugged. "Commissioner Boolin has left for the day. He must have used his private exit."

Poe glanced at his partners. "Not a problem," he said. "We know where he lives."

CHAPTER 5

HEADING NORTH ON the West Side Highway, the GTO's 380-horsepower engine growled as Poe speed-shifted through traffic. Once they passed Riverside Park, he opened it up further.

"Think he'll beat us home?" asked Holmes.

"Only if he took the chopper," said Poe.

The GPS had estimated a thirty-four-minute drive to Riverdale. It took twenty. Poe slowed the car to a crawl as they entered the narrow, tree-lined roads of the exclusive Fieldston enclave. The stately homes were set on natural hills and tucked away in cozy hollows. It was like a charming forest village, where low-end properties went for about two million. Poe drove slowly up Goodridge Avenue.

"I think your car might stand out a bit in this neighborhood," said Marple.

Poe looked around. Marple was right. The curved driveways were dotted with Mercedes, BMWs, and Teslas. He parked the flashy red Pontiac in a shady spot across from the entrance to Boolin's secluded estate, then climbed out of the car. Holmes and Marple followed. They took positions in a grove of fir trees near the stone pillars at the end of the driveway.

Just two minutes later, a black Suburban rolled up the street and pulled to a gentle stop. The rear door opened. Police Commissioner Boolin stepped out. He was tall and imposing, with wavy silver hair. Poe watched from behind a thick trunk as Boolin waved to his driver, who executed a skillful K-turn and drove off.

The commissioner walked to his mailbox and pulled out a small stack of envelopes and magazines, then started up the driveway, flipping through the mail as he went. Poe glanced at his partners and gave the signal. All at once, they stepped out from behind cover. Boolin looked up, startled.

"Anything interesting in the mail?" asked Holmes. "Or just the usual bribes?"

Boolin's expression darkened as the three PIs approached. "What are you doing here? I told my girl to get rid of you."

"Don't blame Samantha," said Holmes. "She did her best." He pulled out a business card. "Holmes, Marple, and Poe Investigations," he said. "When we said we needed to talk to you, we meant it."

Boolin ignored the card. "Why are you skulking around in my woods?" he said, thrusting his square chin forward.

Poe stepped up. "Commissioner," he said, "the information we have concerns Sloane Stone."

Boolin waved dismissively. "Right. You and everybody else in town." He started back up the driveway. "If you've got a lead, call the hotline. Or make an appointment through channels, like professionals—instead of a pack of goddamn stalkers."

Poe glanced at Holmes. This was the moment.

"We know she was murdered," Holmes called out. "And we know where she's buried."

Boolin stopped and turned around slowly. He took a few steps back down the driveway and looked from Holmes to Marple to Poe. "And how the hell do you know that?"

"When you have eliminated the impossible," said Holmes, "whatever remains, however improbable, must be the truth."

Boolin's eyes narrowed. "That sounds like gobbledygook," he said. "But sure. I'll call your bluff." He folded his thick arms across his chest. "Where is she?"

CHAPTER 6

THREE HOURS LATER, Holmes stood with Marple and Poe at the entrance to an abandoned farm about a hundred miles north of New York City. He looked around at the small caravan of police vehicles that had escorted them. Boolin hadn't been ready to call out a full search team on the say-so of three unfamiliar PIs. But he'd agreed to send a couple of rookies and one homicide detective for a preliminary scout.

Holmes could feel his heart racing. The partners had agreed that he would take the lead on this case, but at the moment, he was way out of his comfort zone.

As soon as they'd arrived, the odors of fertilizer and manure had overwhelmed him. They were staggering, almost intolerable, clouding his olfactory sense just when he really needed it. He leaned back against a fence post and pressed his hands against his temples, breathing through his mouth. His superior sense of smell made him part bloodhound, part pointer, and part bulldog. But sometimes, it just made him sick.

He felt Poe's hand on his shoulder. "Brendan, are you okay?"

Holmes nodded. "I just need a few minutes to adjust to the redolence."

"What's happening?" asked Marple.

"He's recalibrating his nostrils," said Poe.

"Not a fan of country air?" asked Detective Lieutenant Helene Grey.

Holmes could tell that she thought this was a waste of time, and he sensed that she was going out of her way to needle him.

Grey was a newcomer to the squad. Holmes estimated her age at thirty-eight, give or take a year. From quick observation, he determined that she was a natural blonde, with just a little salon assist. Normally, he would have been able to detect the level of ethanolamine in her hair dye. But not today. Too much olfactory competition.

"I much prefer the urban miasma," said Holmes.

Grey cocked her head. "Tell me something, Mr. Holmes. How can you be so sure about the location of Sloane Stone's body—unless you had something to do with hiding it?"

Holmes ignored the jab and stalled for time, waiting for his overactive senses to settle. He glanced around the property, from the barnyard to the fence line in the distance.

"If you want to dispose of a body on a farm," he said, "you have several options. You can feed it to the pigs, but they leave hair and teeth behind, so it's an incomplete solution. You can bury the body in the middle of a field, but eventually a plow or some woodland creature will dig it up. You can drop a body in a grain silo, but you'd have to lug the dead weight up the stairs and hope that you don't tumble in yourself and suffocate under the grain."

Grey stood with her arms crossed, drumming her fingers. "Put up or shut up, Mr. Holmes," she said. "Do you know where the body is or not?"

Holmes paused and took a deep breath. His delaying speech had worked. Olfactory adaptation was setting in, desensitizing him to nearby smells. In their place, he began to detect telltale molecules of cadaverine, putrescine, indole, and skatole. Faint and distant, but unmistakable.

The scent of decomposing flesh.

Holmes looked past the barn toward the uncultivated field behind it. "Follow me."

The team walked single file across the muddy furrows, Holmes first, then Grey, then the two cops, then Poe, then Marple—the only one in the posse wearing knee-high Wellington boots.

As he walked, Holmes felt all the ancillary scents disappear. It was like wiping a film of vapor from a pair of glasses. Now everything was clear. *Painfully* clear. His stomach started to turn as he homed in on the odor of death, and it triggered a curious sense of loss. He'd never met Sloane Stone, but he knew things about her that nobody else did. Not even his partners.

At the edge of the field was a mound of compost, five feet high and stretching twenty yards along the perimeter of the property. Holmes walked slowly down the row as the others trailed behind him. About ten feet from the end of the mound, he stopped and pointed.

"She's right here," he said.

Grey glanced at Marple. "Is he sane?"

"Not always," said Marple.

"But he's usually right," added Poe.

Grey turned to the two cops. "Tape it off, guys." Then she pulled out her phone and placed the call to CSU.

CHAPTER 7

MARPLE WATCHED TWO white Crime Scene Unit vans roll to a stop near the barn. Stone-faced and anxious, she stood with Holmes and Poe as Detective Grey briefed the technicians, dressed in white overalls with matching hoods and booties. As the techs gathered their tools, the detective walked over with three extra respirator masks. "If Holmes is right," she said, "you'll want these."

Marple strapped the mask around her face and heard the strange sound of her own breathing from behind the mouthpiece. She hesitated for a few moments while the rest of the team headed across the field.

As much as she trusted her partner's skills, Marple held out a small hope that he was wrong, at least in this case. She preferred to imagine Sloane Stone on a sunny beach with a huge margarita, laughing at the thought of men in hazmat suits trying to dig up her bones in a bean field.

"Margaret! You coming?" Poe's voice was muddled by his mask. Marple waved back and followed the worn path through the furrows.

The CSU team set up a series of metal screens over huge trays. They used small spades, not much bigger than beach toys. Working slowly and deliberately, they scooped small mounds of compost onto the screens and spread it with their gloves and tools. But just a few minutes into the dig, the detailed archeology became moot.

"Christ!" shouted one of the techs, stepping back. A human arm, or what was left of it, protruded from the pile.

Marple turned away for a moment, then forced herself to look. It was part of the job. For her, it was the hardest part—the part where all hope was gone.

The extraction took thirty minutes, and the result was pure horror. The once beautiful young woman was now barely a coherent shape. Only the hair on her scalp still had some semblance of who she had been. Though matted with dirt and refuse, it retained a hint of how it had looked in her official law-firm profile photo.

New pictures were being taken now, detailed and devastating, from every possible angle. Inside her mask, Marple murmured a silent prayer as the team unzipped a body bag and gently enclosed inside it the mortal remains of Sloane Stone. Two of the CSU guys then carefully transported the bag back across the field toward the vans. A second team stayed behind to sift for more evidence.

Grey, Holmes, and Poe walked a few yards away from the scene and yanked off their masks. Marple removed hers too and caught up with them. She could hear Holmes expounding again.

"Don't be surprised if the hyoid bone is intact," said Holmes. "That doesn't mean she wasn't strangled. She was. I believe that the act took some time. Perhaps because the killer had small hands."

"Well, let's see what the autopsy turns up," said Grey. "That might narrow down our suspect list." She looked pointedly at Holmes. "Let's hope it excludes you."

It was clear to Marple that Grey was into procedure and process, and that she was eager to get the case back onto a normal track, firmly under her control. But Marple could tell that, as usual, Holmes had a plan of his own.

CHAPTER 8

AT NINE O'CLOCK sharp the next morning, Holmes and his partners arrived at Gracie Mansion, the official residence of Mayor Felix Rollins. Detective Grey pulled up behind them in an unmarked sedan, then led the way inside.

At a security screening station, the three PIs surrendered their handguns. Grey waved her badge and got a pass for hers.

The Upper East Side mansion was humming, and Holmes noticed that the corridors and cubicles were mostly filled with attractive young women—including the statuesque assistant who walked them to the first-floor parlor.

"The mayor will be with you shortly," she said, showing them into the room.

As he crossed the threshold, Holmes felt as if he'd stepped back into the eighteenth century. Colonial-era furniture. Thick draperies. Crystal chandeliers. Ornate vases filled with white flowers. A mildly fruity aroma filled his nostrils.

"Panicle hydrangea," said Marple, brushing one of the petals. "Lovely." Poe ran his hands admiringly over an antique bowfront sideboard.

"Remember," Grey said firmly, "we're here to update the mayor on the investigation. Nothing more. You're here as a courtesy."

"And because we located the body," said Holmes.

"We still have to solve the crime," said Grey.

"Crime is common. Logic is rare," Holmes muttered. "Therefore it is upon the logic rather than the crime that you should dwell."

"What the hell does that mean?" asked Grey.

"It means you should read more Arthur Conan Doyle," said Holmes. "In fact, his work should be taught at the academy."

At that moment, the mayor appeared in the doorway. Holmes was not surprised to see him flanked by his assistant, Kristin Rove. From what he'd learned, Rollins rarely went anywhere without her.

Holmes took a quick inventory of the mayor. It was the first time he'd seen him in person. Large head. Dark eyes. Slight, almost delicate physique, interrupted by a pronounced belly.

"Why are we here?" asked Rollins. Brusque and arrogant. "You said you've got something new on Stone?"

Grey stepped forward, but Holmes stepped right in front of her.

"That's true, we do," said Holmes.

"Who the hell are you?" Rollins asked.

"He's a PI," replied Kristin. She'd said "PI" as if it were a venereal disease.

"My name is Holmes." Rollins gave him a weak, noncommittal shake. Holmes noted his small, soft hands. "And these are my associates, Ms. Marple and Mr. Poe."

Grey stepped up again, nudging Holmes aside. "Sorry, Mr. Mayor."

Rollins glared at her. "Let's hear it, Grey. Have you got something new on Stone or not?"

"As of yesterday, Mr. Mayor," she said, "it's a murder investigation."

"You have a body?" asked Kristin.

Grey nodded. "Sadly, we do."

"At least that's progress," Rollins replied evenly. "What about suspects?"

Holmes inched closer to the mayor, deliberately violating his personal space. "As a matter of fact," he said, "we're looking at somebody right now." He was being obnoxious and invasive—and he knew it.

It was one of his favorite techniques for rattling his prey.

CHAPTER 9

"*HOLMES!* WHAT ARE you doing?" Grey grabbed him by the shoulders.

Rollins took a step back. "Hold on. Are you saying I'm . . . ?"

"No, we're not!" said Grey.

"Or *are* we?" said Holmes.

Grey looked exasperated. "Mr. Mayor, I apologize. We're only here to—"

Rollins put his hand up. "Shut up. I'd like to hear this." He stared directly at Holmes. "You have something to say about me?" He glanced at his Rolex and perched himself on the arm of one of the parlor's antique chairs. "You have two minutes. Before I have you thrown out. Or arrested."

Holmes glanced at his partners, then walked to the fireplace and rested his arm on the marble mantel, calm and unhurried. Inside, he felt fully alive and totally focused. He *lived* for moments like this. Moments when he was in total control.

"Mr. Mayor, when you prefer not to bother with a security detail, you have a personal car at your disposal. Is that right?"

Rollins shrugged. "You mean do I sometimes go under the radar for some private time? Absolutely. My car, my business."

"The Audi S8," said Holmes.

Rollins turned toward Grey. "Is somebody tailing me? Did you put a tracker on my car?"

"Absolutely not, Mr. Mayor," said Grey. "We'd have no reason to do that."

Holmes pressed on. "Not NYPD, sir. It was somebody on your staff. For security purposes, ostensibly. But I'm sure you're aware, there are many additional ways to deduce a vehicle's travels. Tire prints. Fender well residue. Soil matches. Specifically, silt loam with a pH of 6.5 and traces of *Phaseolus vulgaris*."

Rollins was clearly losing patience. "What are you talking about?"

"Bean leaves," said Holmes. "Mr. Mayor, do you have any reason to visit Dutchess County?"

"Dutchess County?" said Rollins. "I don't go upstate unless I'm meeting with the governor. I haven't been north of Harlem for three months. Kristin can confirm that."

"Your Audi has," said Holmes. "Been north. To Amenia, New York."

"Amenia?" Rollins looked perplexed.

"Rural town," said Holmes. "Conveniently remote."

"Mr. Mayor," said Detective Grey, "Sloane Stone's body was found on a farm near Amenia yesterday afternoon."

"The same location your car visited. Approximately two weeks ago," said Holmes. "Based on tracking. Confirmed by the degree of decay in the vegetation traces in your wheel-well liners."

"This is bullshit!" said Rollins.

Holmes walked back toward Rollins and recited a Gmail address.

"What's that?" Rollins said gruffly.

"Sloane Stone's personal email address."

"So...?"

Holmes glanced up and to the side, as if pulling data out of the air. "There have been, as I recall...twelve messages from your personal email."

"Pure crap," said Rollins. "I never sent any messages to Sloane Stone. I didn't even—"

"Here's one right here," Holmes interrupted, holding his cell phone in front of Rollins's face.

"Enough!" Rollins pushed the phone away and glared around the room. "Listen to me. All of you. I met Sloane Stone once, a year ago, at some legal event."

"Correct," said Holmes. "The Legal Aid Society Benefit. Last May 11th."

"That's right," said Rollins. "I recognized her picture from the news when she went missing. Attractive girl. I talked to her for two minutes at the party. Never saw her again. Never sent her any emails. *Never.*"

Holmes let out a small sigh. "I'm not sure you can prove that, Mr. Mayor." He paused and let the silence sink in. "But your assistant can." He turned toward Kristin. "Am I right, Ms. Rove?" Kristin stiffened. Her composure faded.

Holmes flicked a glance at Marple and Poe. Both were wide-eyed with surprise, as he knew they would be. He felt Grey's hand on his arm. "Holmes! What are you doing?"

"Revealing the truth," said Holmes. "Painful as it may be."

Kristin turned toward the doorway behind her. "Security!"

In two seconds, a plainclothes officer stepped through the doorway. Kristin moved quickly to his side. "I need these people removed," she said. *"Now!"*

"Kristin, calm down," said the mayor. "What are you worried about?"

Kristin whipped her hand inside the officer's jacket and pulled out his handgun.

She took two quick steps back and pointed the weapon at his chest. "On the ground!"

The officer dropped to his knees.

Holmes stepped back to shield his partners. He'd been expecting a reaction, but not this one. As he watched, Kristin whipped the gun toward Detective Grey, who was reaching behind her back. "Go ahead," said Kristin. "Pull it out slowly. And then put it on the floor."

"Hold on," said Grey, moving her hands out to her sides. "Let's talk."

Do it! shouted Kristin. Grey slipped her gun out of her holster and laid it gently on the carpet. Kristin walked over and kicked the butt of the gun, sending it spinning into a corner. Rollins took a step toward Kristin and grabbed her arm. "What the hell are you doing?"

Kristin twisted away and pressed the gun against the mayor's forehead. "Don't fucking touch me!" she said. "Ever again."

Rollins rocked backward. "Kristin, have you gone crazy?"

"She's not crazy, Mr. Mayor," Holmes said calmly. "She's cold and crafty. One of the best I've ever seen. She killed Sloane Stone and almost managed to pin it on you."

Rollins stared at his assistant with a stunned expression.

"Do you want to hear the evidence now, Ms. Rove?" said Holmes. "I can lay it out right here. Or should we wait for your written statement?" He paused. "Or do you plan to kill us all too?"

"Back off!" Kristin shouted. "Everybody just—*back off!*" She swiveled the pistol back and forth, arm extended, and started moving toward the door. The instant she cleared the opening, she turned and dashed out a rear exit and down a set of stairs.

Out of the corner of his eye, Holmes saw a figure bolt after her.

It was Marple.

CHAPTER 10

MARPLE LEAPED DOWN the stone steps three at a time and kicked off her shoes at the bottom. She took off at a sprint, heading across the property and down toward the curved walkway that bordered the East River. She could see Kristin in the distance, about twenty yards ahead, near the far edge of the mansion grounds.

It was obvious that Kristin had shed her shoes too. Nobody could move that fast in heels. But Marple was closing in on her. She was glad she'd chosen wide-legged trousers that morning. Kristin was younger, and had longer legs, but Marple could tell that her tight skirt was cramping her stride. The gun was still in her hand.

In seconds, Marple was on the paved pathway, with the river on her right.

She saw Kristin turn to look over her shoulder. Marple gained a few steps. Now she was just ten yards back. When Kristin turned forward again, a kid on a bike almost knocked into her. She tipped to the left, rocking on one foot. Marple closed the gap. She wrapped her arms around Kristin's shoulders and drove her to the pavement as the gun clattered away.

"Get the hell off me!" shrieked Kristin. *"I'll sue your ass!"*

As the furious woman squirmed and twisted beneath her, Marple heard footsteps coming up from behind.

"Freeze!" Grey's voice.

Marple saw Grey's gun barrel pressing against Kristin's scalp. The plainclothes officer was pinning her legs.

"Okay, Kristin," Grey said between breaths, "let's talk about Sloane Stone."

"You can't prove anything!" shouted the mayor's assistant.

"You just threatened the mayor, NYPD officers, *and* a roomful of civilians with a stolen gun, Kristin. Then you ran. That's both criminal possession of a firearm and consciousness of guilt. We'll start there."

Marple eased herself off Kristin's back and sat on the walkway, panting hard as Grey cuffed Kristin and led her away. The other officer squatted down at Marple's side.

"You okay?" he asked. "That was a mean tackle."

"I'm fine," said Marple, brushing dirt off her slacks. "Murder brings out the bitch in me."

CHAPTER 11

HOLMES HITCHED A ride in a squad car back to Bushwick—alone. Marple and Poe had left without him. Not a surprise. He had fully expected that his partners would be furious with him for keeping them in the dark about the real killer. And deep down, he knew they had every right to be. On their first major case, he had blindsided them.

Maybe it was all those years working on his own that made him so independent. Maybe, like the original Holmes, he considered himself the last and highest court of appeal in detection. Maybe he was self-destructive. Or maybe he just craved the drama.

When he walked into the office, Poe and Marple were sitting at a table in the common area, waiting for him. Poe spoke first.

"What the hell, Brendan!"

"That was completely irresponsible," said Marple. "Your big reveal could have gotten us all shot."

"Well, nobody told you to run off in hot pursuit," said Holmes. "*That* was dangerous."

"I had no choice," said Marple. "When I see a fox, I turn into a hound."

"Look," said Holmes, taking a seat at the table. "It was my case. My lead."

"True," said Poe, "but that didn't give you the right to hold out on us on our first major case. We're *partners*. Remember?"

"Misdirection," said Holmes. "It's one of my gifts."

Poe's expression darkened. "Well, you don't get to misdirect *us*!"

"The truth is," said Holmes, "I was misdirected myself until yesterday. Everything pointed directly to the mayor. The evidence supported it. The car. The tire prints. The emails."

"The location of the body," added Poe.

Holmes nodded. "Everybody knows about the mayor's fondness for young women. It was logical to deduce that he and Sloane had an affair. That she might have become a liability, or an embarrassment, or threatened blackmail. So he killed her and disposed of her body. Classic story. But, as we all know, there is nothing more deceptive than an obvious fact."

Marple leaned forward. "You're saying Rollins and Sloane weren't having an affair—"

"Correct," said Holmes. "*Kristin* and Sloane were. And it ended badly."

"According to whom?" asked Poe.

"According to Samantha."

"The commissioner's assistant?" said Marple.

Holmes nodded. "I could see that Samantha was rattled by our visit. So last night I went to see her in Queens. She and Kristin used to both work in the commissioner's office, before Kristin got promoted. Samantha knew all about Kristin's romance with Sloane. They were keeping it a secret because Kristin didn't think a same-sex relationship would go over well in the mayor's office."

"Rollins clearly prefers mayor-on-girl," said Poe.

"There was an ugly breakup," said Holmes. "This was a few days before she disappeared. Apparently, Sloane wanted to see other people. Men, specifically. That's all Samantha knew. Until we walked in."

Poe leaned back. "So when Kristin realized she couldn't have Sloane to herself..."

"They fought," said Marple, picking up the thread, "and she killed her—with her bare hands."

"Her bare, *small* hands," said Poe. "Just like the mayor's."

"From what Kristin told Samantha," said Holmes, "Rollins has been pawing her in the office from the day she started."

Poe shifted in his chair. "Which is why she set him up to take the fall."

Holmes nodded. "Kristin put a tracker in the mayor's private car. Used the car to drive Sloane's body to the country. Then planted the emails to Sloane from the mayor's account. She had everything she needed to point the finger at her grabby boss. All that was missing was somebody to find the body. So when NYPD dropped the ball, she left us an anonymous tip."

"Thinking we'd stop at the obvious suspect," said Poe.

"Which we almost did," said Holmes.

"That still doesn't excuse your keeping secrets from us," said Marple. "We're partners, not rogue operators."

Holmes could tell she was angry, embarrassed, and hurt. "For the record," he said, "the firm solved the crime. Holmes, Marple, and Poe Investigations. We did it. And we'll all reap the rewards." Holmes reached into his pocket and pulled out a small key. "In the meantime, I'm afraid there's something else I've been keeping from you."

He reached over and unlocked a cabinet next to the table. He pulled out a bottle of wine. A 1992 Screaming Eagle Cabernet. He'd paid twenty-five hundred dollars for it on the black market, and he'd been saving it for a special occasion. Right now, he hoped it might help him get back in his partners' good graces.

"Is that what I think it is?" asked Poe, eyes wide.

"Looks are not always deceiving, Auguste," said Holmes. He set the bottle on the table and reached for three large wine goblets. He pulled the cork and poured.

Marple swirled the wine and sniffed. "You know I prefer sherry," she said. Then her expression softened. "But this bouquet is heaven."

"I propose a toast," said Holmes. "To Holmes, Marple, and Poe."

"To teamwork," said Poe.

"To no more secrets," said Marple.

Holmes smiled as they all clinked glasses. "I'll do my best."

CHAPTER 12

THE NEXT MORNING, Auguste Poe was peeking out from behind a thick curtain in the lobby of One Police Plaza. His heart was pounding. Holmes and Marple hovered right behind him. He could feel that they were just as excited as he was. The scene out front was wild and almost out of control. It was everything they could have hoped for.

Commissioner Boolin had called the press conference for 9 a.m. The place had been packed since 7. News of Kristin Rove's arrest had leaked the previous afternoon, and reporters from every outlet were crowded in front of the podium. This story had everything—politics, sex, murder. Everybody wanted answers.

The DA and his assistants were on hand, but Boolin had insisted on making the formal announcement himself.

Poe and his partners inched out from behind the curtain as Boolin stepped up to the podium, his badge gleaming under the lights. The reporters crowded toward him, thrusting iPhones and mini recorders in his direction. Grey looked over and gave the investigators a polite nod. But they received no acknowledgment from Boolin. Apparently, he was pretending that they didn't exist.

The commissioner did the ritual tapping of the microphone, sending loud thuds and feedback echoing through the lobby. He cleared his throat. The murmurs settled. A hundred camera buttons clicked. He shuffled his note cards.

"Ladies and gentlemen of the press, and all New Yorkers. I am here to announce that we are confident that the case of Miss Sloane Stone's disappearance has been brought to a conclusion." He looked up and paused. Cleared his throat. "While we had all hoped for a positive outcome, we are gratified that the alleged killer is in custody. Kristin Marie Rove, age twenty-eight, until yesterday an executive assistant in the office of Felix Rollins, the mayor of New York, will be arraigned this afternoon on a charge of second-degree murder. Based on our investigation..." Boolin fumbled with his note cards.

"Hold on! *Your* investigation?" A voice from the middle of the press mob. Poe looked over. The voice belonged to Shelbi Scott, Channel 4 News, a sharp young journalist with a reputation as a pot stirrer. "We have reports that the case was actually solved by a team of private investigators," Scott shouted. "Can you comment on that, Commissioner?"

Boolin leaned his beefy torso across the podium. "Sorry. We cannot comment on procedural or investigative matters."

"Is that *them*?"

Poe noticed a Fox News reporter pointing in their direction.

"Over there!"

"Fuck me!" muttered Boolin. The microphones picked it up. He gripped the podium and tried to maintain his power position. "Like many private citizens and professionals who stepped forward with leads and tips, certain private investigators contributed to our—"

The reporters shouted him down. "Give 'em a mic. Let 'em talk!" They pushed toward the trio in a wave. Poe looked at his partners, then squared his shoulders. This was it. The moment they'd been waiting for.

The questions started coming like fireballs, fast and overlapping. "Who are you?" "Are you from New York?" "How did you crack it?"

Poe spoke first, as cameras zoomed in on his somber visage. "Our firm is Holmes, Marple, and Poe Investigations."

The room was buzzing. There were a few titters, and then more questions, as eager reporters tried to out-shout one another.

"Holmes, Marple, and Poe? Are those your real names?"

Marple leaned forward. "Why would you doubt it?"

"Are you mystery-novel fans?"

"Rabid," said Poe.

"What did you figure out that the police couldn't?"

"It's our business to know what other people don't know," said Holmes.

"We simply followed the clues," added Poe. "Sadly, they led to Sloane Stone's body."

Boolin, red-faced, shouted into the podium mic. "Thank you! That's all we have for you right now!"

A squad of uniformed cops surrounded Holmes, Marple, and Poe, as if protecting them from the press. Then, at Boolin's nod, they quickly hustled them behind the curtain. The commissioner walked over, clearly furious.

"What were you *doing* out there," he growled, "running for office?"

"Why?" Marple asked with a smile. "Is there an opening?"

Poe exchanged glances with Holmes. Their plan had worked. The crime was solved. And they were now the most famous private investigators in New York.

But they'd clearly made one very powerful enemy.

CHAPTER 13

BY NINE THAT evening, the headquarters of Holmes, Marple & Poe Investigations glimmered with light and excitement. Marple had initially had reservations about following through with their company launch party just one day after solving a murder, but Holmes and Poe had insisted. And she had to admit that the timing was fortunate.

Just as they'd hoped, the press conference that morning had raised their profile dramatically, and curiosity had enriched the guest list. Anybody who mattered in New York was there. Reporters. Political operatives. And the cream of Brooklyn hipsterdom. The cheerful buzz had temporarily muted Marple's sadness about Sloane Stone. Not that she was ready to get over it. Victims stayed with her for a long time. Especially when the victim was a young woman.

Marple was hearing a lot of compliments about the renovation of the old bakery and the unique use of space. In addition to the open offices, conference area, and chef's kitchen on the ground floor, the partners had put in a lab and a small but fully equipped gym. The light-filled atrium space was ringed by interior balconies, leading to a private library and elegant personal apartments on the second level for each of the three partners. Of course, the living quarters were off-limits to guests, which only added to the intrigue.

For the evening's event, the lower level was illuminated by tiny lights wound through small potted trees in heavy steel bins. Out of respect for her partner's freakish olfactory receptors, Marple had ordered scentless floral arrangements. Colorful combinations of sunflowers, dahlias, and hibiscus decorated every corner and table-top. Marple was definitely more comfortable with flowers than she was with crowds. On the other hand, parties were wonderful oppor-tunities for people watching, which she considered her specialty.

Office furniture had been moved into a back room for the occa-sion. Servers in black vests circulated through the open space with trays of blue cheese focaccia, salmon rillettes, and carrot harissa hummus. Music and lively conversation echoed off the brick walls. Some of the guests were a bit starstruck, not only by their hosts but also by their fellow attendees. Holmes, Marple, and Poe were not the only celebrities in the house.

"Is that . . . ?" a guest asked Marple, pointing across the room.

"It is," she replied.

While building their business over the past year, the firm had done some discreet snooping for some very prominent people. And tonight, some of those clients had come to repay the favor—which is why guests spotted Alicia Keys at the piano and Adrien Brody behind the bar.

Marple saw Holmes holding court on a sofa in the common area. Surrounding him was a crowd of young reporters, including an attentive Shelbi Scott. Marple hoped that Holmes wasn't giving away any inside information on their cases. Knowing her partner, she realized that he was more likely to be sending them all down a rab-bit hole. When she looked over, he gave her a conspiratorial wink.

Poe was on the other side of the room with his companion for the evening, a lithe, dark-haired young woman in a daringly cut dress.

Her name was Dana. Junior associate at Sullivan and Cromwell. They made a stunning couple, and Marple was happy to see Poe distracted, even if it was just a temporary thing. She knew he was still aching over the loss of his late love, Annie—even after ten years. Marple looked at Dana again. The likeness was remarkable.

"Do you always keep your back to the wall, Ms. Marple?"

It was Detective Lieutenant Helene Grey. Hair down. Sleeveless dress. Vodka in hand.

"Don't mind me," said Marple. "I'm just the little old lady in the corner with a book. No life at all."

"That surprises me," said Grey, taking a sip of her drink, "based on the way he looks at you."

"Who?"

Grey nodded toward Holmes. "Your partner."

Marple smiled into her sherry. "Brendan? He's just watching to make sure I don't nod off and fall into a planter."

"Mmm," said Grey.

Marple leaned down to set her glass on a nearby table. "Oh. Actually. While I have you . . ."

Grey frowned. "We're not talking shop tonight, are we?"

"Do you know anything about the history of this building?" asked Marple.

"This building? No." Grey nodded toward the side window. "But I think Vice broke up a meth ring next door."

"Somebody was killed here years ago," said Marple. "A girl."

"How long ago?"

"Nineteen fifty-four," said Marple. "Never solved."

"Not surprising," said Grey. "Our clearance rate on homicides right now is probably about 60 percent, even with all our fancy forensics. That's a piss-poor stat. I can't imagine what it was like back then. Especially in this neighborhood."

"So you wouldn't want to look into . . . ?"

"What? No. Forget it," said Grey. "That case has cobwebs."

"Of course," said Marple. "I understand." She picked up her glass again and clinked it against Grey's. "I guess I'll just have to solve it myself. In my spare time."

"You mean you haven't had enough death and betrayal for one week?" asked Grey.

"Fig with bacon?" A slim young man with slicked-back hair was waving a tray of offerings under their chins.

"No thanks," said Marple.

"Pass," said Grey.

The server nodded politely and turned toward other prospects. Grey polished off her vodka in a gulp. She leaned in close to Marple. "There *is* one mystery about this building I'm dying to work out," she said.

"What's that?"

"How three people were able to get New York State PI licenses without leaving any of their fingerprints on file. Almost as if they were trying to conceal their true identities."

"Well, I try not to make a thing out of it," said Marple. "But we are very good at what we do."

"Right," said Grey. "Whoever you are."

Marple smiled. "Yes," she said. "Whoever we are."

CHAPTER 14

DANA DUFREIGN WOKE up very slowly. She was naked beneath black silk sheets. As she stirred, feelings from the night before started coming back. Good feelings. She'd never been with anybody quite like Auguste Poe. Tender. Giving. And deliciously mysterious. She looked to the side and realized that she was alone in bed.

"Auguste?" she called out.

The door to the bedroom opened and Poe walked through, carrying a bamboo tray with a French press coffee maker and more.

"Do I smell chocolate?" asked Dana. She slid herself up against the headboard and wrapped the top sheet tight across her chest.

"And cinnamon," said Poe, unveiling a basket with two warm croissants.

"And coffee?" said Dana. "You, sir, are a man of distinction and a true lifesaver."

"Like a Saint Bernard in a snowstorm," said Poe.

He set the tray down and leaned over the bed. Then he brushed Dana's dark hair back and kissed her lightly on the forehead. "Nothing but the best for the most glamorous woman at the ball."

"Awww," Dana replied. She'd only known Auguste since yesterday, but so far, he did not disappoint. For a second, she considered lowering the sheet and pulling his body against hers again.

While Poe expertly pressed and poured the first cupful of coffee, Dana looked around the room. All she remembered about her surroundings from the night before was how plush and comfortable the bed was. Now she noticed the exposed brick walls, the sturdy beams supporting the polished wood ceiling, light pouring in through deep-set skylights, stacks of books on the floor, and dozens of filled-in word puzzles piled on a chair. The only thing she didn't see were her clothes. She took a quick peek under the covers.

"Any idea where my party dress ended up?" she asked.

"Fear not," said Poe. "I took care." He handed her a cup of steaming coffee and opened the door of a massive oak wardrobe. Sure enough, her dress was dangling neatly from a cushioned hanger. Her heels were perfectly aligned below.

Dana sipped as Poe poured a cup of coffee for himself. He balanced a plate with both croissants on top of his cup and walked to his side of the bed. He eased down gently, then set the plate on a pillow and let the aromas waft up. This little tableau was almost too good to be true, Dana thought.

"So, tell me again," she said, breaking off the tip of a croissant. "You said you actually live here, above your office, full time?"

"Correct," said Poe. "Twenty-second commute."

"And your two partners live here *with* you?"

"Right," said Poe, sipping his coffee. "Same floor. Separate apartments. Very convenient."

Dana took a nibble of the warm pastry. "You don't find that a bit strange?" she asked. "Like living in a college dorm?"

"My college dorm was nothing like this," said Poe.

"But isn't it awkward?" Dana pressed. "Sharing the same space twenty-four seven? Walking into the hall and seeing each other in your underwear?"

"That almost never happens," said Poe. He smiled. "Although, once in a while, I *do* catch Holmes in his bathrobe."

There was something else on Dana's mind. Something that nagged at her. All evening long, Poe had been the perfect gentleman. Freshened her drinks without being asked. Engaged her in lively, intelligent conversation. Introduced her to Alicia Keys.

But there had been moments during the party—fleeting moments—when Dana sensed Poe's mind wandering. Moments when he was looking at her but seemed to be thinking about someone else. Maybe his attractive business partner, Margaret? The one who was living right down the hall. Dana couldn't exactly put her finger on it, but the whole arrangement felt a little . . . odd.

"If you need sugar, there's some in the nightstand," said Poe.

"You read my mind," said Dana. She leaned over and pulled the small drawer open. Inside was a small tin filled with raw sugar packets. And next to it, a sleek, black pistol case. Underneath the gun was a framed photograph of a young woman with dark hair. Dana nudged the pistol aside to see the woman's face. It looked startlingly like her own. Dana took two packets and closed the drawer.

"You know what, Auguste?" she said. "This has been great. All of it. But I have a huge opening argument to work on. Would it be weird if I took off?"

Poe reached out and tucked a loose strand of hair behind her ear. "There is no exquisite beauty without some strangeness in proportion," he said.

"That's so sweet," said Dana. "I think."

"The shower is right through that door," said Poe. "Whenever you're ready, I'll drive you home." He handed her a plush robe.

Dana put her coffee cup down on the nightstand. She took the robe and deftly covered herself as she slipped out from between the sheets.

"No need," she said. "I'll call an Uber."

CHAPTER 15

AFTER A NIGHT in lively company, Marple always felt the need to recharge her introvert batteries. As a child, she'd often been branded antisocial. She was not. She loved people. Enjoyed being around them. But only in small doses. Afterward, during her recovery time, she usually sought out fictional friends.

Marple walked down the hall from her apartment and pressed the code on the door to the firm's private library. It was her favorite room in the entire building. Maybe in the entire world. The door opened with a gentle burp of released air. Marple stepped inside the sanctum.

The room was climate-controlled to within one degree of optimal temperature and one percentage point of optimal humidity, but the air still held the essence of leather bindings and aged paper.

Marple knew the scents sometimes bothered Holmes, but to her, the room was paradise.

The sensors turned on recessed lights, illuminating walls lined with bookshelves, from floor to ceiling. A pair of wooden ladders stretched to the top rows, eighteen feet off the floor. Three matching reading chairs with ottomans were arranged at one end of the room, but the partners were almost never in the library at the same time. By tacit agreement, this was a place for solitary reflection.

Green-shaded lamps on metal stands provided a cozy halo around the easy chairs. Many of the items here were irreplaceable. A vault in the center of one wall held the most valuable volumes. A secure case on the other wall contained an assortment of rare violins, crafted by the Amati, Bergonzi, and Stradivari families. Both Holmes and Poe were avid collectors. Holmes claimed to be a virtuoso on the instrument, but Marple couldn't recall ever hearing him play.

The bookshelves contained the consolidated collections of all three partners, organized into categories devised by Poe. He found the Dewey Decimal Classification inherently biased against esoterica.

One section held Auguste's books on magic and the occult. Another was filled with Brendan's chemistry texts. There was an entire shelf devoted to weaponry, another to magic and illusions. An array of current medical journals sat next to a bound collection of Da Vinci's anatomical drawings.

Marple headed straight to the back of the room, where the heart of the collection resided. It was the reason the room existed in the first place. One section contained a copy of everything ever published by Sir Arthur Conan Doyle. Over twenty novels, plus dozens upon dozens of collected short stories, plays, volumes of poetry, pamphlets on the spiritual and paranormal, and near-mint copies of nineteenth-century magazines containing his contributions—*The Strand, The Cornhill,* the *British Medical Journal,* and others.

Edgar Allan Poe had his own section, lined with volumes of poetry, magazines featuring his macabre tales, and collections of his essays on science and writing, along with a variety of pamphlets and textbooks, including his thoughts on hypnotism. At one end was an esoteric collection of plays performed by the writer's estranged father, who'd been a touring actor.

Marple moved to the middle shelves. Her belly fluttered as she ran her fingers along row after row of Agatha Christie first editions. Almost a hundred novels and volumes of short stories—all in mint condition, many signed by the author herself. It had taken Marple decades to assemble the collection, and in her mind, it was never complete. There was always one more obscure text or letter to locate.

Perched on a shelf next to a bookend was a framed photograph of Christie herself as a young girl. Her blond hair tumbled in frizzy waves down to her shoulders. Her dark-eyed gaze seemed both sad and knowing. A young lady with secrets.

Marple often came to the library in the early hours before her part-ners woke up or in the late hours before they came home. It was her haven and a source of inspiration. She settled into a chair, closed her eyes, and took a deep, centering breath, preparing for whatever the day would bring. In this quiet room, surrounded by tales of mystery and deception, she felt most like herself.

CHAPTER 16

DOWNSTAIRS, SITTING ALONE at the office kitchen island, Poe was filling in the final squares of the *Financial Times* crossword. No online puzzles for him. Strictly paper and pen. He looked up to see Holmes descending the staircase. A few seconds later, Marple emerged from the second-floor library and followed him down.

Dana was gone. Maybe for good, Poe thought. Or maybe she just needed time to adjust to his idiosyncrasies. On the other hand, maybe *he* was the one with the problem. Maybe he wasn't ready to be loved again—*really* loved—by anybody.

Poe rubbed his temples. He'd had too much to drink last night. Like most nights.

"What a bloody mess!" Marple said as she settled on a stool on the opposite side of the island.

Poe looked around and took in the post-party carnage. The entire first level was littered with empty wineglasses and beer bottles. The sink and counter were filled with plates. Every surface was coated with clumps of damp party sparkles.

"It looks like we were attacked by Huns," said Holmes, shuddering slightly.

Poe could sense his partner's visceral discomfort with the disorder. This was a man who regularly took two showers every day.

"Did we not schedule the cleaning service?" asked Poe. He felt Marple staring at him.

"I believe that was on *your* to-do list, Auguste," she said.

Poe winced. Marple was right. His usual attention to detail had lapsed. Embarrassing. "Maybe we need an assistant," he mumbled. Not the first time he'd thought it.

"Your young attorney must have distracted you," said Holmes. He looked up toward Poe's apartment. "What have you done with her, by the way?"

"Gone at first light," said Poe. "I think our live-work situation may have unsettled her."

"Too bad," said Holmes, brushing some sparkles off the table. "Brilliant legal mind."

The front door buzzed.

"Expecting anyone?" asked Poe. He shuffled slowly toward the entryway. When he opened the door to the visitor, he felt an odd tingle.

"Good morning, Mr. Poe." It was Helene Grey.

Poe blinked. "Forget something, Detective?" he asked. "A glass slipper?"

Grey offered a game smile. "It was a very nice party. But I'm here on business. Can I come in?"

"Why not?" said Poe. "The friendly sunshine smiles."

Grey was in a dark suit with a bulge at her hip. As she stepped into the main space, she looked around and gave a low whistle. "Wow. I guess things got more lively after I left."

"Espresso, anybody?" Marple called out.

"God, yes," said Holmes.

"I wouldn't say no to one," said Grey.

She took a seat on an island stool as Marple fired up the complex Rocket Espresso machine.

"Has Boolin cooled off about the press conference?" asked Poe.

"Not by a long shot," said Grey. "He thinks you three orchestrated the whole thing for your own purposes. If you want some friendly advice, I'd stay out of his way for a while."

"So you're not here to arrest us?" said Marple.

"Believe it or not," said Grey, "I'm here to give you your next case."

CHAPTER 17

MARPLE COCKED HER head, immediately suspicious. She knew that Detective Grey didn't totally trust her or her partners. So why give them a lead? Was she testing them? Tricking them? Trapping them? Marple passed the cups of hot espresso down the island counter.

Grey added sugar and rattled a small spoon in her cup. She leaned forward. "The man you need to talk to is Huntley Bain."

Holmes frowned. "Bain? The media monster?"

Grey nodded and took a sip of her espresso. "That's the one."

Marple wrinkled her nose in distaste. Bain was a legend in New York. Big ego and an even bigger mouth. CEO of a network of internet content providers, mostly second-tier news outlets. The rumor was that his seed money had come from running European-based porn sites in the 1990s. The corporation they'd spawned was now worth billions.

"An insufferable lout," said Marple.

Grey nodded. "And one of the mayor's biggest contributors."

"So who did he kill?" asked Poe.

"This is not about murder," said Grey. "It's about an art theft."

Marple stared at Grey. "Art theft? But you're Homicide."

"I'll explain," said Grey. She pulled out her notebook. "The missing pieces are a Shakespeare First Folio and a 1455 Gutenberg Bible. Bain has only owned them for four months. Now they're gone. Stolen sometime after 6 p.m. two nights ago. No alarms triggered. When he checked his vault the next morning, it was empty."

Marple exchanged glances with her partners.

Holmes wrinkled his brow. "I thought many of the Shakespeare First Folios were in the Folger collection."

"The Folgers have nothing to do with this," said Grey. "Bain acquired the Folio on his own, through his connections in Europe."

"It's authentic?" asked Holmes.

"Certified and documented," said Grey. "He has all the paperwork."

"What about the Bible?" asked Poe.

Grey checked her notes again. "One of twenty-one known copies left in the world."

"*Complete* copies," Holmes corrected. "There are plenty of Gutenbergs floating around. But most of them are partials or have at least one forged page. Even experts get fooled."

"From what Bain says," said Grey, "his copy is totally legit. That's why he's through the roof. He says that First Folios go for ten million. The Bible could be worth—"

"Thirty-five million," said Marple. "Or more. I have a few nice Bibles in my own collection. Worth pennies compared to that."

"You can't put a value on works like these," said Holmes. "They're cultural milestones. Human history on the page. The thought of them sitting in some philistine's garage..." He shook his head in disgust.

"Go see Bain," said Grey. "I told him to expect all of you this morning."

"You're not coming?" said Poe. Marple sensed a bit of disappointment in the question.

"No," said Grey. "At the moment, this case doesn't officially exist." She finished her espresso. "The mayor reached out to me off the record. Bain doesn't want any official police involvement. He's afraid the story will leak and make him look stupid. He hasn't even filed a report. Boolin knows nothing about this." She placed her palms flat on the countertop. "Can I trust you to be discreet?"

"As silent as shadows," Poe whispered.

"By the way," said Grey, sliding off her stool, "Bain donates a million dollars a year to the Police Benevolent Association. Try not to piss him off."

"So you're leaving us on our own?" asked Marple.

The detective nodded. "I was never here."

Marple smiled to herself. Grey was growing on her. She appreciated a woman who knew how to keep a secret.

CHAPTER 18

HUNTLEY BAIN'S FIFTH AVENUE home had none of the gilded garishness of Trump Tower a few blocks away. It was clean, modern, tasteful. What's more, it was even closer to Central Park. Location, location, location.

Marple stood in the entryway with Holmes and Poe while a minion hurried to fetch the master. She watched as Holmes began to examine an elaborately sculpted statuette in a small recess. He pulled a tiny magnifying glass from his pocket. Marple rolled her eyes. "Really, Brendan? Where's your deerstalker cap?"

"Chinese bronze. Buddha Vairocana. At least that's what they tell me." A brash, booming voice.

Holmes tucked the glass back into his jacket as Huntley Bain strutted across his gleaming white floor. Marple felt queasy just looking at him. The pricey European-cut suit, one size too small. The manicured nails. The Botoxed forehead. The air of superiority. For her, it was disgust at first sight. Bain poked a finger toward the trio. "So. Are you my goddamn miracle workers?"

By an earlier draw of straws, this was Marple's case to lead. She sucked in a breath, stepped forward, and extended her hand.

"Margaret Marple," she said, as Bain gave her hand an aggressive shake. "These are my partners, Auguste Poe and Brendan Holmes."

Bain's mouth curled into a cruel smile. "You're the ones who took down that little slut in the mayor's office. Good for you. Never trusted her."

Marple's stomach was turning. When it came to clients, she always tried to keep an open mind, but Huntley Bain offended her senses on every level. She could already feel him sapping her energy. But this was her case. She asked the first question.

"Why us, Mr. Bain?"

"Because the police are useless," said Bain. "I called the mayor, and the mayor had someone reach out to you."

"Where were the items taken from?" asked Holmes.

"Here!" said Bain. "Right here. My apartment. This floor. Weren't you briefed?"

"Where *exactly*?" asked Poe.

"This way," said Bain, snorting with impatience. "Pay attention. I'm only going through this once."

Bain led the way down a wide inner gallery lined with meticulously framed etchings and prints. The hallway opened into a large library. The shelves were lined with books bound in color-coordinated spines. Marple doubted that any of them had ever been opened. When she looked across the room, she stopped mid-step.

"Hold on, Mr. Bain," she said. "I'm confused."

There, sitting in front of her in a rectangular case, were a Shakespeare First Folio and a Gutenberg Bible. She could tell, because they were boldly labeled with engraved brass plates.

"You shouldn't be confused," said Bain. "You should be convinced. Most people would be."

Holmes stepped up to the case. He pulled out his magnifying glass again and leaned in close to the top of the case, examining the pages beneath. "Decoy copies," he said. "About as valuable as fake fruit."

"How can you tell?" asked Marple.

"Absence of watermarks in the Shakespeare," said Holmes. "Facsimile illumination in the Gutenberg, not original. Not the most impressive copies I've seen but solid work."

"Good enough to fool most crooks," said Bain.

"Most people see," said Holmes, "but they do not observe."

"Well, this guy must've been *very* observant," said Bain. "He wasn't fooled for a goddamn second. He went right for the good stuff."

He waved the investigators toward an adjacent room, the size of a walk-in closet. Marple stood in the entryway as the others walked in. She was suddenly claustrophobic; or maybe it was just an aversion to being in a tight space with Bain. The air inside the room felt totally dead.

"Lead-lined walls," said Bain, pounding them with his fist to make the point. "Steel-reinforced floor and ceiling. Motion detectors. Safe carved from a single block of steel. Unbreakable lock."

"And yet . . ." said Marple.

The door to the vault in the wall hung open. She could see two felt-lined shelves inside, both empty.

"There's your crime," said Bain, turning toward her. "Now, what's your plan?"

Marple cleared her throat. "Before we start," she said, "you should know that our fee is two hundred thousand dollars."

Bain cocked his head in disbelief. "Are you *shitting* me?" he said. "You're three gumshoes from Brooklyn who got lucky on a murder case. Find my books and we'll talk about an appropriate fee. If you need an advance for expenses, we can—"

"Two hundred thousand," Marple repeated evenly. "Up front, and no refunds."

Bain's voice turned menacing. "Look," he said. "Just between us chickens, do I really care about some moldy plays or a Bible with type I can't read? No. I just like having them, because it means somebody else can't. And it's embarrassing to have them stolen without a goddamn trace. But two hundred grand? Kiss my ass."

"And another two hundred when we return the pieces," said Marple.

"Get the fuck out of here," said Bain.

Holmes pulled out his cell phone. "Auguste, do you have the number...?"

"Of that reporter at Channel 4?" Poe replied. "Shelbi Scott. Hold on...I have it right here..."

"Hey!" said Bain. "No! No press."

"The media will gobble this story up, Mr. Bain," said Marple. "Pig-headed billionaire who doesn't even appreciate art has two iconic volumes stolen from right under his nose."

"She's paraphrasing," said Holmes, starting to tap numbers on his phone.

"They probably won't use those exact words," added Poe.

Bain grabbed the phone. "Okay!" he said. "You fucking bastards. Two hundred g's. I'll cut you a personal check. But I want your full focus on this thing. No noise. No bullshit. Total attention—from all three of you."

"When you hire one of us, you hire the whole firm," Marple said. "All of us are totally involved. You have my promise."

Marple turned and headed back toward the door. She felt the need to get out of the billionaire's presence before something truly embarrassing happened. There was something about Huntley Bain that made her feel like throwing up.

CHAPTER 19

TWENTY MINUTES LATER, the partners were back in Bushwick.

As Poe pulled the Pontiac into the former bakery's loading bay, he spotted Helene Grey leaning against the brick wall near the entrance, talking on her cell phone. She was wearing aviator shades and her head was tipped back in the midday sun.

"Look," he said. "She can't get enough of us."

"I hope she hasn't been going through our rubbish," said Marple.

Poe couldn't quite explain why seeing Grey gave him a little lift. For some reason, she intrigued him. He already knew there was more to her than met the eye, because he'd run a thorough background check. He wondered why a bright young FBI agent would suddenly quit to become a middle-rank homicide detective. An odd career path. On the surface, she seemed like a total stickler for rules, but there was clearly some wiggle room. The Bain case proved that.

Grey ended her call as the investigators walked up. "I asked you not to piss him off," she said.

"You heard?" asked Holmes.

"About ten seconds after you left," said Grey. "Something about an exorbitant fee?"

"He can afford it," said Poe. "And we're worth every penny."

"I hope you know what you're doing," said Grey.

"We absolutely do," said Marple. "In our own way."

Grey lowered her sunglasses. "I'm sure the mayor will be comforted to hear that."

"The Police Benevolent Association too," said Poe.

Holmes tapped the security code on the pad next to the door. The heavy lock clicked open. He turned to Grey. "If you'll excuse us, Detective, we really need to get to work. Most stolen art ends up in another country within an hour of being taken, and we've already lost two days."

"Right," said Grey. "I'll leave you to it." She started toward the unmarked police Impala at the curb. On an impulse, Poe took a step after her.

"Detective? One question." Grey turned. Poe smiled. "Can I take you to dinner?"

Grey looked at Poe, then over his shoulder at Holmes and Marple, then back at Poe. She shook her head. "I don't think so."

As she resumed walking to her car, she nodded toward Poe's GTO, parked just ahead of her. "But let's drag race sometime," she said. "That would be fun." She slid into her Impala and started the engine, giving it a loud rev before pulling away.

Poe turned back toward his partners. "Not a word."

"I like her," said Marple. "I like her a lot."

As they walked into the office, the partners split up and headed for their individual workspaces, spread out across the huge ground floor. On the way to his desk, Poe saw the red message light blinking on the team's landline phone set in the common area. He pressed Speaker, then Play. A woman's voice echoed through the space. She sounded frantic.

"They're gone! My daughter. My husband. I need you! Now!"

Poe picked up the handset and took the phone off speaker. He stepped to his desk and jotted on a small whiteboard there as he listened to the rest of the message. Holmes and Marple walked over as he hung up. Scrawled on the whiteboard was the name "Addilyn Charles" and a SoHo address.

"New case?" asked Holmes.

"Possible kidnapping," said Poe. "Sounds dark."

"Perfect for you," said Marple. "Your lead."

CHAPTER 20

POE HAD EXPECTED the SoHo building to be a converted industrial space like their HQ, or maybe an artist's loft. But it was nothing like that. It was a contemporary tower with a high-end, designer interior.

When he and his partners stepped off a private elevator into the foyer of the penthouse level, a woman was waiting for them. Mid-fifties. Small boned. Sharp featured. Impeccably coiffed. And obviously distraught.

"Mrs. Charles?" said Poe.

"Yes! Call me Addilyn. Come in. Please!" She turned and walked from the foyer into a cleanly decorated parlor. The investigators followed. Poe went first, making the introductions. "I'm Auguste Poe. These are my associates, Brendan Holmes and Margaret Marple."

"Yes, of course," said Addilyn. "Such interesting names. I recognize you all from the press conference—about that poor young lawyer." She stopped wringing her hands just long enough to shake theirs. Firm and polite.

"Addilyn," Marple said gently, "have you contacted the police?"

"Dear Lord, no!" said Addilyn. "Kidnappers always say not to call the police. Isn't that right? Isn't that what they always say? No police. That's why I called you. Promise me you won't call the police!"

Poe noticed that, upset as she was, Addilyn was still well put together. She was wearing an expensive silk dress and high heels. A string of pearls circled her neck, which was impressively smooth compared to her hands. Brazilian work, Poe surmised. And from the degree of skin tension below the ears, recent. Her makeup was impeccable, but there were small mascara smears under both eyes.

"Tell us exactly what happened, Addilyn," said Poe.

Addilyn kept pacing as she talked, her phrases broken by short anxious breaths.

"They just—*disappeared*! I had dinner with both of them—my husband and daughter—last night at eight. I went to bed early. When I woke up this morning, they were *gone*."

"What makes you think they were kidnapped?" asked Holmes.

"What else could it be?" said Addilyn. "My husband would never be away this long without telling me where he was. Neither would my daughter."

"Was there a note?" asked Poe. "Any signs of a break-in?"

"None," said Addilyn. "We have an alarm system, of course. But there was no sound. Not a peep."

"You've tried their phones?"

Addilyn nodded. "Of course. No answer from either of them. That never happens."

"How old is your daughter?" asked Poe.

"She's eighteen. Her name is Zozi. Zozi Turner."

"And her father?"

"Her father died almost fifteen years ago," Addilyn said. "Zozi is the child of my first marriage. Eton is my second husband. We've been married for ten years."

"Did Eton adopt your daughter?" asked Poe.

"No," said Addilyn. "Eton said he could never adopt another man's child. But we're a family. They get along fine. We've made it work." At that point, her whole body appeared to cave in a bit. "You have to find them. You *have* to. They're all I've got."

Poe started a new line of questioning. "Have there been any—"

"He has enemies!" Addilyn burst out. "My husband. He does business in China, Korea, South America. It could be one of those drug gangs. Those . . . *cartels.*"

Poe glanced at Holmes. Drugs always complicated things. Made people more ruthless. If this was revenge or leverage for some kind of illicit deal, things could get very ugly.

"Is there anything else missing?" asked Holmes, switching to a new path.

"Yes," Addilyn said softly. "The dog."

"The dog?" asked Marple.

"Toby," said Addilyn. "Zozi's dog. He's an English mastiff. Whoever took Zozi took Toby too. Or killed him, probably. He would have defended Zozi. I know that. She and that dog are inseparable. I've always been a bit twitchy around him, to be honest. So strong. He could knock you over in a heartbeat."

Poe glanced toward the hallway off the living room. "Do you mind if Mr. Holmes and I poke around a bit?" he asked.

"Not at all," said Addilyn. "But there's nothing amiss. I've already looked. Everything is just as it was."

"Fresh eyes," said Holmes. "You never know."

Poe watched as Marple touched Addilyn's shoulder and gestured toward a sofa. "Shall we sit?"

Addilyn perched primly on the edge of the cushion and smoothed her dress. Her hands twitched nervously.

Poe knew that in an abduction, minutes were precious. In most cases, kidnappings were solved quickly or not at all. But he could see that Marple was trying to give Addilyn a little time. Time to think. Time to remember. Details were everything, and Marple was a master at fishing them out.

"It's just you and me now, Addilyn," Poe heard her saying. "Tell me everything."

CHAPTER 21

POE LED THE way down the hallway toward the bedrooms. The girl's room was first on the right. The clean lines contrasted with typical teen-girl clutter—clothes, cosmetics, schoolbooks.

Poe reached into his pocket and pulled out two pairs of latex gloves. He tossed one pair to Holmes. Holmes stepped into the crowded closet and began riffling through pockets and purses while Poe opened dresser drawers, feeling around carefully beneath the pricey tops and underthings for drugs, weapons, hidden flash drives. But there was nothing.

He fished deftly through a teak box on the dresser top. It was filled with rings and beaded bracelets. Poe lifted the felt liner at the bottom and pulled out a set of ID cards with Zozi's photo. He studied the craftsmanship—the thickness of the laminate, the quality of the holographic seals. The cards were expertly faked. He couldn't have done better himself.

"Find any electronics?" he called out to Holmes.

"Not so far."

A teenager's room without a laptop or a phone? *Impossible,* thought Poe. "Whoever took her, took her stuff too," he said.

Above a small makeup table, the wall was covered with photo printouts. Poe leaned in close for a look. Zozi Turner was petite and pretty, with shoulder-length blond hair. The pictures showed her with an assortment of attractive friends, especially good-looking boys—preppy, athletic types with perfect smiles.

In one photo, a heavily muscled boy dangled his arm over Zozi's shoulder, his fingers almost touching her right breast. A hint of menace, Poe wondered, or just casual adolescent horniness? From the photo backgrounds, Poe could pick out Mexico, Spain, and the Caribbean. *What a life this girl leads,* thought Poe. Or *led*. He had a tendency to think the worst, then work his way back.

The dog was in a lot of the pictures too, usually with Zozi's arms around him.

Addilyn was right—the mastiff was huge, with thick neck folds and a forbidding face. Not the kind of dog to give up without a fight. Compared to the massive black hound, the girl looked almost like a child.

Holmes emerged from Zozi's bathroom with a little plastic loop dangling from his index finger. It was the size of a small bracelet. "Found this in the wastebasket," he said. "Some kind of friendship trinket?" He slid the loop onto Poe's gloved palm.

Poe was rarely stumped on a search, but this object had him mystified. "Possible," he said. He slid the loop into a small plastic bag and put it into his pocket.

Together, Poe and Holmes walked down the hall to the master bedroom. It was spacious and elegant, with wraparound windows. The massive bed was covered in a plush comforter. Off to each side, matching dressing rooms led to matching bathrooms. A floating shelf along one wall held elegant bric-a-brac and a grouping of framed family photos.

While Holmes prowled the closets, Poe pulled open the drawer to the night table nearest the door. Inside, he found a man's manicure kit and a pair of reading glasses.

He walked to the other side of the bed and pulled open the wife's drawer. His eyes widened. Inside was a cornucopia of sex toys. Clearly, cosmetic surgery was not the only area in which Addilyn was putting in extra effort.

Poe and Holmes walked back into the living room, just as Marple stood up from the sofa. "All set?" she asked. From her tone, Poe could tell that she'd gotten all she could from Addilyn.

"We have everything we need for now," said Poe. He walked up to Addilyn, who was still perched on the edge of the sofa cushion. "Try to stay calm," he said. "If it's really a kidnapping, you'll get a call or a text with a ransom demand or instructions. But I think it's likely that your family will be back soon under their own power. There's probably a perfectly innocent explanation. Either way, call us."

Addilyn nodded absently. "There's nothing else you can do?"

"We'll start digging," said Poe. "But the most important thing you can do is be patient and wait. Call us the minute you hear anything."

Poe handed her a business card as the elevator arrived. The investigators stepped on. The last thing Poe registered as the door closed was the look on Addilyn's face: pained, lonely, scared.

The trio maintained strict silence until they were out on the street. Poe turned to his partners. "What do you think?"

"They weren't taken from home," said Holmes. "No sign of a struggle. And even if the kidnappers bypassed the alarm, the dog would have put up a fuss."

"I'd hate to run into that hound on a dark night," said Poe.

"There's something else going on," said Marple. "Something beyond the kidnapping. Something she's holding back. I haven't put my finger on it yet."

Holmes nudged Poe in the shoulder. "Show Margaret the thing."

"The what?"

"That thing we found."

Poe pulled the bag from his pocket and held it up at Marple's eye level. "Any clue what this might be?"

"Where did you find that?"

"In a bathroom wastebasket."

"No wonder," said Marple. "It's a vaginal ring."

"Body piercing?" asked Poe, cringing.

"Contraceptive," said Marple. "More popular in the UK than here. But quite effective. Addilyn said Zozi spent last summer in London."

"So Zozi is sexually active?" asked Holmes.

"Apparently so," said Marple. "Don't look so surprised."

"Let's divvy up duties," said Poe. "I'll take the husband's business. Brendan, you dig into the marriage. Margaret, you take the girl."

"Should we call Helene?" asked Poe.

"What?" said Holmes. "And have her take over the case?"

"Not yet," said Marple. "In matters like this, sometimes less is more."

Holmes and Poe headed for the GTO, parked in front of a bodega across the street. Marple hung back, checking her phone.

"You two go on ahead," she said. "I have some things to do."

Holmes and Poe both stopped and turned.

"*What* things?" asked Holmes.

"We need to get started on this case, Margaret," said Poe.

"I understand," said Marple. "I've got my brief. And I don't need to be micromanaged by the two of you."

Poe was taken aback. He realized that he was cracking the whip a bit, but he'd also been looking forward to spending the afternoon together, the three of them assembling pieces of the puzzle. Without Marple, the dynamic wasn't the same. But he wasn't her boss. Just her partner.

"No problem, Margaret," said Poe, backing down. "Do what you need to do. We'll catch up later."

Marple started walking up the street toward Greenwich Village. "I might be *very* late," she called over her shoulder. "I have a date!"

Poe looked at Holmes, who seemed as surprised as he was. *A date? Margaret?*

CHAPTER 22

ONE OF THE windows in the small, gloomy bar looked out on the Hudson River. The other looked out on a corner guard turret of the Sing Sing Correctional Facility. Marple sipped her sherry as she waited.

The train ride up to Ossining through the river towns from Grand Central had been pleasant and peaceful, and Marple was grateful for the think time. It was rare to have any time alone at all these days. The last year had been a blur. New business. New living situation. And now, one case after another—bang, bang, bang. *No looking back now,* thought Marple. *Only forward.*

As she watched the sun ease down over the west side of the river, shouts erupted from her fellow patrons around the bar. All men. All watching the Yankees game on the TV over the bar.

A wiry man slid onto the stool to Marple's left. He wore a mechanic's overalls, and his fingers and nails were stained black with grease. "Nice of you to come up to my neighborhood," he said.

"I enjoyed the trip," said Marple. "Shall we take a booth?"

The man signaled the bartender, who nodded back and pulled a bottle of Miller High Life from the cooler under the bar.

"How's it goin', Finn?" said the bartender as he popped the top and set the bottle down.

"Goin' good," the man said. He jerked his head toward Marple. "Found a woman."

"Out of your league, clearly," the bartender replied.

Marple smiled. "We'll be in the booth at the end." She put a twenty on the bar as she stood up. "Take the beer out of this and keep the change."

The bartender grinned. "If he tries to steal your purse, just yell."

Marple slid onto the narrow wood bench on one side of the booth. Finn slid onto the bench across from her. There was a small candle inside a thick glass bowl in the middle of the table. Marple pushed it to the side and leaned forward. Finn's dark collar hung open to expose a small patch of his white T-shirt. In the dim light, it almost looked like the neckline of a vicar.

"Did you get what I sent?" Marple asked.

Finn put the bottle to his lips, took a sip of his beer. "Got it. Studied it."

"And . . . ?"

"It's impossible."

"Well, it happened," said Marple. "I saw the safe myself."

"No marks on it?"

"Pristine."

"Then it's an inside job. The guy stole his own books."

Marple sipped her sherry. She was hearing exactly what she had expected to hear. But she wasn't about to leave it there. "What about one of the new kids? Somebody with twenty-first-century skills. And advanced tools."

Finn took another sip. "My tools always did me fine."

"Your tools got you five years in the pokey."

"True." Finn sighed. "Pretty sunsets, though."

"What about the design?" asked Marple.

"Maybe the Bahnhof guy," said Finn.

"Bahnhof?"

Finn nodded. "Bahnhof's the internet provider that used to host WikiLeaks' servers—in an old nuclear bunker under Stockholm. One of the guys who designed their security system makes vaults and safes on the side. Sells them on the dark web. Maybe he built this one."

"Somebody got into it in under ten minutes," said Marple.

"Like I said, not possible. Not without a nuclear bomb."

"Interesting," said Marple. Finn was still on his game.

The bartender appeared with a fresh glass of sherry and a second bottle of Miller. "On the house," he said. He picked up the empties and walked away.

"Is he your parole officer?" asked Marple.

"I fixed his mom's transmission," said Finn. "How about you? Still bird-watching?"

"I swear I saw a bald eagle from the train," said Marple.

"Oh, yeah, they love the tracks," said Finn. "Lots of rail kill."

It was dark by the time Marple emerged onto the streets of Ossining. She was a little unsteady on her feet, and so was her companion.

"I'll drive you to the station," said Finn.

"And add another DWI to your sheet?" said Marple, her lips slightly numb. "No thanks. I'll walk."

Finn nodded and braced one arm against a storefront. "Good to see you, Maggie," he said.

"You too," said Marple. "Believe it or not, you've actually given me useful information. Exactly what I came for."

"I'd hug you good-bye," said Finn, "but you'd have grease prints all over you."

"In that case," said Marple, "just blow me a kiss."

<label>74</label>

CHAPTER 23

AT TEN THIRTY the next morning, Marple stepped out of an Uber in front of Saint Celeste's, an all-girls school a few miles north of Manhattan. The campus was classically gorgeous, with groomed lawns and stately brick architecture—fitting for one of the most exclusive prep schools in the state.

Marple had timed her arrival for the midmorning break. The manicured grounds were filled with roving clusters of students in matching plaid skirts and white polos, mostly untucked and draped insouciantly over the hip.

"Wait for me right here," Marple told the driver.

Marple spotted a group of three students walking toward her on the sidewalk.

One had shiny black hair with bangs. Another had her dark-brown hair wound into a single tight braid. The third had Titian-red tresses that caught the sun like copper.

The girl with the braid held her phone in front of her as she walked. Her friends leaned in from either side to see the screen. Marple headed straight toward them, pretending not to notice the wide crack in the sidewalk. She intentionally jammed her toe into the crack and tumbled forward, landing on the pavement with a loud groan.

"Omigod!" shouted the braid. She tucked her phone into her pocket and ran over to where Marple was lying. "Are you okay?"

The other two girls crowded around. "Should we call somebody?" asked the redhead. "Did you break anything?"

Marple pushed herself up onto her knees and then stood up. "I'm fine, I'm fine," she said with an embarrassed grin. Cheap trick, but effective. Instant empathy.

"I'm here looking for my niece," she said. "Zozi Turner. I'm in town for a visit."

"Zozi?" said the girl with bangs. "You mean The Legend?"

"The Legend?" asked Marple, mirroring the girls' casual slouches and head tilts. "So my niece is famous?"

"Absolutely," said the braid. "Campus hero."

"For what?" asked Marple.

"For everything," said the redhead. "Sports. Clubs. Student government. The Legend never stops."

"She got accepted at Stanford, Harvard, and Oxford," said the braid. "It's embarrassing how smart she is."

Marple nodded. This fit with what Addilyn had told her. Zozi was definitely an overachiever.

The redhead was looking from side to side. "I didn't know Zozi had an aunt."

"I haven't been around much, I'm afraid," said Marple.

"*Love* your accent," said the girl with bangs.

"You sound like *Bridgerton*," said the braid.

"Flattering," said Marple, looking from one girl to the other. "So where would I find Zozi?"

The girl with bangs shrugged. "I don't have any classes with her today."

"Me neither," said the redhead, looking down at the sidewalk.

"We have History together," said the braid, "but she wasn't in class this morning."

"What about yesterday?" asked Marple.

"We were all off yesterday," said the braid. "Teacher conference."

"But none of you have heard from her?" asked Marple. "What about her social media?"

The braid tapped her phone. "She hasn't put anything on her Insta story for a couple of days," she said. Another few taps. "And nothing new on TikTok."

"That's not weird for Zozi," said the redhead. "She's into social, but she's not obsessed."

"Bogey. Three o'clock," the braid muttered. She jerked her head toward the main building. In the distance, a stout woman in a business suit and a short black veil was heading their way with a purposeful stride.

"It's Sister Monaghan from the office," said the redhead. "She's very suspicious of strangers on campus."

"No problem," said Marple. "I'll wait for Zozi at home. I'm sure she'll turn up."

"Should we tell her that her aunt was here?" asked the girl with bangs.

"Please don't," said Marple. "I'd like to surprise her."

She walked back to the Uber and hopped into the back seat just as the administrator closed in.

"Back to Bushwick, please," Marple told the driver. She looked over her shoulder as the car pulled away. The girls had already scattered in three different directions. Marple studied their body language from a distance—the length of their strides, the direction of their glances. Her hobby was human nature, and her conversation had already told her a few things for certain. The girl with bangs and the girl with the braid had been honest and direct—at least as direct as teenage girls ever are.

But not the other one.

The redhead was nervous about something.

CHAPTER 24

"LET'S GO THROUGH it again," said Holmes, taking immense plea-sure in Huntley Bain's discomfort.

The billionaire was clearly out of patience. "I thought you assholes were coming with new information! What the hell is this? Where's your list of suspects? And where's your better half?"

"Better *third*," said Poe.

"Ms. Marple is engaged in another matter this morning," said Holmes. "We didn't want to delay the investigation."

"Delay for *what*?" asked Bain. "Who did it? Where's my stuff? That's all I need to know."

Holmes leaned across the elegant coffee table in Bain's impeccably designed living room. "Mr. Bain, I have to be honest with you. Based on all the information we've gathered so far, the most likely suspect in this case . . . is *you*."

Bain brought his fist down on the glass table, jostling a thick stack of art books. "What the hell are you talking about? Is this what I'm paying you for? Why in Christ's name would I steal my own art?"

"I can think of a few reasons," said Holmes. "Insurance, for one.

Where were you the night before last?" He enjoyed getting under the skin of guys like Bain. No. He *loved* it.

"I was upstairs with my girlfriend. In bed. All night."

"Been dating her long?" asked Poe.

Bain stretched his arms back over his lush leather sofa and stuck his chin in the air. "Let's just say we've been seeing each other regularly for a while."

"Do you mind if we talk to her?" asked Poe. "Your girlfriend?"

"Yes, I *do* mind," said Bain. "Leave her out of it."

"May Anurak," said Holmes.

Bain's face went blank. "Who?"

"That's her birth name," said Holmes.

Bain looked perplexed.

"Marianne," said Poe. "Your girlfriend."

"Born in Bangkok," said Holmes. "Nineteen years ago."

"She's in esthetician school," said Bain. "I pay her tuition."

"She's also a professional escort," said Poe.

Bain shook his head and let out a loud huff—part exasperation, part grudging admiration. "Okay," he said, "so what? What do I care what her real name is? With her skills, she can call herself Little Miss Muffet for all I care. How the hell do you know this stuff?"

"You're paying us a lot of money, Mr. Bain," said Holmes. "You should expect us to be thorough."

"We're thinking maybe the young lady was a decoy," said Poe.

Holmes leaned in. "Or an accomplice."

Bain exploded. "That's it! *Out!* Widen your goddamn search! Widen it beyond my fucking bedroom!"

Bain stood up and practically shoved the investigators into the elevator. As the door slid closed, Poe turned to Holmes. "He's riled."

"Good," Holmes said with a smile. "The game, as they say, is afoot."

CHAPTER 25

"DO Y'ALL EVER get used to that noise?"

A few blocks south, on Madison Avenue, a lanky young woman sat at the edge of her chair in a small reception area. She was nervous, just trying to make conversation. But it was an honest question. Even ten stories up, she could hear the clash of car horns, air brakes, and siren squawks from the street.

"You filter it out after a while," said the stylish assistant behind the desk. She eyed the young woman from head to toe. "New to New York?" she asked. As if it weren't obvious.

"Second day," said the visitor. She was a little nervous, but she told herself she didn't need to be. Back home in Texas, she'd been thrown off broncos and chased by bulls. How hard could a modeling interview be?

The young woman tugged her blue cotton dress over her knees, covering a small whitish barbed-wire scar. She was way more comfortable in Wranglers, but the short skirt showed off her legs—and her legs, she had been told more than once, were money. Her sun-streaked hair hung loose, brushing the tops of her shoulders. For footwear, she had chosen her favorite black boots, the ones with the red leather inlays on the side—in the shape of Texas. They'd always brought her good luck.

There was a soft buzz on the phone console. The receptionist looked over. "She's ready for you."

The young woman straightened up to her full five-foot-ten-inch height and smoothed her dress over her narrow hips. She took a deep breath and walked past reception and down a short hallway. *Game on.*

The woman waiting for her in the sunny office looked instantly familiar. Her magazine covers hung in a row along one wall; her face had hardly changed at all since her first swimsuit issue twenty years ago.

"Hello, there," she said. "I'm Betsy Bronte."

"I know," the visitor replied, trying her best not to stare. She held out her hand.

"I'm Lucy. Lucy Ferry."

Betsy leaned over her sleek glass desk for a quick handshake and then came around to the other side. She moved with a model's ease, and her trademark curls were still full and wild. She gestured toward two elegant leather chairs facing each other at the other end of the room. "Over here, honey," she said. Lucy walked to the chair on the right and turned to sit.

"Not yet," said Betsy. "Look this way."

Lucy straightened up again. She looked at Betsy, who was standing about four feet away with her hand on her chin. Betsy wiggled her index finger in the air. "Turn, please."

Lucy put her weight on the ball of her right foot and did a quick pirouette. At least that stupid ballet class had been good for something.

"And smile," said Betsy.

Lucy knew the trick. Do it with a little laugh. More natural. She still wasn't used to being looked at this way. But she knew it was part of the game. And, after all, here she was, a ranch girl from the Texas Panhandle, standing in front of one of the most famous models in the world—now running one of the hottest boutique modeling agencies in New York.

"Lovely," said Betsy. She gestured toward a chair. "*Now* sit."

"Thanks," said Lucy. She eased herself onto the seat gracefully, back straight, instead of just flopping down, which was her usual style. Betsy sat down across from her and leaned forward.

"I loved the samples you sent," said Betsy. "Sometimes it's hard to tell with local photographers, but you shine. You really do. Even in the catalog work. And you just turned . . . ?"

"Nineteen," said Lucy. "Last week."

"So here's the good news," said Betsy. "You've got an interesting face. Very commercial but different. You've got the height for runway work. And your figure is terrific."

Lucy shifted awkwardly in her seat. She felt like she was being scored like an Angus heifer.

Betsy plucked two business cards from a table. "Here's what I need you to do. First, get a decent haircut. Second, get that chip on your front tooth fixed."

Lucy took the cards. "These people are the best," said Betsy. "Tell them I sent you. They'll know what to do. I'll see what I can find for you in the meantime. Sound good?"

"Sounds . . . *great!*" Lucy broke into a huge grin, chip and all.

Betsy stood up. Lucy did too. She realized that the interview was over. Short but sweet.

"You have real potential," said Betsy, "but you'll have to put in the work."

"Oh, don't you worry," said Lucy. "I will! I promise!"

Betsy walked Lucy toward the door, then stopped. "Now that I think of it—do you have a middle name?"

"I do. It's Lynn."

"*Lucy Lynn Ferry,*" said Betsy, turning the sound over in her head. "Better. We'll use that." She smiled her stunning model smile. "And keep the drawl. It worked for Jerry Hall."

"Sorry, who?"

Betsy sighed. "Google her, sweetheart."

There were two businessmen and a FedEx guy in the down elevator. Otherwise, Lucy Lynn Ferry would have screamed for joy at the top of her lungs. By the time she stepped back out onto the street, she was practically floating.

It had been hard leaving home. Naturally, she missed her parents, her friends, her horses. Her boyfriend hadn't wanted to let her go. But they wanted different things. He was content in small-town Texas, for one thing, and Lucy definitely wanted more than that. But all that drama was behind her now. She'd taken a big chance by coming all the way to New York on her own. Now it looked like exactly the right choice.

Her life was about to begin. Her *new* life. And there was nobody holding her back.

CHAPTER 26

"HE LOOKS LIKE an upstanding citizen," said Holmes.

"Behaves like one too," said Poe, "at least on the surface."

After returning from their heated visit with Huntley Bain, Poe was flicking through the file he'd assembled on fifty-five-year-old Eton Charles, bringing up photos and documents on a large screen for his partners in the middle of the office.

"He's been a principal at Burns and Manning Architects for the past fifteen years. Big firm. International clients. Big money," said Poe. The pictures, an assortment of profile pics and candids, showed a handsome man with greying temples. He wore fashionable, black-framed glasses and well-tailored suits.

"Looks TED Talk ready," said Marple, watching intently from a side chair.

"Any girlfriends?" asked Holmes.

"Any boyfriends?" asked Marple.

"Not that I can find," said Poe. "He doesn't even drink at office parties."

"What about the overseas business?" asked Marple.

"He travels a lot," said Poe, bringing up a world map with pin markers in Singapore, Hong Kong, Berlin, Amsterdam, and Cambodia. "This is just the last six months. Flies first class. Five-star hotels. Not unusual for him to be out of touch with the office for a day or two."

"Any shady dealings?" asked Holmes. "Drugs? Payola?"

"You can't work in the building trades without getting your hands dirty, especially in certain corners of the world," said Poe. "For example . . ." He clicked to a grainy image of Eton Charles conferring with a group of grim-looking Asian men on an urban construction site. "These are the guys whose palms you need to grease for a building permit in Phnom Penh."

"Let's hope he didn't cross them," said Marple.

Poe turned to Holmes. "What did you find on the marriage?"

"Nothing leaps out," said Holmes. He clicked his laptop and took over the large screen. It filled with an image of a fit-looking middle-aged couple in bathing suits. Eton and Addilyn. "They met on Sint Maarten over ten years ago. Addilyn was a widowed single mom with a six-year-old. They got married in Cancun." The screen clicked to a picture of the happy couple, with Zozi as the adorable flower girl.

"Addilyn already had the apartment from her first marriage," Holmes continued. "Eton sold his condo and moved in. His business kept growing. No money worries on either side. Zozi's got her own trust fund."

"I bet the dog does too," said Poe.

The whole time they talked, all three of their iPhones were vibrating on the table, like a small electronic riot. By mutual agreement, they were letting all calls go to voice mail. It was the only way to get any work done.

Calls had been coming in nonstop since the launch party. Their secure email server had already crashed twice. Most of the messages were junk. But they hadn't even had time to follow up on the promising prospects. Not with a possible abduction on their plate and Huntley Bain to manage.

Poe looked down at the devices humming on the table. "I think we overdid the publicity," he said. "We can't handle the onslaught." That week alone, he'd had to skip his regular session at the firing range. And for the first time in years, he hadn't finished the *New York Times* crossword. There were times that he wished he were on his own again—working lean, mean, and under the radar.

"Maybe we need to hire someone to winnow the chaff," said Holmes.

"My thoughts exactly," said Poe. The main phone in the center of the table started ringing with its own chirpy tone. Poe grabbed the handset, rubbing his eyes with his other hand. He made a smooth switch to his telephone voice.

"Holmes, Marple, and Poe Investigations, Poe speaking..."

He tucked the handset under his chin and started jotting notes on a scrap of paper. He looked up. "It's Helene," he whispered. "Another case." He pressed the Speaker button and caught Detective Grey mid-sentence.

"...human skeletons," she was saying. *"We're still counting."*

CHAPTER 27

THE AIR IN the abandoned subway tunnel felt dank and stale, as if it hadn't stirred in a century. The curved tile walls were glistening with moisture. Holmes had brought along his own high-filtration face mask to ward off the odors, but he could still detect a faint scent of human decay. It disgusted him—and excited him.

Poe and Marple used standard-issue police masks. A cop in a bright yellow safety vest pointed them toward where Grey was standing, silhouetted by the glare of powerful scene lights. When she spotted the investigators, she walked back toward them.

"Goddamn nightmare," she said. "Edgar Allan Poe himself couldn't make this up."

Poe raised his eyebrows. "You mean my great-great-great grandfather?"

Grey's eyes narrowed. "What? *Seriously?*"

Marple winked as she walked past. "Don't listen to a word he says."

"But is he telling the truth?" asked Grey.

"That's the thing," Marple replied. "You never know."

Ten yards down the tunnel, a small crew of MTA workers and

uniformed cops stood at the edge of a mound of dirt. An area the size of a studio apartment had been staked out and marked with yellow tape.

"Where are we exactly?" asked Marple. They'd driven about two miles west from Bushwick to the tunnel entrance, but once they were underground, it was hard to stay oriented.

"Under Atlantic Avenue," said Grey. "This tunnel was only in operation for a few years in the early 1900s." She started leading the way toward the dig. "An engineering student rediscovered it in 1982 and started giving tours, then the city sealed it up again about twenty years ago. But obviously somebody's been getting in—maybe through another access point. Somebody who knows the tunnels."

Grey held up a plastic evidence bag with an irregular grey disk inside. "An inspector was down here taking soil samples this morning," she said. "He pulled up a kneecap."

They reached the edge of the mound. When Holmes looked down, his whole body began to tingle. The powerful lights illuminated a flat excavation about five feet deep. It was littered with isolated piles of human bones and skulls.

"Bare bones," said Grey. "I mean literally. No flesh remaining. No traces of clothing. At first, we thought it might be Native Americans or a slave burial site, but they wouldn't be this deep. We're seventy feet below street level."

A CSU team in white suits was sorting through the piles, brushing off dirt and placing the bones in rough anatomical positions. There appeared to be dozens of skeletons, in various stages of assembly. One of the techs held a femur up to the light. Actually, *half* a femur.

Poe nudged Holmes. "Look at the edge. Saw cut."

Holmes nodded. "No question." At the same moment, he noticed something else.

A tech just beneath where he and Poe were standing was gently extracting a skull from a small depression. As he pulled, the mandible separated and dropped back into the dirt.

"Show me that skull!" Holmes called down.

The tech looked up at Grey.

"It's okay," she said. "He's with me."

"The jawbone too," Holmes said impatiently. He took a pair of rubber gloves from his pocket and slipped them on.

The tech picked up the bony curve and held it up in one hand, while balancing the rounded skull in the other. Holmes squatted at the edge of the hole and pulled out his magnifying glass. He examined the arc of the jawbone and the lower edge of the upper jaw.

He looked around as other techs began turning the other skulls over, one by one. The techs looked at one another with puzzled expressions. All the jaws, including the one Holmes was holding, had one thing in common.

There was not a single tooth in any of them.

Holmes experienced what felt like an electric shock from head to toe. He was practically trembling with excitement. "This isn't a burial ground," he said from behind his mask. "It's a dumping ground. These people were all murdered."

Then he jumped down into the pit.

"Holmes! What the hell?" shouted Grey.

"He can't help himself," said Marple. "He has a passion for knowledge."

"Bones are kind of his thing," added Poe.

CHAPTER 28

IT WAS MIDNIGHT. Marple was back in her apartment, still blowing her nose. It had taken her two hot showers to get the taint of the subway tomb off her body. The scent still lingered in her nostrils, though. She couldn't get rid of it—or the vision of all those bones in the dirt.

As always, Marple had been dazzled by Brendan's on-site analysis. Even before the medical examiner showed up, he had identified the skeletons as a mix of male and female, all adults aged between twenty and thirty years old. No children or infants. No seniors. None of the craniums, vertebrae, or limbs showed any pre-mortem trauma. No bullet holes, fractures, or stab marks. Just neat separations made by sharp surgical blades, turning long bones into short ones.

According to Holmes, it appeared that dental pliers had been used to neatly remove the teeth, roots and all, leaving the sockets intact.

Somewhere at this very hour, Marple was certain, forensic scientists were attempting to date the bones and trying to extract DNA from the marrow. From what Holmes said at the scene, the bones definitely weren't ancient. In fact, some were quite fresh. The thought gave Marple a chill. The skeleton tunnel was less than two miles away. Whoever buried them could be still walking around, maybe even in this neighborhood.

As she settled into bed, Marple decided to distract herself in the best way she knew how: with another murder.

She set a black cardboard storage box on top of her quilted bedcover and pulled out a black-and-white photograph of a pretty, dark-haired girl standing with two coworkers in front of the bakery window.

Since the day she and her partners purchased this building, Marple had been collecting every scrap of information she could find about the young woman killed just one floor below.

Her name was Mary McShane, a nineteen-year-old Irish immigrant. From a passenger ship manifest, Marple determined that Mary had traveled across the Atlantic alone three years earlier, at age sixteen, without parents or relatives. She'd found work in the bakery, prepping supplies and staying overnight to make sure the ovens were at the right temperature when the bakers arrived for work at 3 a.m.

Mary's name did not appear on the bakery payroll records, which told Marple that she was probably paid off the books, in cash and food. And maybe given a free room above the bakery.

Maybe, Marple realized, the same room where she was sitting right now.

Then, in 1954, sometime between 8 p.m. on June 10 and 3 a.m. on June 11, Mary McShane's throat was neatly slit, and she was left to bleed out on the floor in front of the massive ovens. That's where she was found by the first baker to arrive for work in the morning. Both he and the owner had been cleared, and no other suspects had ever surfaced.

Marple knew that if the girl had been working as a nanny or housemaid in an Upper East Side mansion, the investigation might have been more thorough. But down here, in the steaming stew of postwar immigrants, Mary had been just another statistic. Nobody had even claimed her body.

The Mary McShane case couldn't possibly be any colder. And that was what drew Marple in. She was going to solve it. All by herself.

Marple adjusted her bedside lamp and sifted through the yellowed papers, looking for anything she might have missed. Mary had become real to her. As real as a daughter. And she wanted to bring her justice.

As she pulled another news clipping from the pile, she froze.

A noise. A soft thumping sound.

It was coming from the darkest corner of the room.

CHAPTER 29

IN HIS APARTMENT on the other side of a five-inch-thick wall, Holmes pushed aside a row of freshly pressed suits to expose a small safe set into his closet wall. He tapped in the combination. The spring-loaded door popped open. As Holmes reached in, he heard a high-pitched scream through the wall.

Marple!

Heart pounding, Holmes slammed the safe shut and ran out through his living room, then into the hallway. He saw Poe emerging from his apartment down the hall with his .45. They reached Marple's door at the same time. Holmes took a position to the right, Poe to the left.

"Margaret?" Holmes shouted.

Silence from inside. Then another scream. Louder.

Poe nodded at Holmes. "Do it!"

Holmes rammed the door open with his shoulder. Poe spun past him into Marple's apartment and crouched in shooting position. He swept the living room with the barrel as Holmes headed for the bedroom. The door was open. He stepped in and felt Poe at his back. They both froze at the entrance.

Margaret was crouched on the windowsill, clutching a knitting needle like a dagger. A pot of flowers had been knocked over, and a large black storage box was upside down on the floor, its contents spilled onto the carpet.

"Margaret!" shouted Holmes. "What is it? What happened?"

Margaret pointed to the dark space behind the door.

"It was there!" she said, her voice trembling. "It was right there!"

"*What* was?" asked Poe, swinging the .45 toward the corner.

Marple's face reddened. She looked terrified and embarrassed at the same time.

"A mouse."

Poe holstered his weapon and looked behind the door. "Gone now," he said. "Back to his hole."

As Marple sat shaking on the windowsill, Holmes slid up next to her.

"I'm sorry," she said. "Rodents simply undo me."

Holmes wrapped his long arm around Marple's shoulder. "Not to worry, Margaret," he said. "We all have our weaknesses."

CHAPTER 30

THE NEXT MORNING, Margaret was still shaking it off.

Walking down Thompson Street near the Charles family's apartment, she felt chagrined by her scare. She hated showing fragility of any kind in front of her partners. Fear, Marple believed firmly, was incomplete knowledge. But she didn't care to know anything more about mice. Unless it was how to exterminate them.

As she passed Addilyn's building, she tried to blot out the incident and focus on the task at hand, which was finding Zozi Turner and Eton Charles alive.

She had already scanned through the surveillance footage from the building garage and exterior for the day of the kidnapping. Time-stamped video from three days earlier showed Eton's Lexus heading uptown as usual at 8 a.m. and returning at 6 p.m. Zozi left for school in her sporty Miata at 7:30 a.m. and returned at 4:30 p.m. the same day. Neither car had moved since.

The video showed the comings and goings of other residents and delivery people but nothing suspicious. Marple hadn't spotted anybody surveilling the building, and according to Addilyn, nobody but the family and the dog had entered the apartment that day.

It was time for canvassing. It was a task most cops and detectives hated. So did Holmes and Poe. Canvassing was a low percentage game and a notorious time suck. Marple loved it. In fact, she got up early for it.

As she walked down Thompson Street, she had a gallery of new photos on her phone—a few of Eton Charles, swiped from Poe's presentation, and a few of Zozi Turner, lifted from her Instagram page. A lot of those photos included Toby.

Her first stop was a small bodega, kitty-corner from the Charleses' apartment building. The entrance was covered in thick strips of clear plastic and the interior smelled of ripe fruit and fresh coffee. An air conditioner dripped rusty water onto the tile floor in the corner. A few customers wandered through the narrow aisles. Two senior citizens huddled near the coffee machine. Marple headed straight for the front counter, where the owner was stocking cigarettes.

Marple had found the proprietor's name in the city licensing records. She knew that Balam Ahn was fifty-five years old, widowed, with two grown children, and that she'd purchased the bodega from her uncle eighteen years ago, the year Zozi was born.

"Mrs. Ahn?" Marple asked as she stepped up to the counter. She knew better than to use the proprietor's first name. To a native-born Korean, that would've been unforgivably rude, especially coming from somebody younger. Marple prided herself on her cultural etiquette. She considered it a dying art.

The tiny, black-haired woman placed the last pack of Salems into the slot behind the register and turned around. Her face was lined and friendly.

"You want coffee?" she asked.

"Do you have tea?" asked Marple. "Chamomile?"

Mrs. Ahn nodded.

"Lovely," said Marple. "Thank you."

The tea came with the tag hanging out of a lidded to-go cup.

Marple put a five-dollar bill on the worn counter, and Mrs. Ahn handed her the change.

"Can I ask you a question?" said Marple.

The proprietor rested her arms on the counter.

Marple pulled out her phone and swiped to a picture of Eton Charles. "Does this man look familiar?"

Mrs. Ahn took the phone in her hands and studied the screen carefully.

"Sorry, no," she said. She paused and held the phone out at a distance. "Wait. Maybe." She handed the phone back. "You cop?"

"Family friend," said Marple. She swiped to a picture of Zozi. "What about her?" Mrs. Ahn didn't even have to look twice.

"Zozi!" she said cheerfully. Her smile exposed a missing incisor. "Every day she come here. Nice girl."

It took only a few more exchanges for Marple to learn that Zozi had been a regular at the bodega since she was old enough to cross the street on her own. She liked Snickers, Ben & Jerry's, Diet Coke, and, more recently, Red Bull. Never tried to scam cigarettes or beer. Never shoplifted. Mrs. Ahn had seen Zozi after school on the day before she disappeared. About 5 p.m. She was sure of it.

"Anybody with her?"

"Just the dog. Toby," said Mrs. Ahn. "Always waits outside." She pointed to a handwritten sign over the counter. It read NO PETS PLEASE!

"Do you have a security camera?" Marple asked. Maybe there'd been somebody else in the bodega, or somebody waiting on the sidewalk.

Mrs. Ahn pointed to her eyes and opened them wide. "No camera. Just these. And good memory."

"What did Zozi buy when she was here last time?" asked Marple.

Mrs. Ahn gave it some thought. "Diet Coke. Fruit bars. And cold boxes."

"Cold boxes?" asked Marple. "You mean juice boxes?"

Mrs. Ahn turned and pointed at a row of cheap vinyl coolers on a high shelf over the cigarette slots. "Cold boxes," she said. "Like for picnic. Two of them."

Marple's phone vibrated in her pocket. She pulled it out and saw the caller's name on the screen. She pressed Accept.

"Addilyn?" she said. "What's going—?"

"I just got the call!" Addilyn wailed.

"*What* call?" asked Marple, heading out onto the sidewalk.

"The kidnappers! How soon can you come?"

"Hang on, Addilyn. I'm already here."

CHAPTER 31

MARPLE RACED ACROSS the street, waving cars aside. She shot past the building doorman into the lobby and jumped into an open elevator just as the door was closing. Thirty seconds later, she was standing in Addilyn's living room.

Addilyn was frantic. Her hair and makeup were already done to perfection, but under the eye shadow, her eyes were red.

"Who called?" Marple asked, perspiring slightly from her dash. "Male? Female?"

"Female," said Addilyn, dabbing at her nose with a tissue.

"Any accent?"

"Hard to tell," said Addilyn. "But I think ... American."

"Okay," said Marple. "Now tell me exactly what she said. Her precise words, if you can."

Addilyn wiped her nose delicately and sniffed. "Can I just play it for you?"

Marple stepped forward. "Play it ... ? You mean you *recorded* it?"

"Yes. It's right over here." Addilyn walked to an elegant desk in an alcove just off the living room. Sitting at the edge was a cordless phone in its base. A small Olympus voice recorder was attached to the handset with a short black cable.

"My husband used it to record business calls," said Addilyn. "I haven't played it back. I didn't want to erase it by mistake. I'm not even sure I pressed the right button."

"Fingers crossed," said Marple. She pulled the jack out of the recorder and checked the tiny screen. It indicated a full battery and a single recording. Marple pressed the silver button in the center of the device. There was a crackle of static from the tiny speaker, and then:

"Hello?"

"Who's this?"

"This is Addilyn Charles. Who is this?"

There was a brief pause and then—

"I'm the one you need to talk to. We have your husband and your daughter and your dog."

Marple leaned in. The voice did sound female, but it had been passed through a voice-changer app. Impossible to know for sure.

Next on the playback was a loud gasp from Addilyn. After a couple of seconds, her voice returned, shaky but clear.

"Are they alive? Is my daughter alive? Is my husband alive?"

"For the moment, yes."

"Can I talk to them? I need to talk to them!"

"No."

"What do you want?"

"We want five million dollars."

"What?"

"I'll speak more slowly. Five. Million. Dollars. For your husband and your daughter's safe return."

"Dear God . . ."

"One more thing. About the detective."

"Detective? What detective? I haven't called the police. I promise you!"

"The detective. The lady. The one with the English accent. Tell her to back off or everybody dies. Badly."

Then the line went dead.

CHAPTER 32

AT 11:44 THAT night, Holmes arrived at the designated location. His contact had been very specific about the timing. After the Uber drove off, he was the only one left in the vast parking lot in Bayonne, New Jersey. In front of him sat a massive warehouse, weather-beaten and rusted, like dozens of others on the huge lot.

For a few seconds, Holmes wondered if he was in the right place. He looked up. A faded unlit sign near the edge of the roof said J.E.H. ENTERPRISES. Holmes smiled. The joke cinched it. He imagined that, somewhere, J. Edgar Hoover was smiling too.

At 11:45 exactly, a truck-sized cargo door on the front of the warehouse began to open. Holmes expected it to creak and groan as it moved along its track. Instead, it glided smoothly to the side with a gentle hum.

Holmes walked through the entrance into a space half the size of a soccer field, lit only by yellow security lamps. Row after row of metal storage racks ran down the entire length of the building, almost disappearing into the gloom. The huge door closed behind him with a gentle thud.

"That you, Mr. Holmes?" A voice echoed from the shadows somewhere above.

"Who's asking?" Holmes called back.

There was a loud bang, and suddenly long light banks on the ceiling popped on, bathing the space in bright fluorescent light. Holmes heard a metallic whine overhead. He looked up. A man in blue was descending from a scaffold in a bucket at the end of a huge mechanical lift. As the bucket touched the concrete floor, the man unhooked his safety belt and stepped out.

"Forgive the deus ex machina," he said. "I love to make an entrance." He extended his hand. "I'm Essen Blythe."

"Brendan Holmes. Thanks for meeting with me."

"No problem. I understand you need some artistic insight."

In his baggy coveralls, Blythe looked like a neighborhood mechanic or gym coach. But Holmes knew better. Essen Blythe, he'd been assured, was one of the world's foremost authorities on art—more specifically, art *theft*—and a highly decorated special agent in one of the FBI's most clandestine operations. If anybody could help find the culprit responsible for the Bain heist, this was the guy.

"Hop on," said Blythe.

Holmes looked to the side and saw a small electric vehicle—like a golf cart, only sleeker. He took the seat on the passenger side while Blythe took the wheel. There was a click and a hum as the shuttlecraft started moving down the aisle.

Rising high on both sides, the industrial shelves were filled with large wooden crates, some as compact as briefcases, others as big as highway billboards. Holmes felt his olfactory bulbs coming alive. Above the stale scents of concrete and factory dust, he could pick out dozens of odors—turpentine, hydrocerussite, plumbonacrite, and other components of aging paint. The smell of fine art.

"What's all this?" he asked.

"War orphans," said Blythe.

"Pardon?"

"Everything in that section was reclaimed from the Third Reich," said Blythe. "Hundreds of thousands of pieces were stolen. Hard to establish provenance after all these years, but we do our best to get the art back home."

As the cart neared the end of the aisle, Blythe rolled to a stop facing a metal wall. Holmes assumed it was the inner side of the building's exterior. Blythe pulled a small device from his pocket and clicked a button. The wall separated in the center, leaving a space just wide enough for the cart to pass through. As the vehicle bumped over the threshold into another huge space, Holmes looked up, stunned.

He wasn't in a New Jersey warehouse anymore.

He was in the Sistine Chapel.

CHAPTER 33

"MY GOD! *INCREDIBLE!*"

Holmes was awestruck. The space was a perfect replica of Vatican City's architectural masterpiece. Patterned marble floor. Arched windows. Overhead was the famous vaulted ceiling with its iconic frescoes, replicated down to the last figure.

One section featured *The Trials of Moses* and *Descent from Mount Sinai*. Another, *Baptism of Christ* and *The Last Supper*. And those were just the appetizers. In the center, God the Father reached out, finger extended across the sky. As Blythe stopped the cart, Holmes squinted. One detail in the fresco was off. Instead of reaching to touch the hand of Adam with his index finger, God the Almighty was dangling a neon-colored yo-yo.

"Sacrilege, I know," said Blythe, following Holmes's gaze. "Sometimes the team likes to cut loose."

It was only then that Holmes realized the room was filled with men and women—dozens of them—silently at work on tabletops and easels spread out across the vast space. Some looked like fine artists, wearing smocks and holding traditional palettes and brushes. Others, in T-shirts and shorts, looked more like Silicon

Valley coders. But what they were producing was unbelievable. And they were doing it right in front of his eyes.

"You're looking at the finest art forgers in the world," said Blythe. "Some kinesthetic savants. Several on the spectrum. A sprinkling of ex-cons. They all work for me."

The two men stepped from the cart, and Holmes looked up again at the impeccable replica of the chapel ceiling. "These people did *that*?"

Blythe nodded. "Good practice. I find that once you can fake Michelangelo, you can fake pretty much anything."

He led Holmes to a large easel near the center of the room. A young woman with a pink-streaked ponytail chewed gum furiously as she applied yellow highlights to a faux Monet pondscape, using quick, flicking strokes of her brush.

"That work would pass anywhere," said Holmes. The woman didn't respond, didn't even react. Just kept working.

"Close enough for our purposes, at least," said Blythe. "Most of the buyers we need to deceive are drug lords or arms dealers. They use art purchases to launder their money. We bait the hook. El Chapo had quite an extensive collection, you know." He paused for a satisfied grin. "All ours."

As they walked, Holmes did a slow 360, taking it all in. Along one wall, a huge press was pumping out vivid Warhol prints. Other workers were busy creating replicas of Picassos, Pollocks, and Van Goghs. It was like an adult-ed art class where every student was a master.

"Let's talk," said Blythe, heading toward a metal staircase. Holmes followed him up to a loft office that looked out on a fresco of Michelangelo cherubs. Even this close, it was hard to believe they'd been painted in the twenty-first century, not the fifteenth.

Blythe slumped down on one end of a worn leather sofa. Holmes took a seat across from him on an upholstered chair. The cork-lined wall was covered in color swatches, paint formulas, and clips of all kinds of artwork, from Renaissance tapestries to Bob Ross landscapes.

"I've had my experts look into your case," said Blythe. "The disappearance of the Bible and the Shakespeare."

"And . . . ?" asked Holmes, leaning forward.

"They all tell me it's impossible."

"So I've heard," said Holmes. "But it did happen. My question is, where did the pieces go? Who wanted them? What's the market?"

"Fine art is still a mysterious world, Mr. Holmes. The basic rules haven't changed much since the Middle Ages. Buyers often don't know where a piece comes from, and sellers aren't always sure where it will end up. Sales and profits are hard to trace. It's not like buying a share of Home Depot. A lot of people aren't willing to ask probing questions. In a way, they *like* the shadows. The shadows are part of the mystique."

"And a license to steal," said Holmes.

"A time-honored tradition, I'm afraid," said Blythe. "And the people in pearls and tuxedos are often the most accomplished thieves of all."

"Huntley Bain, for example?"

Blythe shook his head. "You can cross him off your list. Bain is a devious businessman but not nearly skilled enough to cover his tracks on something like this. If it was him, we'd know it. You're looking for a genius. Somebody with high-class larceny bred into his bones."

Blythe pulled a large binder from a table alongside the sofa and laid it open on a low table in front of Holmes. "Take a look," he said. The binder was filled with enlargements of photos taken at a Venetian-style mansion, alongside yellowed clippings from Boston newspapers.

"This is the Gardner Museum near Fenway Park in Boston."

"I've heard of it," said Holmes.

"It was robbed in 1990," said Blythe. "Thirteen works, valued at about five hundred million dollars. To this day, not a single piece has been recovered. You'd think that it would be impossible for that much art to simply disappear into the ether, but it did—along with the thieves."

Holmes detected a slight flicker in Blythe's eyelids. A tell.

"But you know who was behind it," said Holmes.

Blythe offered a small, appreciative smile. "I have a pretty good idea. But he's dead. Murdered by associates. Died for his art, you might say."

"Unfortunate," said Holmes. "I would love to have consulted with him."

Blythe closed the binder. "His death wasn't the end of it. The man in question had a relationship with a married Boston art curator. Ten years before the Gardner job, they had a son. The relationship was a well-kept secret, but the son is very much alive, and active in the family trade."

Blythe pulled a folder from the table and opened it. Inside was a surveillance photo of an elegant-looking man leaning against a wall near a European street. A stamp on the margin of the photo read "Amsterdam / 10.4.2019." The man was slim, handsome, early forties. He wore a stylish, tightly fitted shirt, collar open.

"This is Luka Franke," said Blythe. "Or so he calls himself at the moment. Don't bother looking for a criminal record, because he doesn't have one. Never been caught. For a theft that was impossible to pull off, he could be the man you're after."

Holmes picked up the photo and studied it carefully, staring into the eyes of the stranger in the image. He felt a twinge of excitement. And maybe a touch of kinship. He was always intrigued by people who worked in the margins.

CHAPTER 34

THE NEXT MORNING, Auguste Poe paid a completely unauthorized visit to the New York City morgue, with Helene Grey as his accomplice.

"Five minutes," said Detective Grey. "And do not touch *anything*— or I swear I'll put *you* on one of those slabs."

Fortunately for Poe, Grey knew the medical examiner on duty. And right now, according to Grey, the ME was on the fourth floor in a weekly status meeting.

The detective, of course, had a free pass to look at dead bodies, but visitors were not welcome, unless they were there to ID a decedent. Poe understood that he was trespassing on city property. For him, that only heightened the experience. He'd always felt most alive in places where he didn't belong.

Grey led the way through the tiled entry corridor to a large room filled with stainless-steel tables, where the subway skeletons lay like partially reassembled puzzles. And Poe loved puzzles—the harder, the better.

He leaned over to peek at the edges of one of the large bones. "Holmes was right about the saw marks."

Grey nodded. "Every single one, butchered the same way. Transverse cuts midway along the humerus and femur. Same with the smaller leg and arm bones."

"Some hand cut, some by a power blade..." said Poe, almost to himself.

He moved to another table, looking closely at one of the skulls and its accompanying jawbone. He fought the urge to pick up the specimens and turn them over in his hands.

"The teeth were removed first," he said. "Then the flesh and hair were stripped off with some kind of acid," he said. "Probably hydrochloric or nitric. Soon after death."

"Okay," said Grey. "So why not just dissolve the bones too?"

"That would take a stronger acid, like sulfuric," said Poe. "The stench would be tremendous. You'd need an isolated spot or a hermetically sealed lab. It would take *weeks* to do a thorough job. Whoever did this was just being efficient. Pull the teeth. Cut up the corpse. Get rid of the soft bits. Bury the bones."

"What the hell are you doing in here?" said a short Black woman with a commanding presence and a booming voice with a marked Mississippi accent. Poe glanced at Grey. It was Medical Examiner Verna Crown. The status meeting had apparently ended early.

Crown was dressed in black slacks and a bright pink blouse. A city ID tag dangled from her belt.

She pointed at Poe. "Who's he?"

"Sorry, Verna," said Grey. "He's with me."

Poe extended his hand. "Auguste Poe, private investigator."

"You don't want to shake my hand right now," said Crown. She wiggled her fingers, which glistened with a viscous liquid. "I got maple syrup all over me."

She walked to a deep stainless-steel sink at the side of the room and pressed the water lever on the floor. She pumped soap from a huge dispenser and ran her fingers under the stream. "Your name's

Poe?" she asked, turning her head toward him as she washed. "Is that for real?"

"I can show you my driver's license."

Crown turned off the water and shook her hands over the sink. "Didn't Edgar Allan Poe write a book about a morgue . . . ?"

" 'The Murders in the Rue Morgue,' " said Poe. "Short story. But there's no morgue involved. Rue Morgue is the name of a street in Paris."

"No shit. A real one?"

"Actually, no. He made it up."

Crown held her hands under an industrial air dryer and shouted over the roar. "So who's the perp, Mr. Poe? Who's the murderer in the Rue Morgue?"

Poe waited for the dryer racket to stop. He cleared his throat. "An orangutan did it."

Crown shot him a look. "You messing with me?"

Poe shrugged. "I didn't write it."

"You mean one of those big hairy orange monkeys?"

"Technically, an ape."

Crown pulled on a blue paper gown and a pair of purple surgical gloves. "So *technically,* Mr. Poe . . . what are you doing in my place of business?"

"He was at the burial site," said Grey. "He's helping out with the case."

"Okay, then," said Crown. "That's fine." She raised her eyebrows at Grey. "You need all the damn help you can get."

"Have you figured out how old they are?" asked Poe. "The bones, I mean. How long ago were the victims killed?"

"Well now, Mr. Poe, that's a very perceptive question," said Crown, walking to one of the tables. "Because we've got ourselves a real chronological variety here." She picked up one of the skulls. "This woman met her end, I'd say, about sixty years ago."

She turned to another table and picked up a second skull. "This fellow, he's only been gone a few months." She held out the skulls as if she were getting ready to juggle. "You know what that means?"

"We're not talking about a single killer," said Poe. "We're talking generations."

Crown glanced at Grey. "Sharp assistant you've got here." She nudged the detective in the shoulder. "Not a bad looker either."

Grey ignored the hint. "Let me know if you get any DNA matches," she said.

"Will do, Detective," said Crown with a mischievous smile.

Poe felt Grey starting to push him toward the door as Crown's voice echoed against the tile walls. "What's the story, Helene? You guys a couple? 'Cause you could *definitely* use some help in *that* department!"

As Grey hustled him down the corridor, Poe could hear the ME calling from the doorway.

"Come back anytime, Mr. Poe! Read me a bedtime story!"

CHAPTER 35

AT NOON, HOLMES and his partners were nearing the top floor of the Bain Building in Hudson Yards, one of a cluster of spectacular structures on Manhattan's West Side. The glass-fronted elevator faced the Jersey side, with a stunning view across the Hudson River.

From this height, thought Holmes, even Hoboken looked picturesque. He knew there were urgent tasks waiting on the subway murders and the Charles abduction, but this was a command performance, and Huntley Bain had demanded the entire team.

Holmes had filled Poe and Marple in on his late-night meeting with the FBI art maven, and now they were on their way to give Bain an update on the case.

Thanks to Blythe, they had a new person of interest in the art theft. The mysterious Luka Franke. But Holmes had no intention of revealing that fact to Bain. He enjoyed watching him twist. Besides, Holmes suspected the businessman had set this morning's meeting at his office as just another way to impress them with his money and style.

"Good Lord," Marple said softly as they stepped out of the elevator into the executive-level lobby. Holmes could see her eyes widen at the sight of the lush flora that decorated the space. Fresh lilies and orchids in elegant glass pitchers. Huge vases of colorful mums. And, more to the point, a row of potted money trees.

"Bubinga!" Poe said in a low voice.

Holmes and Marple turned.

"The paneling," said Poe. "Bubinga wood. From Western Africa. Obscenely expensive. Endangered and highly restricted."

For a few seconds, all three stood like kids in a museum, running their hands over the smooth, beautifully whorled surface.

"All ethically harvested, of course," Huntley Bain claimed as he appeared around the side of the tall partition and slapped one of the thick vertical panels. "If you care about that tree-hugger shit." He turned to the impeccably groomed young man behind the lobby desk. "I'll be with these three in my office, David. No interruptions."

The young man nodded. "Of course, Mr. Bain."

Holmes followed his partners into the executive's sanctum, which carried through on the spare, elegant design of the lobby. No desk. Just a long glass table cantilevered from a side wall so it seemed to hover in space. The view from the floor-to-ceiling windows covered almost the whole length of the Hudson. The décor was sparse. A few terra cotta figurines on the table. A large fluted vase on a pedestal. Nothing on the walls.

Bain planted himself in the center of the room, arms folded high across his chest, Mussolini style.

"So . . ." he said. "What've you got?"

"Well, Mr. Bain," said Holmes, "you'll be relieved to know that we no longer consider you a suspect."

Bain's expression darkened. "That's it? Your update is that I'm not going to jail for stealing my own stuff? How about finding out how some creep got past the most expensive security system this side of the Louvre!"

"We've spoken to experts," Marple said.

"I thought *you* were the experts," said Bain.

"Think of us as *conduits* to expertise," said Holmes. He knew the circumlocution would drive Bain nuts. Which was his main reason for using it.

"One call to City Hall," Bain said coldly, "and you'll all be looking for other employment."

Poe looked at Marple with a wry expression. "Maybe we could get jobs in the mayor's office."

"He *is* short an assistant," Marple said with a mischievous twinkle.

"How's your typing?" asked Poe.

"Abominable," said Marple.

"Mine too."

Holmes kept his eyes on Bain. He sensed that the banter was pushing him close to his limit but decided to taunt him just a bit more. "Progress is often painfully slow on these matters," he said. "Nothing substantive to report at the moment."

That did it. Bain exploded.

"All right, dammit! I've had enough of this clown show! I should *fire* you phony overpriced asswipes!"

Holmes smiled serenely. "We completely agree. Unless you don't care about actually getting your books back."

"Also," said Marple, "as we emphasized in our first meeting, we have an airtight no-refund policy."

Bain backed toward the pedestal. "That's it. Get the hell *out!*" As he jerked his arm abruptly toward the door, his wrist brushed the lip of the tall vase. The vase rocked precariously, then fell to the floor, shattering with a loud crash. There was a brief moment of silence, before Bain's enraged shout. "*Good Christ!* Do you know what that thing is *worth*?"

"*Was* worth," Poe said solemnly.

Holmes bent down and picked up a small ceramic shard. He turned it over carefully in his hand, then held it up to the light.

"Chinese," he said. "Fourteenth century. I'd say about half a million. Assuming it wasn't a fake, of course."

"Of course it's not a fake, you moron!" shouted Bain. "I brought it back from Beijing myself."

"In that case," said Holmes, "you should really be more careful with your things."

Bain stiffened, red-faced and speechless, clenching and unclenching his hands.

"We'll let ourselves out," said Marple.

As the investigators walked briskly past the reception area, an angry cry came from the office. *"Fuuuuuuckk!"* Holmes turned to the young man behind the desk.

"Pardon me, David. I believe Mr. Bain needs a broom."

CHAPTER 36

ACROSS THE BROOKLYN BRIDGE and into Bushwick, Poe was taking his Torino Talladega out for the first time in months. In some ways, he liked it even better than the GTO. It rode smoother, and the fastback gave it a sleek, aerodynamic look. He knew that most collectors wouldn't think of taking a car this precious out on a city street, but Poe enjoyed the admiring stares.

He had hand-washed the Ford the previous evening and buffed it to a high-gloss shine. It practically glowed as he pulled into a space in front of the Wycoff Animal Shelter—a one-story building with a worn redbrick facade and a big SPCA logo near the entrance.

Poe stepped out of the car and walked the few steps to the front door. A small electronic chime announced his arrival. Not necessary. Poe had seen the young female attendant looking out the window when he parked.

"Nice whip," she said as he walked in. "Sixty-nine?"

"Dead on," said Poe. *Impressive.* The only vehicles most kids recognized were the drift cars from the *Fast & Furious* movies.

The attendant sat on a high stool behind the worn laminated

counter. She was in her early twenties, Poe estimated, with neon-streaked hair and a small silver ring through her right nostril. A colorful snake tattoo emerged from under the right sleeve of her T-shirt and wound its way down to her wrist.

The air smelled of disinfectant. From behind a pair of metal doors at the far end of the space, Poe could hear muffled yips, mews, and howls.

The young woman hopped off her stool. "Looking to adopt today?"

"I need a cat," said Poe. "A good mouser." Marple needed protection, and he was determined to provide it.

"Follow me," said the attendant, tapping her name tag. "I'm Virginia."

"Auguste," said Poe. "My pleasure."

Virginia walked out from the far end of the counter, then placed her hip against one of the doors and bumped it open. "Come meet my buddies."

Poe slid past her into the back room, raw space with cinder-block walls and a concrete floor. Rows of cages lined a wide center aisle with a rusted drainage grate in the middle. The smell of disinfectant competed with the odors of sawdust, wet paper, and fresh animal excrement. Poe was glad he hadn't brought Holmes along. This was no place for a super-smeller.

The basic housing arrangement was simple: dogs on the left, cats on the right. "Take your pick," said Virginia. She was backing down the aisle like a tour guide, pointing at a row of small, elevated cages. In each cage was a scruffy cat or kitten. Some were pawing at the thin metal bars. Others were busy gnawing at tattered toys. One kitten was missing an eye. Another had only three legs.

Poe ran his fingers lightly across the enclosures. Some of the tenants looked up. Others couldn't be bothered.

"I need a hunter," said Poe. "Killer instinct."

Virginia stopped in her tracks. Her eyes narrowed and a knowing expression crossed her face. Her voice lowered to a confidential whisper. She crooked her finger. "Come with me."

She led Poe around a corner to a row of larger cages. Most were empty, but Poe could make out a shadowy shape in the enclosure at the far end. As he got closer, the shape turned in his direction. Poe felt a small flutter in his belly. He stepped up to the wire mesh. The resident of the cage was a large midnight-black cat with bizarre yellow-orange eyes—knowing and slightly sinister.

Virginia placed one arm protectively over the enclosure. "Nobody wants her," she said softly. "She freaks people out." The cat emitted an eerie screech that settled into a strangely ominous purr.

"What's her story?" asked Poe.

"Abandoned," said Virginia. "They found her in a basement apartment when the building was getting demolished. She was starving and dehydrated. Almost gone."

Virginia stuck two fingers through the bars. The cat rubbed its head against her knuckles. "I brought her back to life."

Poe stared at the cat. "Even in the grave, all is not lost," he said.

Virginia raised her eyebrows. "'The Pit and the Pendulum'! Great story."

Poe stepped forward and leaned down toward the cage. The cat shifted her attention to him, looking straight through him with those strange eyes. Now Poe felt like the one being appraised.

"She's been here for a month," said Virginia, her tone turning slightly mournful. "If nobody takes her by tomorrow, they'll put her down."

Poe smiled. He knew a good sales pitch when he heard one. But no matter. He was sold already.

And not just on the cat.

"Virginia," he asked, "would you ever consider office work?"

CHAPTER 37

IT WAS NEARLY midnight. Walking alone down the city street, Brendan Holmes could feel his heart pounding under his suit. His senses were on high alert, and the hedonic hot spots in his brain were tingling in anticipation of a very guilty pleasure.

As he walked past closed noodle joints and dim sum restaurants in Manhattan's Chinatown, garish neon signs reflected off the wet pavement. A late-night rain had dampened some of the odors, but others still cut through. Food, vehicle exhaust, perfume, beer.

As Holmes made his way down Mott Street, he passed groups of teenagers leaning against the storefronts, laughing and smoking. A young couple kissed in a darkened doorway.

The door Holmes was looking for was down a short alley lined with trash bins. He breathed through his mouth to minimize the sickening fumes of shrimp and chicken decomposing in plastic bags.

He pressed the bell in the required pattern: one long ring, two short. A lock clicked. The door opened. The smells of human sweat and cooking oil seeped out, along with the sound of hip-hop music from a tinny speaker.

Holmes could only see enough of the kid in the doorway to

recognize the familiar twisted lip. No need for words. He focused on the slender extended hand, the open palm, the tightly wrapped product. Holmes took the packet and replaced it with a wad of neatly folded bills. The door closed again. The lock clicked back into place.

Holmes walked to the end of the alley and carefully opened his prize on top of a discarded plastic play table. He felt like a kid unwrapping a Happy Meal.

In his coat pocket, he carried his personally designed reagent kit, capable of testing the purity of the product within a percentage point. But he didn't feel the need. His source, one of the few to evade the tentacles of the South American cartels, could be counted on. In this challenging business climate, repeat business was everything, and Holmes was an excellent customer. He had faith that his purchase was about as clean as a regularly fatal street substance could be.

Holmes felt the familiar thrill as he tapped a tiny hill of powder into the hollow between his curled thumb and forefinger. His heart thudded even harder. His pupils dilated. All his fight-or-flight responses were activated and firing. In some ways, this was his favorite moment. The anticipation of the rush. The delicious danger of being discovered. And the intensely heightened awareness of his multiple personas.

Business partner. Crime fighter. Drug fiend.

CHAPTER 38

HOLMES KNEW IT would take about five minutes for the high to set in—just time enough for him to reach the Canal Street subway station and head back to Bushwick. Holmes savored the interval between intake and onset. A delicious bit of delayed gratification. Over the years, he had calibrated the exact amount to inhale in order to produce the desired effect within the desired interval.

As the heroin molecules attached to his opioid receptors, he took on the groggy look of a sleepwalker. With his olfactory senses altered, he saw and smelled the city in a whole new way. He understood the risk of damaging his nasal passages—and threatening his hyperosmia—but also took pleasure in dulling his occasionally overwhelming sensitivity. His natural fastidiousness faded and he reveled in the grit of the streets. The bold colors of the store signs, the distant wail of sirens—it all felt magical.

As Holmes descended the subway steps into the thick air of the underground station, he heard the rumble of the approaching J train. He heard it as thunder, then as pounding hooves, then as a hurricane. He *loved* it. As the train slowed, he walked alongside and positioned himself directly in front of a door.

He stepped inside. He could smell the bleach from the previous night's cleaning, but it registered as pleasantly floral. He grabbed a support pole as the train lurched forward and rolled toward Brooklyn. The racket of the wheels on the rails felt soothing, and he was delighted by the passing mosaic of the tunnel walls—blurred but beautiful.

His fellow travelers included a woman slouched in a seat across from him, turban askew, purse gripped tightly in her lap. At the other end of the car, a young man with a shaved head rocked to the beat in his earbuds. Behind the bleach, Holmes picked up the acidic overtones of stale vomit, but it washed over him like a gentle wave. A delightful experience, the New York subway system, he thought—if you're in the right state of mind.

Holmes exited the train at the Gates Avenue stop. He was alone in the station. By the time he reached the top of the staircase to the street, he felt inexplicably winded. Suddenly, his legs felt wobbly. He staggered over to a building and leaned against the front wall. This never happened. Had he miscalculated the dose? Had the product been laced? His mouth felt dry. His tongue felt thick. He stared at a beer sign in a bar window, trying to focus. The colors spun like a kaleidoscope, then faded to black. Holmes felt himself starting to drop, and then...nothing.

He was in an alley when he came to. That much he knew. His head was pounding with pain. He was propped against a wall, as if somebody had placed him there, like an abandoned doll. There was a small streak of dried saliva on his jacket collar.

As his senses returned, he anxiously patted his pockets, then tipped his head back and let out a loud, angry grunt. His pockets were empty. His stash was gone. Also his cash, his keys, his penknife, and his testing kit. He was relieved that he'd left his cell phone, wallet, and ID at home. Otherwise, somebody, right now, might be in the process of stealing his identity.

He stroked his face and checked his fingers. No blood. He gently palpated his aching skull, feeling for lumps or lacerations. Nothing. Whoever had rolled him had not knocked him out. Holmes had taken care of that all by himself.

As his olfactory bulbs fired up, he could smell liquor and mayonnaise from a glass recycling bin. And, much closer, the smell of dried urine. He looked down, startled—then disgusted. A dark stain ran from his crotch to his knees. The urine odor was all his.

CHAPTER 39

AUGUSTE POE'S BEDROOM glowed with exactly one hundred candles. He was slightly out of breath from hurrying to set up and light them all while she was taking her shower. The amazing woman in his life. He wanted her to be surprised and excited—as excited as he was about her. She was the one. He was sure of it.

He heard the shower tap turn off. The bathroom door opened. For a moment, she was silhouetted by the bathroom light, her slender figure outlined beneath the negligee.

"Wow," she said, glancing around the room.

"Do you like it?" Poe asked, leaning up against a pillow.

"I love it," she said with a laugh. God, he adored that laugh. "I just hope the sprinklers don't go off."

She was kneeling on the sheets now, smelling like jasmine soap and smiling her incredible smile. "It's beautiful, Auguste," she said softly. "Just beautiful." She leaned over and kissed him, slow and deep. Her dark hair fell across his face. She pulled back slightly, stroking his forehead. "Everything's beautiful with you," she said.

He ran his fingers over her shoulders and teased the flowered straps of the negligee down her arms.

She gave him a playful frown. "Wait. Did I put this on just so that you could take it off?"

"So silly," said Poe. "Seems like a wasted step."

"I can always wear it for breakfast," she said, pulling it over her head with one graceful sweep. Her hair fell in damp curls around her pale shoulders. Her body glowed in the candlelight. Poe actually gasped at how beautiful she was. She leaned forward. Her bare breasts brushed his chest. Poe felt his heart beating faster. He couldn't believe how much he loved this woman, needed her, wanted her. Especially right now. He reached for her. Touched her tenderly.

"Not yet," she said. "Close your eyes."

He did.

The next thing he felt was a drip of hot wax on his bare chest. It stung, then instantly cooled. Another drip, this time on his belly. Then two more, on his abdomen. Incredibly arousing. He felt her pulling the sheets lower. She leaned forward, her lips brushing his ear. "Let me know if I'm hurting you," she whispered.

"You're not," Poe said softly. "You never could."

Poe gasped and woke up, clenching his pillow in both hands. He looked around the room slowly, bringing himself back to the present. Back to reality. Back to a world without her. Then the guilt flowed in again, dark and swirling.

If it weren't for him, he knew for a certainty, Annie would still be alive.

Poe sat still for almost a minute, just breathing. Then he leaned over the side of the bed and reached between the mattress and the box spring. He worked his fingers in and swept his hand back and forth—until he felt the familiar flask.

CHAPTER 40

AS HOLMES STUMBLED toward home, his body ached and his mind spun with guilt. If he'd spent the night huddling with his partners instead of indulging himself, none of this would have happened. This was the worst possible time for a clouded brain. And his brain was what he needed most. His logical, analytical brain. Sometimes, as Sir Arthur Conan Doyle had described it, the rest of his body felt like a mere appendix.

Poe had told him about his visit to the subway skeletons in the morgue. That case alone deserved his complete focus. And what about Eton Charles and Zozi Turner? Holmes imagined them sweating and praying in some dank basement, waiting desperately for ransom. He realized that he wasn't doing nearly enough on that investigation either. There were killers and kidnappers on the loose, and what was he doing? Chasing his own demons. He just couldn't help it. And he hated himself for it.

Holmes crossed the street in front of the office and walked to the main entrance. Security lights glowed from the first-floor interior. The second floor was dark. He walked up the two steps to the door and punched in the code on the small panel to the side.

He heard a discordant beep. Wrong digits. He tried again. Same result. *Dammit!* Had somebody changed the code without telling him?

Furious, Holmes reached for his cell phone, then remembered he didn't have it. He raised his fist to pound on the door, then stopped. He decided to turn his problem into a challenge—a way to test himself, mind and body. And to maybe punish himself a little too. A bit of penance for the night's misdeeds. Code or no code, he was getting in.

He rounded the corner to the side of the building facing the abandoned tattoo parlor. In spite of many calls to the city hotline, the ground was still littered with rotting crates and rusted equipment.

Holmes placed his foot on a sturdy emergency water connection sticking out from the side of his building. He stepped up and reached for the concrete sill of the first-floor window. Sturdy bars blocked the opening, and a lace of sensor wires ran across the pane. He needed to get to the second floor, where the windows were alarmed but not barred. There, he might have a chance.

Holmes placed the tip of his shoe into a small crevice above a course of bricks and pressed himself up, free-climbing onto the slender first-floor window ledge. He glanced to his right. A narrow black drainpipe, marked with scabs of rust, rose from the ground all the way to the roof of the building. Holmes tugged on it. The pipe was anchored too tightly to the wall to shimmy up, but there were thin metal brackets every few feet, good enough for toeholds.

After a few strained maneuvers, Holmes was spread out like an insect against the wall—one foot braced against a pipe bracket, another resting tentatively on the corner of a brick, both hands gripping the second-story windowsill. Every muscle in his body was burning, and his breaths were coming in short gasps. He glanced down. If he fell now, he could crack his head open on the water pipe or impale himself on a piece of rusted metal. But it was too late to turn back.

Slowly, meticulously, he walked his feet up the side of the drainpipe, pulling himself up until his face was even with the lower pane of the industrial window. Only one sensor there. Maybe he could disable it or short it out.

Holmes reached instinctively for his penknife, before remembering that it was now in somebody else's pocket. Suddenly, his foot hit a patch of scaly rust on the pipe and slipped off. His leg flailed in midair. A loose bracket fell to the ground and bounced against a metal tin with a loud bang.

Then Holmes heard another noise—this one from above.

He looked up as the window opened. The barrel of a Glock 45 poked over the sill and hovered an inch from his nose.

"Auguste! For Christ's sake, don't shoot!" said Holmes. "It's me."

Poe leaned out over the edge and gave a shaky wave. "Welcome home, Brendan," he said. Even in the open air, Holmes could smell the liquor on his partner's breath. This gave him a bit of solace. In the realm of bad habits, at least he had company.

CHAPTER 41

WHEN HOLMES WOKE up in his apartment a few hours later, his head was still clouded, and he felt filthy. He realized that he'd fallen into bed in his soiled suit. He rolled out, stripped himself naked, and stuffed his clothes into a garbage bag. He did the same with the bedsheets. Then he stepped into his shower and let scalding water stream over his body.

Steam filled the enclosure and cleared his nasal passages. He pressed his palms against the smooth tile walls and took long, deep breaths. Fully sober now, he realized that he was lucky to be alive.

That's it, he vowed. *No more distractions until all the firm's current cases are solved. Every single one.* He owed it to his clients. He owed it to his partners. He owed it to himself. He stepped out of the shower. Dried himself thoroughly. Then stepped back into the stall and showered again.

As he walked downstairs in a freshly pressed suit, Holmes immediately sensed something different in the office. A new presence. It was the hair product that struck him first—primarily the acrylic acid and the light citrus additive.

He walked around the edge of the office and saw a young woman sitting at a desk. A total stranger. She was tapping on a keypad, with a stack of reports and files by her side. Now the scent of hair gel mingled with the aroma of Native body wash.

"Good morning, Mr. Holmes!"

Holmes stared at her, puzzled. "Sorry. You are . . . ?"

The young woman stood and held out her hand. "I'm Virginia." Her dark hair was streaked with pink. The stud in her nostril glinted in the light. "Mr. Poe hired me to help out with operations. I started yesterday afternoon. I guess you'd already gone out." Her grip was firm and professional.

"Of course," said Holmes, masking his confusion. Had he missed a memo—or just been left out of the loop? It wouldn't be the first time Poe had gone rogue on office matters.

"I'm so glad to be here," said Virginia. "Very exciting." She sat back down in her chair and swung around to face her desk. "Ms. Marple will be right down. Mr. Poe is sleeping in," she said. "And the coffee is on. Sumatra dark roast. Mr. Poe said you were an early riser. Same with me. Up with the birds."

Holmes started toward his workspace on the other side of the room, then turned back. He scratched his head. "And what was your previous experience . . . ?"

"I worked at an animal shelter."

"I see," said Holmes. "Well, I expect this will be quite different."

"So far, so good," said Virginia. "Nobody's bitten me yet."

"Wonderful! I see you and Virginia have met." It was Marple, coming down the stairs with a huge black cat nestled in her arms.

"We have," Holmes said pointedly. "Just now. At this very moment." As Marple approached, Holmes stared at the cat, who looked back at him with strange yellow-orange eyes. Unsettling. "And who is this?"

Marple rubbed the cat gently behind the ears. "This is Annabel. A gift from Auguste. She is my avenging angel. Not a rodent in sight."

She set Annabel down on the floor. The cat immediately leaped up onto Virginia's desk and settled into a Sphinx-like pose next to her computer.

"Virginia is an absolute gem," said Marple. "She's already located a crop of unpaid invoices and merged our contact lists." Marple leaned in toward Virginia. "No rush, but when do you think you might get around to . . ."

"Updating the security?" said Virginia. "Done. I sent you all an encrypted email with the new temporary codes last night. That's just until I order the new iris-recognition system."

Temporary codes? *Of course,* thought Holmes. He would have received them if he'd had his phone. Embarrassing.

Virginia's desk phone rang. She picked up. "Holmes, Marple, and Poe Investigations. This is Virginia." Smooth and friendly. As Holmes watched, Virginia's eyes widened and her mouth gaped.

"Yes. Of course," she said softly into the handset. "I'll tell her right away."

She put the call on hold and looked straight at Marple. "It's Addilyn Charles. She said she just got a bloody shirt in the mail."

Marple looked at Holmes.

Holmes looked at Virginia.

"Welcome to the firm," he said.

CHAPTER 42

THE CHARLES APARTMENT was swarming with plainclothes NYPD and federal agents. The special agent in charge was questioning Addilyn on the far side of the room.

Marple stood with her partners in the opposite corner. Poe still looked groggy from sleep. Holmes just looked irritated. Helene Grey crowded in close. "I could have your licenses for this!" the detective hissed. She was clearly furious. "Five days these people have been missing?? What the hell were you thinking??"

"Addilyn trusted us," said Marple. "She was afraid that calling in the police would spook the kidnappers. But the instant we heard about the shirt—"

"We called you," said Poe, interrupting. "You're here now."

"Right," said Grey. "And so is the FBI. And I hope to hell we're not all too late."

The bloody evidence was already on its way to the lab. Marple had only gotten a glimpse of it—a white undershirt with a reddish-brown stain running down from the neckline. Addilyn had confirmed that it was her husband's brand and size. She broke down when she sniffed it. It smelled of his cologne.

Marple saw the agent hand Addilyn a box of tissues before heading in their direction. The agent's name was Brita Stans. She was the first person they'd met when they arrived, and it had not been a cordial greeting. Stans was petite but sturdy, with a no-bullshit manner. She planted herself and looked from Marple to Poe to Holmes.

"Okay, you three—listen to me. From now on, everything on this case runs through my office. No contact with Addilyn Charles. Any information you have, any leads you get, you give directly to me. Got it? You messed up big by not calling us in at the start. You might have caused a kidnapping to turn into a homicide—or two."

Marple took a deep breath and hoped that Holmes and Poe would keep their mouths shut for once. Stans looked over at Grey.

"Keep these loose dicks on a leash, Detective. Can you do that for me?"

"No problem," said Grey, her voice tight.

"But it's our case!" Holmes protested. "Addilyn called us first."

"That was her mistake," said Stans. "Don't make it worse."

"So we're supposed to do *nothing*?" asked Poe. "What if we uncover new information?"

"Detective Grey has my number," said Stans. "She'll pass along anything you find. Otherwise, don't call us—we'll call you."

CHAPTER 43

THE SPIRITED WHITE stallion stood a solid seventeen hands. Nobody on the fashion shoot except Lucy Lynn Ferry knew that metric. Everybody else just called it "a fucking big horse."

Lucy was so excited. Betsy Bronte had really come through for her. Just three days after the interview, she had her first legit modeling job! For Stella McCartney, no less. She hadn't even had time to get her tooth fixed. But no matter. All the photographer wanted were serious faces and somber pouts. No smiling required. After an hour in the hair-and-makeup tent, Lucy barely recognized herself. Now she was standing barefoot in the warm grass of Central Park, dressed in an elegant one-shouldered, wide-leg jumpsuit they told her retailed for sixteen hundred dollars. The diamonds dangling from her earlobes were worth even more. She was a long way from the Texas Panhandle. Even if she was living in a lonely basement apartment.

Lucy hadn't met the other two models before, and they seemed kind of stuck-up. Or maybe they were just skittish. They were both city girls, and they'd probably never been this close to a half ton animal.

The photographer was wiry and intense, with a shaved head and a Scandinavian accent. As he crouched and scurried around, setting up his shots, all three models stood silently with their backs to the massive horse, his pale hide and blond mane contrasting dramatically with their all-black outfits.

A crew member held a large reflective card to bounce the midday light into the girls' elaborately styled faces. McCartney's rep hovered anxiously nearby with his iPad, watching every move.

The photographer knelt on the grass about ten feet away and stared into his viewfinder. He waved his hand without looking up. "Nina! Kayla! Rest your hands on the horse."

Lucy could tell that the other models were nervous.

"What if he kicks me?" Nina whispered.

"He won't," said Lucy. "Just stay clear of his hindquarters."

"His what?" asked Nina.

"His ass," Lucy replied.

Nina and Kayla turned in profile and placed their palms tentatively on the horse's side. The photographer lay flat on the ground, lens angled up. "Lucy! Half step right. Good. Left leg out, please."

Lucy put her hands on her hips and thrust her long leg forward. Her black satin pants billowed slightly in the breeze. "And...*look*!" Lucy knew what that meant now. She'd had lessons. She pressed her chin forward. She turned her head and closed her eyes for a split second, then whipped her head forward and looked straight into the lens. Like she wanted to eat it for lunch.

"Fantastic! Great!" the photographer called out. He reached out to the side. His assistant placed another camera in his hand. "Now—I need one of you girls *on* the horse."

"No way," Nina mumbled under her breath. Kayla looked away and shuffled her feet.

"Quickly, please! Before the sun moves."

"I'll do it!" Lucy called out.

"Great," said the photographer. "Somebody give Lucy a lift, please!"

A horse handler hurried forward with a step stool.

"I'm good," said Lucy. She turned, grabbed the horse's mane, flexed her knees, and jumped, swinging her right leg up and over the horse's bare back. Suddenly, the horse reared, pawing the air with his front hooves, his massive head almost ten feet off the ground. Lucy leaned forward and brought the horse down, settling him with a gentle pat to his neck. She sat up straight, hips square and facing front.

"Holy shit," said Nina. The kid with the reflector card just stared. McCartney's rep almost dropped his iPad.

"All right, then," said the photographer softly.

For the next five minutes, Lucy turned and stretched on horseback as Nina and Kayla vogued alongside. When the photographer called a wrap, an assistant grabbed Lucy's waist to help her dismount and checked to make sure her pants hadn't split. Lucy walked around to give the horse's muzzle a quick kiss. "That was fun," she whispered.

Back in the tent, Lucy stood in front of the mirror as a stylist carefully removed the pricey earrings. As she slipped out of her black outfit, she heard a soft *bing* from inside her backpack. She dug past her wadded-up street clothes and pulled out her phone.

There was a text message on the screen, and it sent a cold chill right through her.

FOUND YOU, it said.

CHAPTER 44

SITTING IN HIS Upper West Side apartment, Luka Franke was both baffled and impressed. He'd been in the art world for a long time, and he'd never seen anything quite like this.

It was 8:15 p.m. and the sun was setting. Franke had a spectacular view from his high-rise. But right now his eyes were locked on his laptop screen. He held a lit cigarette in his left hand as he moved the middle finger of his right hand over the track pad, back and forth.

The images were authentic all right. And out there for the whole world to see. A complete Shakespeare First Folio and a 1455 Gutenberg Bible. The same pieces his contacts had told him were missing from an impregnable residential vault, right here in the city.

What kind of savant could get through a setup that tight? And what kind of thief would post his priceless loot on the internet? Franke had spent hours trying to decode the source of the images, but the IP address had been masked by the most sophisticated VPN he'd ever seen. Impossible to crack. There was simply no way to tell where the images originated, or who had curated them. All Franke knew was that the quality was way beyond what any museum or collector had ever displayed.

Whoever had done this didn't just steal art; he wanted the world to appreciate it—even at the risk of exposing his crime. Bold move.

Franke sat back and took a slow drag on his cigarette. He had to admit he was a bit jealous. If anyone had been able to crack that safe across town, it should have been him. But he certainly wouldn't have posted pictures of his swag after he took it. Not his style. He hadn't lasted this long by showing off. No. He would have moved the items quickly over the Canadian border, then loaded them onto one of his trusted cargo ships to Iceland, where they would rest in his vault until the heat died down.

Franke closed his laptop just in time to see the final rays of the sun fade in the distance. He checked his Rolex and felt a fresh tingle of anticipation. His appointment that evening concerned art far less impressive than the works he'd been admiring. Just a few minor Rembrandt sketches and an early El Greco. He had held them for over a decade, letting the steam run out of the investigations. Now it was time to cash in. This was the part of the game that he loved most.

Franke was as picky about his buyers as he was about his targets. It was easy to turn a quick buck from some nouveau riche sheik or a crime lord with dirty money to launder. He knew that his father had sometimes used masterpieces as leverage to get Mafia sentences reduced. But Franke preferred to deal at a higher level. He scoffed at collectors like Huntley Bain, who only used art as an expensive form of Viagra.

His contact for that evening sounded like the real deal. Franke prided himself on being an impossible man to locate, and somehow she had pinpointed him. That alone showed admirable initiative. He hoped this mystery woman would have the funds to match her gumption. Or at least be attractive enough to be worth bedding.

He loved that part of the game too.

CHAPTER 45

WHEN SITTING AT a bar by herself, Margaret Marple usually brought a book, one of her favorite mysteries—often one with the original Miss Marple in the lead. But that would have been totally out of character tonight.

The woman she was pretending to be didn't read much at all, and definitely not in bars where she wanted to attract attention, not deflect it. This woman had learned how to collect two things in her life: art—and men. And she was an expert at both. The name Marple had assumed for the night was Lucinda Sadler. Poe had picked it for her off a gravestone.

Marple stroked her fingers through the blond waves that cascaded over her shoulders. She shimmied to adjust her silk dress, tight across her breasts and hips. She did a quick makeup check in the mirror behind the bar. Lipstick, mascara, blush. All perfect. Her pretty little mask.

"Excuse me. Is this seat taken?" A young man with a neat beard was standing behind the empty chair next to her. Marple had claimed it when she arrived by placing her small purse on the cushion. Since then, the cocktail lounge had filled up, and the empty place was valuable real estate. Marple checked her watch—a Cartier for the occasion: 10 p.m.

"Sorry," Marple said. "I'm afraid it is. I'm waiting for someone." At least it was a chance to practice her accent. She had worked on making it virtually unplaceable, a modified Southern-Western twang, appropriate for an Air Force brat raised on bases from Fort Rucker to San Antonio—one of her most detailed backstories, which she considered airtight.

"Can I buy you a drink in the meantime?" the man asked. He had a charming smile. There was brandy on his breath, and expensive cologne on his neck. Marple felt a little flush in her cheeks, and a prickle of heat under her wig. It had been a long time.

She took a sip of her sherry and lowered her eyes before glancing up at him again. "Still working on this one, thanks," she said.

"What if I just keep the seat warm?" he said.

"I'll warm it myself, thanks." A new voice. Deep and silky.

Marple turned. "Luka?"

"Lucinda?"

He was a bit older than he looked in the pictures but even more attractive. The bearded man sized up the competition quickly and glided back down the bar.

"May I?" Franke asked, gesturing toward the empty chair.

"Please," said Marple. She quickly swept the clutch onto her lap. Franke eyed her glass.

"What are you drinking?"

"Harvey's," said Marple.

"You like sherry?" said Franke.

"It was my mother's favorite," said Marple. Her inflection turned "my" into "mah."

"We can do much better." Franke leaned forward and eyed the

young woman behind the bar. One glance was all it took. In a second, she was standing in front of him, wiping an errant streak of moisture from the mahogany surface.

"Good evening, sir. What can I get you?"

"We'll each have a González Byass. The Matusalem oloroso, if you have it." Franke picked up Marple's half full glass with two fingers. "And you can take this away."

The bartender raised her eyebrows appreciatively and nodded. Franke shifted in his seat. Marple felt his thigh press against hers, and not by accident. She adjusted her clingy little cocktail dress and patted the outline of the .22 Beretta in her bag. As a rule, she avoided firearms, but Holmes had insisted.

Franke moved closer. One way or another, it was going to be an interesting night.

CHAPTER 46

"YOU DID NOT lie, Luka," said Marple. "This was worth the limo ride." She was admiring the beautifully lit display in Franke's penthouse living room—shelf upon shelf of exotic pieces from all over the globe. African tribal masks. Colorful Egyptian pottery. And an Aztec fertility statue with a prominently erect penis.

"And how exactly did you manage to assemble all this?" asked Marple. "On loan from a museum?"

"*Several* museums," said Franke. "And a few private collections. And 'on loan' is one way to put it."

Marple knew hubris when she heard it. It was exactly what she'd expected. Men like Franke couldn't help flexing their egos. He was letting her know that everything she was looking at had been stolen.

"You're not worried about somebody recognizing one of these pieces from an Interpol notice?" she asked.

"I'm very selective about my visitors," said Franke. He held up a fresh bottle of Lustau. "More sherry?"

"I shouldn't," Marple said, settling back onto an elegant sofa, "but since when has that stopped me." They'd had several rounds before leaving the bar. But thanks to Marple's prior arrangement with the attentive bartender, all of her servings had been radically cut with iced tea. With each drink, Marple had deliberately loosened her drawl until she appeared pleasantly, pliably looped.

Franke pulled two snifters from a cabinet and poured. He made a little toast. "To art."

Marple lifted her snifter in return. "How have you done it, Luka?"

"Done what?"

"Slipped the noose all these years?"

He took a sip. "Luck."

"Nobody's that lucky."

"And friends."

Marple looked across the gallery. "You must have very tasteful friends."

"These are nothing," said Franke. "Minor pieces. Any thug with a fake passport and a duffel bag could assemble a collection like this."

Marple took a small sip of her sherry. "I hear you're trying to unload some Rembrandt sketches. And what else? An El Greco?" Marple let out an exaggerated sigh. "I have to tell you, Luka, the man does nothing for me."

Franke flashed a conspiratorial smile. "I agree," he said. "I find his work exhausting." He put down his sherry. "Come with me."

Marple stood up, pretending to lose her balance a bit. "Don't tell me you're about to show me your etchings."

Franke smiled. "Just . . . come."

He led the way down a short corridor and through an archway. Marple followed, sherry in hand, her purse under one arm. She was not the least bit surprised by the destination, but she was impressed by the décor.

The massive bed was mounted on some sort of central pedestal that made it seem to float in midair. Three walls of the room were glass, with stunning views of the sparkling city below. The side facing the bed held a massive flat-screen TV. Marple set her sherry snifter down on a small glass table.

"Luka. Really?" said Marple. "Do you just *assume* this is where your evenings will end up?"

"Of course," he said smoothly. "But not always like this."

He pulled out his iPhone and tapped a code. A small servomotor whirred. The slim TV screen began to flip slowly on a seamless panel.

"Very Austin Powers," said Marple with a slight grin. Franke's lips twitched. She could tell that he didn't like being needled by a woman—especially a woman he was planning to seduce.

When the panel came to rest, the kidding stopped.

The backing was black velvet. Affixed to the fabric was an antique painting—bright yellow flowers bursting from a round, brownish vase. Marple sucked in a quick breath. She recognized the work. Holmes had covered it in his tutorial.

The flowers were yellow poppies. The painting was a Van Gogh—the same painting that had disappeared without a trace from the Mohamed Mahmoud Khalil Museum in Cairo back in 2010.

CHAPTER 47

MARPLE CLEARED HER throat. "What a lovely surprise."

She pretended to be blasé, but she couldn't resist approaching the piece.

She leaned in, astonished at the exquisite work on the petals and the amazing colors, still brimming with life after more than a century on canvas. She felt Franke move in beside her, his shoulder brushing hers. She noticed that he had shed his jacket.

"Shall we talk price now?" he said. "Or shall we wait...?" His hand slid down the smooth silk of Marple's evening dress and over the upper curve of her left buttock. "You might get a better price."

Marple flinched and angled her body away from him. She concentrated on maintaining her accent. "Luka. Please. I'm flattered. But no. Not interested."

Franke moved in again, eyes flashing. "In me? Or in the painting?"

He placed his large hands on her shoulders and moved in, his lips suddenly on her neck and moving insistently down toward her chest. Marple twisted free. She reached back with one hand and found her glass. With a quick thrust, she tossed the sherry in Franke's face. He staggered backward, furiously wiping his eyes.

"Knock it off," Marple said tersely.

"What the hell is *wrong* with you?" Franke shouted. He lunged for her. Marple reached into her purse and whipped out her pistol. Franke froze. Marple moved toward him. She backed him onto the bed and rested the barrel against his crotch.

"I'm only interested in two items," she said calmly. "The Shakespeare and the Gutenberg. Where are they?" She glanced up. "Maybe under the ceiling mirror?"

Franke shook his head. "Why not just go online and print them out?" he snarled. "Like any other tourist."

"I was told that you could deliver the originals."

"You were misled."

"That's a shame." Marple stepped back. "But at least I know where to find a stolen Van Gogh when I need it. Maybe I'll tell some of *my* friends."

She turned and walked briskly out of the bedroom and down the short corridor to the living room. She could hear Franke's footsteps behind her. She tapped the elevator button with one hand and raised her pistol with the other, stopping him cold.

"Good night," she said.

The elevator opened. Marple quickly backed in and pressed the Down button. She flicked the pistol toward the display wall and squeezed the trigger. The bullet blew the erect penis right off the fertility statue.

Franke stood frozen in the hallway.

"You were right, Luka," Marple said as the doors closed. "A very minor piece."

CHAPTER 48

MARPLE PRACTICALLY JUMPED out of the Uber when she arrived home at 2 a.m. Her heart was still racing. She couldn't wait to tell her partners about her evening. As the car drove off, she looked both ways before crossing to the building. But no need. The street was deserted.

As she walked up to the entrance, she heard a loud pop. A chunk of brick blew off the building, inches from her face. Marple ducked, but there was no cover. Just bare stone stairs.

Then, another pop.

The second shot zinged off the wall and struck the door, blasting a small divot into the thick oak. Marple crouched, hands over her head. A few seconds later, the door burst open. Poe ran out, a pistol in his hands. Holmes was right behind him. He grabbed Marple by the arm and pulled her into the vestibule. He pushed her to the floor and sprawled on top of her, shielding her with his body. Marple had never seen him this panicked.

"Margaret! Are you hit?"

"I'm fine," she wheezed. Holmes was pressing down so hard she could barely catch a breath. She felt his body relax and ease back. He helped her to her feet and wrapped his arms around her. Through her silk dress, she could feel his heart pounding.

"Sonofabitch!" Poe was back, gun held low.

"Anything?" asked Holmes.

"That last shot clipped my Pontiac!" he muttered. "My fault for not putting the GTO back into the garage with the Torino. The paint match will be impossible!"

Holmes sat Marple down gently on the sofa in the dimly lit office and wrapped her in one of her knitted blankets. "Don't move," he said. "I'll get you some tea." He hurried off toward the kitchen. Poe was crouched alongside one of the front windows, scanning the street.

Marple slipped her fingers under the liner of her blond wig and eased it off her head. Underneath, her real hair was pinned into a tight bun. She tossed the wig onto a table, then plucked a tissue from a box and started wiping off her lipstick. "Franke was the shooter," she said, nodding toward the street. "Or somebody he sent."

"I guess the disguise didn't fool him," said Poe.

"I think he appreciated the accent, though," said Marple, reverting momentarily to her fake twang.

"I don't blame him," Holmes called out from the kitchen. "It's very seductive."

"We should have followed you," said Poe. "The man is a menace."

Marple shook her head. "He's a pro. He would have made a tail in two seconds. And if he really wanted to kill me, I'd be dead."

Holmes walked back to the sofa with a steaming mug. He handed it to Marple and sat next to her. "So what did you learn?"

"Your FBI friend was right," said Marple. "Franke looks like a prime suspect. And he's accumulated some very interesting loot." Marple realized she hadn't even mentioned the stolen Van Gogh. But first things first. She took a sip of her tea and reached for her cell phone. "Excuse me," she said. "I need to send a text."

She held the phone in her lap as Holmes peered over her shoulder.

She entered the restricted number that had been so hard to come by. Luka Franke's number. Her thumbs tapped out a short message:

Not scared. R U?

She sent it.

Holmes grabbed the phone out of her hands. "Margaret, enough!" he said. "You're playing with fire."

Marple picked up her mug and nestled back on the sofa. She looked at Holmes. "I know," she said. "Isn't it fun?"

CHAPTER 49

THE NEXT NIGHT.

"Auguste," said Helene Grey, "I need to ask you a serious question."

"Go ahead," said Poe.

"Exactly how many cars do you *own*?"

"More than five, less than ten," said Poe.

"Evasive answer," said Grey. "As usual."

She was sitting in the passenger seat of a clean-lined sedan as Poe drove north through Westchester County. She was still furious with Poe and his partners about the kidnapping case. It had put her in a bad light with the FBI, which was the last thing she needed in her life.

So why had she given in to Poe's persistent invitation for a date? Out of curiosity, she realized. Curiosity about him, and about the place he was taking her.

"My GTO is in the shop," Poe explained. "Bullet scratch." The car surged forward with a growl. "This is my Oldsmobile 442—'65. A little tame in the style department, but a total beast."

"Wait," said Grey. "Somebody *shot* at you? When??"

"To be honest," said Poe, "I was just an innocent bystander."

"Did you file a report?"

"I hate paperwork."

"You should be more careful."

Poe turned and smiled at her. Grey hadn't seen him smile very often. But when he did, she had to admit, he was hard to resist. "I look out for myself," he said. "And I always come prepared."

Grey assumed that he was referring to the gun strapped under his jacket. It was the same model she had in her purse. The difference was that hers was licensed, and his was not. She'd checked. Nobody with the name Auguste Poe had ever registered a firearm in the state of New York. In theory, that made him a dangerous man.

Grey wondered if he was dangerous to her.

Poe exited onto a dark two-lane road. Grey shifted in her seat, adjusting her dress. She hoped Poe wouldn't notice that it was the same one she'd worn to the launch party six nights ago.

"Hungry?" asked Poe.

"Starving," said Grey.

"Too bad. I hear this place has very small portions."

He downshifted as they approached the sign. It was unlit. Just a small rectangle with the restaurant name: Harlowe Farm. Poe turned the sedan onto a gravel drive that wound through a pasture and past a series of geodesic greenhouses. A small farmhouse glowed amber in the distance.

As Poe pulled up to the entrance, a young man in a crisp white shirt and black slacks hurried to the driver's side.

"Good evening, sir. Welcome to Harlowe." He looked down the length of the car, clearly impressed.

Poe left the car running and stepped out. Grey exited the passenger side. The young man slid into the driver's seat and put his hands on the steering wheel. He shifted into gear and headed toward the parking area with a spin of the rear tires.

"You just made his night," said Grey.

Poe smiled and slipped his arm through hers. Grey felt a slight tingle run through her. She wasn't entirely sure what to make of it.

They walked through the stone vestibule, lit by a thick candle on a sturdy wrought-iron stand. Poe pushed open the heavy wood door. They stepped inside. The initial impression was stunning.

The main dining room was lit only by candles, which gave the whole place a shimmering glow. A glass wall looked out on neat crop rows that extended into the darkness. The other three walls were made of heavy fieldstone. The room was filled with low murmurs of conversation. The aromas floating through the air were amazing.

A maître d' in a crisp suit approached and nodded warmly. "Mister Poe, Lieutenant Grey. So glad to have you with us. Follow me, please." He led the way toward the back of the room, past an impeccably neat server station and through a heavy swinging metal door.

Suddenly, they were in a whole different world—the disciplined intensity of a five-star kitchen. Wiry young cooks in striped aprons hovered over flaming stoves and squeezed past one another with bins of ingredients. White clouds of steam rose from skillets. Pots clanged against iron burners. The space was filled with the urgent cadence of commands and responses, all in French.

Here, the aromas were even richer and more visceral. Oil sizzling. Herbs roasting. Meat searing. At the edge of a low counter at the far end of the kitchen was a small wooden farm table. Just one. Set for two. Grey looked at Poe in amazement. The maître d' pulled out one of the chairs for her.

"The chef will be with you shortly," he said. *"Bon appétit."*

Grey took the thick cloth napkin from the table and slid it onto her lap. She looked across at Poe. He had never looked more eager, or more charming. All his usual moodiness seemed to have dissipated. Now she was more curious than ever.

Poe reached across the table and put his hand on hers. She hadn't expected it. Her instinct told her to pull back. But she didn't.

"Relax, Helene," said Poe, flashing that devastating smile. "Life is short."

CHAPTER 50

"'OAK-BARK BISQUE with saffron-infused acorns'!"

"'Cottage-grown ferns with sea-salt glaze'!"

Grey and Poe were practically giddy as they recited items from the tasting menu they'd pocketed when leaving the restaurant. Yes, the descriptions were off-the-charts pretentious. But the flavors had been incredible. Dizzying. Mind-bending. Like no food Grey had ever tasted in her life. Fantastic night.

Poe had seemed steady after two glasses of Merlot. But Grey made sure he stayed under the speed limit the whole way back to Brooklyn. She certainly wouldn't have gotten behind the wheel herself. The Chablis had gone to her head, with a textbook loosening of inhibitions. If not for her second glass, she probably would have already been home, securing her Glock in her closet lockbox.

Instead, she was in another place she never expected to be.

Auguste Poe's bedroom.

"Make yourself comfortable," he said. "I need to use the facilities."

As Poe closed the bathroom door, Grey began to assess her surroundings. Even buzzed, she felt her detective instincts stirring. She could have predicted the shelves of books, on esoteric subjects from medieval armor to the occult. She was not surprised by the fencing foils or the expensive liqueur assortment. After all, she had been mentally profiling Poe since the day they met. Everything fit.

Everything except her.

She recalled Poe's date from the evening of the launch party. Slender, young, sophisticated. Grey did not place herself in any of those three categories.

Maybe Poe had merely invited her up here to chat about their mutual interest in the subway skeletons. Or to try to wheedle his way back into the Charles kidnapping case.

Grey ran her fingers over a drawer pull, fighting the urge to tug on it, fantasizing about discovering an old passport, a bank statement, a diploma. Anything revealing.

Suddenly, Poe was behind her. She hadn't even heard the bathroom door open.

"Detective Grey," he said gently. "Are you investigating me?"

As she turned, she felt his hand behind her neck.

And then . . . a kiss.

Unexpected. Thrilling. Tender. Poe's hands slid down to her waist. As Grey angled her head, their noses bumped, like clumsy teenagers. They both pulled back slightly with awkward grins. She touched his face, running her fingers over his dashing moustache.

"I assure you it's real," he said.

Grey realized that her heart was pounding. "What's happening here, Mr. Poe?"

"Whatever you *want* to happen," he replied. He leaned forward and kissed her again. She kissed him back, then gently pulled away.

"Another evasive answer," she said. She could feel a flush rising across her cheeks and throat.

"What can I say?" he whispered. "I have an elusive soul."

So now it was her call. Her choice. She pulled Poe down onto the bed and reached for his belt. She felt his hand behind her back, his fingers on the zipper of her dress.

As they both wriggled free of their clothes, Grey had a flash of insecurity. She couldn't help it. She worried about being compared to a twenty-five-year-old. Poe pulled the clip from her hair and let it tumble around her neck. She closed her eyes. He kissed his way from her cheek down to her collarbone and kept going.

Somewhere along the way, she quit worrying.

Afterward, Grey slept deeper and longer than she had in years. Four straight hours. It was 3:30 a.m. when she found herself blinking in the darkness. The room was quiet except for the ticking of an antique clock on the bookshelf. As steady as a heartbeat.

As her eyes adjusted, she saw Poe's bare back facing her from the other side of the bed. She could make out the lines of his muscles as his torso rose and fell. She reached out and lightly traced her finger along the slope of his shoulder. As soon as she touched him, his body began to shake. She loosened the covers around her body and slid closer to his, pressing softly against him. She leaned over to peer at his face, pulling a lock of dark hair off his forehead.

Poe's eyes were shut tight. His lips were working, as if trying to form words. Suddenly, tears spilled down his cheeks onto his pillow, and the words became clear.

"I'm sorry!" he moaned softly in his sleep. And then, "Don't leave me! *Please!*"

CHAPTER 51

AT 7 A.M., Marple sat at her desk, stroking a purring Annabel and watching as Helene Grey tiptoed down the steps from the apartment level and moved along the inside wall toward the door. She was holding her strappy heels in one hand, her purse in the other.

Marple had worried that the kidnapping case might have doused the spark she'd detected between Auguste and Helene. Apparently not.

"Good morning, Detective!" she called out brightly.

Grey froze. Caught.

Virginia stood up from another desk and smiled at her. "Well, I guess all the ladies are up early this morning!"

"I'm sorry," said Grey, her voice low and hoarse. "I was just . . ." She started moving toward the entryway.

"No need to explain, Detective," said Marple. "People come and go at all hours around here."

"It's true," added Virginia. "I've noticed that too."

Grey stopped again and exhaled in a breathy sigh. Clearly surrendering any pretense of a smooth escape, she walked over to Marple's workspace in her bare feet and plunked down in an office chair.

Her wrinkled dress sagged low on her chest. Virginia stepped over and handed her a PETA sweatshirt. "It's chilly in here before the sun comes up. Coffee?"

Grey took the sweatshirt. "Yes, please."

"One sugar, right?" said Virginia.

Grey nodded.

Virginia walked off toward the kitchen. Grey slipped the sweatshirt over her head and whispered to Marple. "Who's that? Is she psychic?"

"You mean Virginia?" said Marple. "Sorry. I should have introduced you. A new office hire. She started a few days ago. One of Poe's discoveries."

Grey tugged the sweatshirt down to her waist. "Don't tell me she lives here too."

Marple shook her head. "She just comes in *very* early."

Grey lowered her head and pressed her fingers against her temples.

"Are you okay, Detective?" asked Marple.

"Fine," said Grey. "I'm fine."

"Anything on the kidnapping?" asked Marple. She knew it was a touchy subject, but she had to ask.

Grey looked up, frowning. "You know I can't talk to you about that." She paused for a second. "But no. Nothing more from the kidnappers. No proof of life. And no leads. If it was an international job, they're probably somewhere out of the country by now. The FBI has taps and surveillance on the apartment and Eton's office phone."

Marple caught Grey looking across her desk. She had her eyes on a map of Hart Island, the site of New York City's potter's field.

"What's that about?" asked the detective.

Marple quickly slid the map into a file folder. *Sloppy*, she told herself. She shouldn't have left it out. "Probably nothing," she said.

"Nothing?" Grey asked.

"I spend most of my days on dead ends," said Marple. "Nights too.

Believe it or not, that's how I tend to solve cases. It seems to work. Surprisingly well, actually."

"Do you have a lead on something?" asked Grey.

Virginia stepped close and handed Grey a huge mug. "Careful, it's hot."

Grey took the mug. "Thank you, Virginia. I'm Helene, by the way."

"Detective Lieutenant Helene Grey. Badge number 1514. Of course. I was just looking at your file."

Grey looked at Marple. "You have a file on me?"

Marple smiled. "Just the basics. Precinct. Contact info. Last known address. SAT scores. Favorite color..."

Grey stared at Virginia as she walked back to her desk, then she turned again toward Marple. "Sorry. You were saying? About Hart Island? Anything I should know about?"

"Not at the moment," said Marple.

Grey took a sip from the mug. Her eyes widened. "God, this is delicious." She raised her voice and said, "Excellent coffee, Virginia!"

Virginia nodded. "Cubano whole bean. It's in your file."

Grey took three more sips and then stood up. "I really need to get out of here before..." Her voice trailed off. She cleared her throat and started again. "Will you please tell Auguste..."

"That you got called in early on a case. Of course."

Virginia smiled. "I already ordered you a car, Detective. It's out front." She returned to her work.

"Damn, she's good," said Grey.

Marple nodded. "Poe has very high standards."

Grey started toward the door, then paused and looked back. "Nobody in the department needs to know about this, right?"

Marple looked up. "About what?"

Grey smiled. "Thanks, Margaret. I owe you."

"Don't worry," Marple said sweetly. "I plan to collect."

CHAPTER 52

"WHO DIED THIS time?" The ferry captain tucked the fresh packet of bills into his pocket.

"Who knows?" said Marple. It was her standard answer. And as usual, it ended the conversation. The captain shuffled back across the deck and climbed the stairs to the bridge. A minute later, the lumbering metal craft was on its way across the channel. Marple was left staring down at the grey water churning past the hull, thinking about all the times she'd made this sad trip, and afraid of what she was about to find.

Hart Island was not an easy place to get to. There was no bridge or causeway. The only access was by water, and visitors were not allowed, except in "managed visitations" under the careful watch of park rangers. Unless, of course, you had a connection—and a stack of cash. This was definitely an unmanaged trip, and Marple was the only paying passenger.

She hadn't been totally bullshitting earlier when she blew Grey off about her morning's mission. Sometimes her information was solid, sometimes just a hunch. No need to swarm the island with police until she had more clarity.

All Marple knew from her source was that an unidentified young woman was being buried on the island that morning. And she was hoping—for Addilyn's sake—that the young woman would not turn out to be Zozi Turner.

The trip took only ten minutes. As the ferry settled against the dock, Marple walked off the metal ramp and down the short road that led to the center of the island, a jagged puzzle piece of land about one mile long and a third of a mile across. She passed through a metal gate and onto a grassy expanse that had been accepting the city's unclaimed dead for more than a century.

In a field across the island was a plot of small markers. Not headstones, just rectangles of white concrete sticking out of the ground. Dozens of them, widely scattered. Below each marker lay the bodies of a thousand unnamed infants. Marple quickened her pace as she walked past.

Toward the south end of the island, Marple spotted a man in the distance. He was busy with a shovel. Marple waved. The man waved back. As Marple came closer, he stopped digging and rested his arms on his shovel handle. He was tall, Black, and made of muscle. There was a silvery glint in the close-cropped hair over his temples.

"Morning, Stephen," said Marple.

"Morning, Margaret." There was still a hint of the bayou in his voice. Behind him was a backhoe and a fresh hole deep enough for three coffins. Two were already stacked in the ground. A third coffin rested on the lip of the hole. It was simple white pine with straight sides, as unadorned as a shipping box.

"Is this the one?" asked Marple, her heart pounding.

"It is," said Stephen. "Jane Doe. They found her in Rosedale a few days ago."

He put down the shovel and picked up a huge hammer. "You ready?"

"Go ahead," said Marple. She mouthed a simple prayer.

Stephen jammed the claw of the hammer under the coffin lid, working it around the edge, inch by inch. Slowly, with loud squeaks, the wooden top began to lift. When it was mostly free, Stephen grabbed it with both hands and pulled it all the way off. Marple leaned forward and peered inside, then leaned back with a sigh of relief. The body in the shroud was tall and slender, with narrow hips and long legs. Nothing like the petite and curvy teenager in the pictures from Zozi's bedroom.

"Not her," said Marple.

"That's good," said Stephen, wiping sweat from his forehead. "That means there's hope, right?"

"Possibly," said Marple. "Or she could just be buried somewhere else." She reached under her jacket and pulled out the customary carton of Marlboros.

Stephen took the box and smiled grimly. "These'll put me in the ground too, soon enough."

"But not here, Stephen," said Marple. "At least it won't be here."

The gravedigger looked past Marple, squinting. "Friend of yours?"

Marple turned. About fifty yards back, a young man—late teens or early twenties—was standing in the middle of the walkway, staring in their direction. He looked slim and fit. He was wearing jeans, a denim jacket, and a white ten-gallon hat. Not exactly a New York look.

"Nobody I know," said Marple. "I didn't see him on the ferry."

Stephen shook his head. "Sometimes they come over on kayaks. They all think they're gonna see something freaky—like *Ghostbusters*." He started to refasten the coffin lid.

"Thanks again, Stephen," said Marple. She headed back down the path.

"Take care now, Margaret," said the gravedigger. "See you next time."

As Marple watched, the cowboy turned and started walking quickly toward the dock road.

Then he started running.

CHAPTER 53

MARPLE DECIDED NOT to spook the kid with a full-on chase. But she kept her eyes on him. She watched him run past a stand of trees and the ruins of an old building. From that point to the dock road, there was no other cover. She saw him pass through the metal gate and head toward the ferry slip.

When Marple reached the dock, the young man was nowhere in sight. As she walked up the ferry ramp, a deckhand in a Yankees cap emerged from under the metal superstructure.

"Excuse me," Marple called out. "The boy in the cowboy hat. Where did he go?"

"Sorry. I was in the head. I didn't see anybody."

The Yankees fan and a second deckhand—a tall kid with a red bandana across his forehead—moved to the stern and raised the ramp. The engines fired up. Marple steadied herself with one hand on the rail and moved forward. Her heart was starting to pound. Where did the cowboy go? He had to be here somewhere.

The ferry was mostly one level, with a large open space in the middle. The only vehicle aboard was a battered DOT pickup. Marple walked over and checked the front seat and footwells. As she moved back along the side of the truck, she saw a thick tarp covering the cargo bed.

There was a large bulge in the middle.

Marple felt her adrenaline rising. She inched her way to the back of the truck, grabbed a corner of the tarp, and flipped it over.

Underneath were two fat sacks of sand. Marple moved quickly to the port side. A narrow cabin with thick plastic windows ran half the length of the deck. She pushed the door open and saw a large wooden bin against the wall. She jerked the lid open. Inside was a pile of musty life jackets. She leaned over and swept her arm through the pile. Nothing.

Marple ran to the starboard side and looked out over the rail. Suddenly, she spotted an object bobbing in the grey water about twenty yards away.

She squinted.

It was a white cowboy hat. Floating upside down.

Marple shouted at the two deckhands. "Over there! He must have jumped!"

"Holy shit!" said the Yankees fan. He grabbed a red rubber donut off the wall and heaved it over the rail. It landed about ten yards short of the hat.

"What's going on?" the captain called down from the bridge.

"Man overboard, Cap!" shouted the second deckhand. "Midship! Starboard side!"

"I'll come about!" The captain ducked back into the wheelhouse.

Marple heard the ferry engine strain as the boat started to make a wide right turn. She leaned back over the rail and scanned the choppy water, from the bobbing hat to the City Island dock, now just a few hundred yards away.

Then she saw a shape moving toward shore.

"There he is!" Marple shouted.

The Yankees fan ran up with a pair of binoculars. Marple grabbed them. She brought the eyepieces up and looked toward shore.

"Hey, look!" The second deckhand was shouting from the stern. Marple turned. He was pulling a length of thick rope from the water. It was tied to the stern rail and knotted at the lower end.

The Yankees fan leaned over the rail, squinting into the distance. "Jesus! He must've been hanging on to the rope the whole way! He's lucky he didn't get sucked into the screws."

Marple lifted the binoculars again. She saw a male figure swimming the last twenty yards to the other side of the channel. He stood up in the shallows, waded out of the choppy surf, and staggered up the landing toward the road.

Marple watched through the eyepieces as the kid slid into the driver's side of a white pickup truck. The rear tires spun in the gravel as the truck pulled away from the curb. Marple tried to adjust the focus knob, but the truck kept bouncing in and out of view.

The license plate was white with black letters, but the image was too shaky for a clear read. *Dammit!* Marple held tight on the rear window as the truck sped away. Even with the blur through the eyepiece, she could make out a large white decal on the right side of the glass.

A lone star.

CHAPTER 54

AN HOUR AFTER losing the cowboy on City Island, Marple was sitting with Holmes and Poe in the common area of their first-floor offices. She was antsy and impatient for answers.

"Four point two million!" Virginia called out from her desk.

Not what Marple had been hoping to hear.

"What does that mean?" asked Holmes.

"Apparently, that's how many pickup trucks are registered in the state of Texas," said Marple.

"You said the truck was white," said Poe. "That should narrow it down."

Virginia called out again: "One point one million of those trucks are white!"

Marple let out a long sigh.

"Margaret, let it go," said Poe. "Maybe your cowboy just freaked out when he saw the coffin opening. Maybe he realized that he was in a restricted area and was afraid of getting caught."

"Or maybe he was following me," said Marple. "Once I spotted him, he was crazy enough to take a swim in the middle of Long Island Sound."

"Should we report him to Helene?" asked Poe. "She could put out an APB on the pickup."

Marple shook her head. "She already knows I had a tip about Hart Island. If she finds out I was looking for Zozi Turner..."

Holmes leaned forward. "Look. The body wasn't Zozi—and we've been told to take a back seat on that case. Let's focus on more fertile areas."

"Such as..." said Poe. He pressed a remote to turn on a large flat-screen monitor. The screen filled with a color map of New York City, from Manhattan to the Bronx and east to Brooklyn and Queens.

"What's this?" Marple asked.

"Auguste's latest creation," said Holmes. "A new view on the subway case."

The map was covered with tiny icons, thousands of them, overlapping in some places into a single solid mass.

"Take a look," said Poe. He sat at the edge of the sofa, iPhone in his palm. "On average, thirty-five people go missing in New York every day. Most of them turn up within forty-eight hours." Poe tapped his phone screen with his thumb. Icons started popping off, leaving a scattering across the map. "These people are still gone."

"Where did you get this data?" asked Marple.

"I assembled it," said Poe.

"Don't be modest," said Holmes. "He did it by hacking into the NYPD database."

"Once I got past their deep packet inspection," said Poe, "it was pure silk. They haven't updated their software significantly since 9/11. Plenty of gaps if you know where to look." He zoomed in on Brooklyn, where a pattern of pins dotted several neighborhoods from Clinton Hill to Greenpoint.

"The ME report says the oldest bones from the subway dig may be about sixty years old," said Poe. "The newest are less than one year old. And the ages of the victims are so far all between twenty and thirty." He pointed at the screen. "Here are all the local disappearances in that age range since 1950. Cold cases, without resolution, including a few recent disappearances. All with one thing in common."

"What's the pattern?" asked Holmes.

"The pattern is, no known relatives," said Poe. He flicked through page after page of missing person reports, usually filed by friends or employers. "All people on the margins—sex workers, restaurant dishwashers, hotel housekeepers—people without nearby relations. Or none at all. No family to pester the police or the media year after year. Nobody to keep their cases alive."

"These people weren't like Sloane Stone," continued Poe. "The tabloids weren't clamoring over them."

"Invisible victims," said Marple. She thought about Mary McShane, alone in New York, with nobody to claim her after she died.

Along with his diagrams and missing person profiles, Poe had assembled a gallery of Google Maps images.

"These are the locations of last-known sightings," he said.

Marple looked up at the street views of city parks, apartment complexes, storefronts, nightclubs, restaurants, brownstones, and private houses. Poe scrolled slowly through the pictures, a mundane gallery of urban locations. *Nothing in common,* thought Marple, *except that somebody was last seen alive near each of them.*

Suddenly a flash of red and blue lights flickered across the windows. Next came the sound of vehicle doors opening and slamming shut. Then heavy footsteps.

Virginia turned her head toward them. "I think we're being invaded."

She and Marple both moved to the front door. On the security screen, Marple could see a cluster of uniformed cops gathered outside, along with a few officers in plainclothes. Helene Grey was in the pack, flanked by a couple of other detectives. The group parted as a bulky man thrust his way to the front and pounded his fist on the door.

"Police! Open up!"

Marple turned to her partners. "It's Boolin."

Virginia had her finger on the release button. "Should I open the door?" she asked.

"Might as well," said Marple, "before they break it down."

CHAPTER 55

THE LATCH CLICKED. Commissioner Boolin shoved the door open and pushed his way through. The rest of the posse followed him through the vestibule and into the common area.

Feeling violated, Holmes stepped forward to defend the firm's turf. "I wish you'd called ahead, Commissioner. We would have put out some donuts."

Boolin planted himself a few inches from Holmes's face. "Go ahead," he said. "Dig yourself in deeper."

Poe looked at Grey. "Helene, what's this about?"

Boolin held up his hand, claiming the floor. "What this is about, in addition to failure to report a kidnapping, is unauthorized access to the New York City morgue and illegal excursions to Hart Island. Interference in police procedure. Possible obstruction of justice." He leaned in even closer toward Holmes. "Did they cover that concept in private-investigator school? Or did you three just take the online course?"

Holmes exchanged looks with his partners.

"I've got eyes too," said the commissioner. "I've got eyes in the back of my ass." He turned to the monitor screen. "What the hell is that?" he asked. "What are those markers?"

"Chinese restaurants," said Holmes. "We were just planning to order takeout." He could see Grey glaring at Poe.

Poe hesitated for a second. Then he tapped his phone and enlarged the view of Brooklyn. "Patterns of unsolved disappearances cross-matched with subway victim evidence."

"This is NCIC stuff," said Boolin. "How did you get this?"

"It's my own software," said Poe. "Independently developed."

"Bullshit!" said Boolin. "These are restricted files." He turned to look Grey in the eye. "You were right, Detective. They have a very nice space here."

"Yes, sir," said Grey.

"Good. Because until this subway perp is caught, I think your team should use it as an annex. Get yourself set up and pool your resources with these three . . . experts. From now on, whatever they know, *we* know."

"Hold on!" said Holmes. "This is a private business office. You can't just . . ."

Boolin pointed at the screen. "Or I could just go ahead, charge you with theft of proprietary government files."

Holmes could see Virginia watching the whole spectacle from her desk, her head swiveling back and forth to follow the action. She caught his eye and passed him a folded note. He opened it.

Should I order cots? it said.

CHAPTER 56

BY THE NEXT night, Poe was about to go completely out of his mind.

"*Assholes!* I can't function in this atmosphere! I can't *work*! I can't *think*!"

He was looking over the balcony rail outside his apartment to the office space below. The firm's once-neat headquarters was now crowded with folding tables and whiteboards. Soda cans and half eaten deli sandwiches littered the tabletops. The air reeked of stale onions and kosher pickles and overused restrooms. Even for his normal human nostrils, it was a lot. He imagined that Holmes must be nauseated.

Most of the task force, including Grey, were out following up on leads. A couple of uniforms leaned against the kitchen island, drinking coffee. A detective in wrinkled khakis slouched and snored on one of the reception chairs. Poe could see Virginia at her desk, answering calls to the tip line.

He turned and walked back through the open door into his living room, shutting the door firmly behind him. Holmes and Marple sat in armchairs near an open window. Holmes sipped from a goblet of wine. He looked morose. Marple stirred a cup of tea. Annabel was curled up under her chair, hiding out from the task force. The investigators had been holed up together for nearly thirty-six hours, like prisoners in their own castle.

"Can they really commandeer our space like this?" Poe asked. "We should take them to court!"

"*Exactly!*" said Holmes. "Illegal confiscation. Malicious loitering. Something like that."

Marple took a slow sip from her cup. "There's only one way to get rid of them," she said softly. "Solve the case."

Her phone dinged with a text message. As she put down her tea and looked at the screen, her mood instantly brightened. "Look!" she said. "It's on!"

"The exhibit?" asked Holmes. He moved over to look at Marple's screen. Poe slipped in on the other side. Marple clicked to an elegant electronic invitation from a small gallery in Williamsburg—the very artsy neighborhood nearby.

"Looks like they put together an interesting show," she said. "Some minor pieces...and..." Marple scrolled to an image of the exhibit's big draw. She whistled softly. "And a *very* nice Picasso."

Holmes grinned. "I told you my friend Essen Blythe would come through."

"How do we know Franke will be interested?" asked Poe.

"Because he's already cased the gallery four times," said Marple. "He's jealous about the Shakespeare and Gutenberg. Also, I insulted his manhood."

"He needs to score," said Holmes.

Marple nodded. "So. Are we ready to take the great Luka Franke down?"

She was obviously eager to get into the details of the sting, but Poe couldn't muster the interest. Through the door, he could hear two cops downstairs guffawing at a crude joke.

"You two work it out," he said. "I need a break from these Neanderthals."

CHAPTER 57

TEN MILES AWAY, in his Manhattan penthouse, Luka Franke was using the Van Gogh he'd lifted in Cairo for practice. By coincidence, it was almost exactly the same size as the Picasso he intended to steal from the Williamsburg gallery the next day.

He had built a replica of the gallery's display case, complete with alarm system. He had also laser measured the dimensions of the gallery floor, the height of the ceiling, the distances to the exits. Everything. Down to the centimeter.

Disconnecting the alarm would be child's play. A simple wiring bypass. The same panel contained the connections for the surveillance cameras. Careless but convenient. And not totally surprising. This was a pop-up gallery, after all, not the Smithsonian.

He had already hired his shills, a Swiss couple with impeccable credentials who would create a diversion at the right moment. He had ordered a uniform for himself to match those of the gallery guards, two of whom were now on his payroll. Now it was just a matter of making the switch—and making it undetectable. For that, he would rely on his own sleight of hand, and the wizardry of his Japanese technicians.

Franke had supplied the refractive index and gradient for the Plexiglas case, along with the lumens and positions of the gallery lights. His young freelancers at Hitachi had done the rest.

Franke stared at the Van Gogh from the front, then from 30 degrees to each side, the most extreme angles available to the gallery viewers. Amazing. At every point, the illusion held up.

He opened the case and gently touched the surface of the painting, which was not a painting at all. It was an electronic image on a finely textured screen, as thin as a coat of varnish, mounted on canvas and powered by a battery the diameter of a hair. The resolution was rated at 4,000 dpi, much higher than what the human eye could actually discern. A comfortable margin, thought Franke. And worth every penny. A Picasso, even a lesser-known piece, could fetch tens of millions.

Franke stepped back two and a half feet, the exact distance from the case to the gallery's visitor barrier. He looked back and forth from the image to the stolen original, which was sitting on an easel alongside. The difference was undetectable. Franke pressed a button on a slim controller in his pocket.

On the impossibly slim screen, the image of the Van Gogh dissolved, replaced by an image of the Picasso, every bit as perfect.

Franke smiled. He liked things to be precise. Safer that way. He had learned early in life that art theft was no game. It was a demanding and dangerous profession. Sometimes deadly. And there were only three things that made it worth the risk.

Money. Cred. Payback.

CHAPTER 58

AT 2 A.M., Poe was slumped on a barstool, staring into an almost empty glass.

"Sir, do you need a ride somewhere?"

"Last call already?" asked Poe, looking up slowly from his ice cubes.

"It is for you, my friend. Sorry."

Poe stared at the bartender with bleary eyes. This was the last place he expected to be cut off. In general, he spent his leisure time in high-end establishments. But he preferred to do his serious drinking in spots like this, the divier and more forgiving the better. He'd found this place on a quiet corner a few blocks from the Brooklyn Navy Yard and immediately felt at home. The décor was dark wood and red vinyl. The playlist was late '90s. There were no craft cocktails.

"I'll be fine," said Poe. He tipped his glass back, letting the last of the cold vodka drip down his throat. He slapped an extra twenty on the bar and stood up.

"Get some sleep, buddy, okay?" said the bartender.

Poe placed both hands on the bar and leaned in, lowering his voice to a whisper. "'Sleep—those little slices of death!'" He leaned back. "Do you know where that's from?"

"Sorry, I don't," said the bartender.

"*A Nightmare on Elm Street 3*," said Poe.

The crowd had thinned considerably since he'd claimed his stool. There were only two couples left on the tiny dance floor. Poe weaved past them and headed for the door.

He liked drinking by himself. Gave him time to think. And he'd been thinking hard. About Sloane Stone. About Huntley Bain. About the subway murders. About the kidnapping. But mostly about Helene Grey. He was wondering if he'd made a mistake by getting close to her, especially now that she and her team had rudely intruded on his space. Not her idea, he realized, but awkward none-theless. They hadn't spoken in two days, except to exchange possible leads. In the office, it was all business, all the time. Like nothing had ever happened between them.

Maybe it shouldn't have, thought Poe. Maybe it had been a mis-take. Maybe he still wasn't ready.

The night air was sticky. There were no cabs in sight. Poe didn't mind. He felt like walking. He took a couple of deep breaths and headed east. At least he *thought* it was east. After two blocks and a couple of turns, he realized that he was headed in the wrong direc-tion. Nothing looked familiar.

He looked toward the street signs marking the next intersection. He recognized the street names from his map of pilfered NYPD data.

Poe had his bearings now, even if his perception was a bit wobbly. He turned around and headed in the opposite direction. The street was lined with brownstones fronted by wrought-iron gates. Some stoops were decorated with flower boxes, the blooms illuminated by streetlamps. He looked across the street and stopped.

He was looking at a large detached house in an elevated yard. A nineteenth-century mini mansion. It was redbrick, covered in vines, with a three-story turret facing the street. A distinctive house. And strangely familiar. Where had he seen it before?

Then something clicked. He'd seen it in his own photo gallery. Somebody had disappeared near this house. He remembered sticking a digital pin on this very spot. But who? Which one of those invisible victims was it? Poe flicked through his mental files. Right. It was one of the more recent disappearances. A hotel maid on her way home. About a year ago.

Poe heard the rumble of a car engine behind him. He recognized the sound before he even turned around. A Lamborghini. The sound of the naturally aspirated engine was unmistakable. As the car passed, he saw two men inside: one behind the wheel and another in the passenger seat.

The low-slung car turned the corner and pulled into the driveway of the mini mansion, then reappeared in front of the detached garage in the rear. Poe walked up the slope beside the house. He was a little unsteady on his feet, but he wanted a closer look at that magnificent machine.

The automatic garage door opened. Poe watched. The two men emerged and headed for the back of the house as the garage door slid shut. They both were mid-thirties, stylishly dressed. Poe watched them go inside.

As he walked back toward the street, he heard a loud metallic click and then the sound of a compressor turning on. Poe's mechanical mind started to whir. *How much does AC cost for a house that old?* he wondered. Bad insulation. Single-pane windows. The ConEd bill would be obscene.

He stopped in the middle of the lawn and looked toward the back of the house. Sure enough, there was the circular AC unit sitting on a concrete base. But that wasn't where the loud hum was coming from. That noise was coming from behind a row of hedges. Peeking above the foliage were two huge aluminum rectangles. Exhaust fans? Heat pumps?

Something about the house felt strange. Poe couldn't explain it. Or maybe he was just being paranoid. Maybe because he'd had too much to drink. Maybe because the place reminded him of the House of Usher. He needed a calmer head. He pulled out his phone and scrolled to a number, steadied his hand, and texted four characters:

U up?

He hoped Grey wouldn't take the message the wrong way.

CHAPTER 59

JUST SEVEN HOURS later, Marple settled into a booth with Poe and Holmes at a neighborhood diner, a few blocks from the office. It was a chance to debrief away from the clutter and the occupying task force. Marple was especially eager to hear more about Poe's overnight adventure. She buttered her English muffin, and leaned across the table. "So? The mystery house. What did you find out?"

Poe lifted his coffee cup with shaky hands. "Helene ran the property records for me," said Poe. "The house is in the name of two brothers. Richard and Nelson Siglik." He pushed his iPhone to the middle of the table and swiped through a few images. "Virginia just scraped these from their social accounts. No question. They're the two guys I saw last night."

"You mean early this morning," said Holmes. "While you were totally inebriated."

Poe scowled. "I saw what I saw."

The shots were nothing unusual, Marple thought. Two good-looking thirtysomething guys, almost twins. Richard had a trendy stubble. Nelson was clean-shaven, with longer hair. In the Instagram shots, they were sometimes together, sometimes in separate pairs or groups. Always with attractive companions, male and female. Both brothers were fit and smartly dressed, the type who'd look at home in any Manhattan investment firm or high-end nightclub.

"Does either of them have a record?" asked Marple.

"Squeaky clean," said Poe. "They pay their taxes, donate to the neighborhood association, rent a bouncy castle for block parties. But look at this..."

Poe scrolled to a photo of a young woman in a dancer's leotard. It was a studio portrait, carefully posed and beautifully lit. The subject looked like a young Nicole Kidman, with pale skin and auburn curls.

"Who's this?" asked Marple.

"Anna Sofia. The brothers' mother. Professional dancer. Disappeared without a trace almost thirty years ago. The dad was investigated, but nothing came of it. He claimed she was unbalanced and just ran off. Nobody could prove otherwise."

Marple got a sick feeling in her gut. "Did they question the boys?"

"Sure," said Poe. "But they were only about six or seven when it happened. They couldn't offer anything useful."

He turned back to a photo of the mansion. "The house has been in the family since the 1930s," said Poe. "The grandfather owned a funeral home a few blocks from where we're sitting. He specialized in deceased immigrants. His son moved the business to Park Slope and started burying rich people."

"The brothers are *undertakers*?" asked Holmes.

"Nope," said Poe. "They sold the business to a funeral home consortium when their dad died. Cashed out for millions."

"Do they work?" asked Marple.

"Don't need to," said Poe. "Trust fund. Plus the profit from the sale of the funeral business."

Marple took a sip of her tea. "What about all the fancy equipment you saw outside?"

"Air scrubbers for mold mitigation, according to the permits," said Poe. "All legal and up to code."

"Not exactly like finding a wood chipper in the backyard," said Holmes.

Poe signaled the waitress and pointed to his empty coffee cup. "Helene said she'd have patrol do some drive-bys."

"Useless," said Holmes. "We should stake it out ourselves."

"No stakeouts," said Marple. "We need to get inside."

"Helene says we'll never get a warrant," said Poe. "No probable cause."

Marple admired her two partners. But she was happy to have resources of her own—and favors to call in.

"Don't worry," said Marple. "Leave that to me."

CHAPTER 60

BY THAT AFTERNOON, the weather had turned ugly. As Poe sat alone in the back seat of a town car, the clouds through the tinted roof panel swirled ominously. Before long, the car was being pelted by a steady drizzle.

He was riding through a part of New Jersey that looked more like rural Pennsylvania, filled with rolling fields and horse farms, ninety minutes south of the chemical plants that gave the Garden State a bad rap.

The woman he was on his way to see had led him to long-buried secrets before, and he was hoping she would come through today. Besides, it would be good to see her. It had been too long.

Poe asked the driver for a classical station and made it clear he wasn't in the mood for chat. For most of the ride, he kept his eyes closed, head back, listening to *La traviata*. Verdi was a perfect match for the weather.

When Poe looked up, the car was rolling down a narrow country road. The driver slowed at the entrance to a rutted dirt driveway with a battered mailbox at the end.

"This is it," said Poe.

The car pulled to a stop. "Need me to wait?" asked the driver.

"Not necessary," said Poe. At least that's what he hoped.

As the car drove off, Poe put up his umbrella. He started walking up the muddy driveway for thirty yards or so, past a ramshackle farmhouse and toward an even more decrepit barn behind it. The whole structure had a rightward lean to it, as if it were just longing to lie down.

As Poe got closer, the barn door slid open. A woman stepped out wearing a plastic poncho and rubber boots. Her black hair, grey streaked, was pulled back into a ponytail that poked out behind her John Deere cap. She looked her visitor up and down, then laughed. "Amazing," she said. "Only Auguste Poe would wear a three-piece suit to visit a farm in a torrential downpour."

"Sorry," said Poe. "My hip waders are at the cleaners."

The woman walked up and gave Poe a long, strong hug. She smelled of hay and gasoline. Poe was always amazed at how much she looked like her sister.

"Good to see you, Jacklyn," said Poe. "Where is she?"

Jacklyn pulled back from the hug and nodded toward the barn.

The rain was coming down harder now. Thunder rolled in the distance. "How long has she been here?" asked Poe.

"Long time," said Jacklyn.

Poe followed her into the barn and dropped his umbrella on the floor. A pair of swallows fluttered off a beam high overhead.

"Nobody else has been down here?"

"Nope. Nobody but me."

Jacklyn led him to a walled-off section with its own door, some kind of storage room or stall with its own padlock, already open. Poe's heart started pounding.

Jacklyn pulled the lock off the latch and wrestled the wooden door fully open. She stepped aside. Poe walked into the stall, lit by a single naked bulb. He rocked back, stunned.

Sitting there, surrounded by storage bins, was a Dodge Shelby Charger, all black. It looked a little dusty but otherwise mint. Poe felt a flutter in his chest. It was exactly what he'd been hoping for.

"You sure it's the right year?" he asked.

"Why do you think I called?" said Jacklyn.

Poe dropped his head for a moment and let out a sigh. He ran his palm gently over the hood and side panels. Not a scratch or a dent anywhere. Even the wheel covers looked intact. He wiped a clear patch in the window grime with two fingers and peered inside.

"Original upholstery?" he asked.

Jacklyn nodded. "Factory all the way."

"Battery good?"

"Fresh from AutoZone."

"Think she'll fire up?"

Jacklyn tossed him a set of keys attached to an STP tag. She smiled. "For you, they usually do."

Poe opened the car door and slid behind the wheel. He put the key into the slot, pumped the gas pedal twice, and turned the key to Start. There was a whine and a cough from under the hood, then a thin rattle. On the second try, Poe heard a low grumble, and then—amazingly—a loud roar. A plume of vapor burst from the exhaust pipe. The turbo engine vibrated with power. Poe glanced down at the odometer. Only 60,000 miles.

Plenty of life left in her.

CHAPTER 61

A HALF HOUR later, the mighty Dodge idled gently outside the barn. It had taken that long to clear the junk away around it so that Poe could drive the car out.

The rain had mostly stopped. A few scattered drops dotted the dust on the hood and roof. Poe leaned against the front side panel with the folded title in his hand. Jacklyn leaned next to him, the check in her pocket. They'd run out of things to say about the Charger's gear ratio and engine specs.

Jacklyn shifted awkwardly against the car and stared out over the wet, empty field. Finally she spoke up again. "Seeing anybody?" she asked.

"Now and then," Poe said softly.

"Still working?"

"Like a madman."

"Still drinking?"

"On and off."

Jacklyn nodded. She scraped a divot in the mud with the heel of her rain boot. "You can't change what happened to Annie, Auguste. You can't keep torturing yourself."

Poe dipped his head. "So people keep telling me."

"Dammit," said Jacklyn, her voice cracking slightly. "I miss her too. Every day." She turned and patted the car. "I thought maybe this would help."

Poe pushed himself off the car. He put his arms around Jacklyn's shoulders and squeezed her tight. "Thank you for finding this one, Jacklyn. It's special."

"If it helps you remember her," she said, "it was worth the hunt."

Poe opened the door and slid into the driver's seat. He put the Shelby into gear and waved through the window. Jacklyn waved back.

The car swerved in the mud on the way to the main road, but once the tires bit into the pavement, it practically begged to race. Poe gave it more gas, feeling the surge from the powerful machine. The car was built the same year she was born. His lovely, lost Annie. The woman he was still having dreams about. And sometimes nightmares.

He glanced over toward the passenger seat and imagined her there, window open, laughing into the wind, begging him to go faster.

God, she would have loved it.

CHAPTER 62

THAT NIGHT, LUKA Franke rode up in his building's padded freight elevator with a satisfied smile on his face. The gallery theft could not have gone off any smoother. The Swiss couple had started a spat so convincing that the staff convened to usher them out onto the sidewalk. Franke made a note to wire them a bonus.

As he and the other faux guards closed the security curtain in front of the Picasso during the ruckus, Franke himself had opened the case and made the switch. The alarms had been temporarily disabled. For that same interval, the video surveillance record would show only black.

As Franke entered his apartment, the sensors automatically brought the lights up to a warm, flattering glow. He set the case down on the sofa and opened the lid.

And there it was.

Even in the dim light, the Picasso was stunning. Franke took a deep breath and exhaled slowly. Relieved. Proud. Triumphant.

Then it hit him. Subtle but distinctive.

The smell of stale tea.

Rising from the case.

Franke felt a swell of nausea. Sweat prickled his scalp. He lifted the painting out of the case and turned it over. He bent down and pressed his nose close to the wooden frame. No question. A subtle tell. Wet tea bags had been recently applied to the pine. A short-cut to simulate aging. Not every thief would recognize the trick. But Franke did. He'd learned it from his father.

He reached for a remote and dialed the ceiling lights up to full. The room lit up like a stage set. Franke opened a small drawer and pulled out a jeweler's loupe. He placed the glass over the canvas and peered through the round eyepiece.

Goddamnit!

He let the loupe drop onto the floor.

The artwork was superb. Nearly flawless. Which made Franke even more furious. Whoever had painted this canvas was a technical master.

But it wasn't Pablo Picasso.

Franke looked up. He sensed rustling outside in the hallway. Then he heard three loud pounds on his door—like hammer blows.

"Police!"

CHAPTER 63

FOR THE FIRST time in two days, Virginia was alone in the office. Her three bosses were out. So was Detective Grey. The rest of the task force had been called out for support on a drug raid. It had taken her an hour to make the place presentable again. Like cleaning up after a frat party. It was way past time to go home.

She made one last pass through the space, picking up fast-food containers and scraps of paper. As she walked back to her desk, she heard a soft rustle from the rear of the office.

"Annabel?"

Now there was something else.

An aroma.

Molasses?

Virginia walked over and opened the microwave. Empty. Same with the oven.

The sound came again. More defined.

Like shoes shuffling on a stone floor.

Virginia looked toward the back wall, lined with black metal file cabinets. She felt a tingle shoot through her and heard her pulse throbbing in her ears.

"Hello? Anybody there?"

As Virginia stepped away from the last desk, she found herself about ten feet from the back wall. Then she heard the sound again. Somebody walking.

She jumped.

The footsteps were right next to her.

She turned slowly toward the black metal file cabinets. Suddenly, she saw a shape. Or a shadow. Just for a second. It was moving from one side of the cabinet row to the other.

Virginia blinked. The shadow was gone.

Eyestrain, she thought. *Definitely eyestrain.* She really needed to take more breaks from the computer. She took a deep breath and exhaled.

Wait.

The smell was back. Getting stronger. Filling the room.

Virginia recognized it now.

It was the aroma of baking bread.

CHAPTER 64

HOLMES, MARPLE, AND Poe were delighted. Especially Marple. This was better than *The Great British Bake Off*.

On the other side of the one-way mirror, Luka Franke sat at a small metal table, his fingers twisting through his thick hair, muttering obscenities into the bare, fluorescent-lit interrogation room.

"Look at him," said Marple. "Wilted like a weed."

The door from the hallway opened. Helene Grey walked in with a tall woman in a business suit.

"This is Catherine East from Art Crimes," said Grey. "Her team made the arrest."

"We appreciate the tip," said East. "He's a big fish."

"We appreciate the takedown," said Marple. "He's a real prick."

"I have to ask," said East. "Where did you get the fake Picasso? It sure as hell would have fooled me."

Silence.

Then Poe spoke up. "Paint by number," he said. "Took forever."

Grey scowled at him. "No. Really."

Holmes just smiled. "Friend of a friend."

For the moment, Grey didn't push it. Neither did East. They

both seemed more interested in the captive than the bait. At Marple's request, Grey had remanded Franke to one of the city's most depressing holding areas—a bleak basement built in the 1960s. Cinder-block walls. Concrete floor. Oppressively low ceiling. The air was thick with half a century of body odor and cigarette smoke.

"I'd say he's a bit out of his comfort zone," said Grey.

"He's miserable," said Marple. "It's magnificent."

CHAPTER 65

SUDDENLY, FRANKE STOOD up from the table and walked straight up to the mirror, pressing his face against it from the other side. "I want my *lawwwyerrr*!" He stretched the last word out as if he were speaking to a toddler. Then he walked back to his seat and drummed his fingers on the tabletop.

Marple smiled. It was a pleasure watching him stew.

Just then, a slim man in a well-tailored suit and wire-framed glasses walked into the viewing room carrying a leather briefcase. He looked through the glass. "Is that him?" he asked bluntly.

Helene looked up. "I'm Detective Lieutenant Helene Grey," she said. "This is Catherine East, Art Crimes. Have we met?"

"Roger Gow, DA's office," said the new arrival. "Antiquities Trafficking Unit."

"You're an attorney?" asked East.

"JD, MFA, PhD. Take your pick." Gow nodded toward the investigators. "Who are they?"

"Holmes, Marple, and Poe," said Grey. "They're private investigators."

Gow cocked his head and repeated the names. "Holmes, Marple,

199

Poe. Funny." He wasn't smiling. He nodded toward the interrogation room. "Shall we?"

Grey unlocked the door. Gow pushed through first.

Franke stared up at him. "Where the fuck is my lawyer?"

"Mr. Franke? I'm Roger Gow, assistant district attorney." Gow held out his hand. Franke ignored it. Grey and East followed the lawyer into the room, just ahead of Holmes and Poe. When Marple walked through the door, she saw Franke's face twitch.

"Hello, Luka," she said.

"No wig today?" said Franke. "I should have known! *You set me up!*"

"Settle down now," said Marple. "You just got greedy."

"You were blinded by love," said Poe.

Holmes looked admiringly at Marple. "Who could blame you?"

"Where's my lawyer?" snarled Franke. "Nothing from me until he gets here."

"Of course," said Gow. "Don't speak. That's your prerogative. In the meantime, I highly recommend that you *listen*. I'm actually here to help you."

"I don't need any help," said Franke. "The Picasso is worthless. I took nothing of value. Your experts will tell you the same thing."

"So they have," said Gow. "A curiosity item. Petty larceny at best. Maybe throw in B and E for the alarm work. Still, minor charges." Gow reached into his briefcase. "I'm far more interested in *this*."

Marple saw Franke's eyes twitch.

Gow pulled out an iPad and tapped the screen. It filled with an image of Van Gogh's *Poppy Flowers*.

"Can we agree that *this* has value?" asked Gow.

Franke stared at Marple, slowly clenching and unclenching his hands. Marple smiled back.

"We don't have a final estimate yet," said Gow. "But *considerably* north of a million. As I'm sure you know, that's a very significant threshold."

"That's grand larceny," said Holmes.

"First degree," added Poe.

"Class D felony," said Marple.

Gow turned back to Franke. "You've kept your record clean so far, Mr. Franke. But even a first-time conviction could get you several years. That's enough to significantly cloud your future. A lot of your clients might avoid doing business with a convicted felon. Am I right?"

Marple looked at Grey. She could tell the detective was holding her tongue, waiting to see where Gow was headed.

The attorney leaned in, inches from Franke's ear. "You're trapped, Mr. Franke. But—as they say in the movies—there's a *twist*. It turns out the mayor of New York has a special interest in your case. A close friend and supporter of his also happens to be the victim of an art theft. Mr. Huntley Bain. Apparently, he lost a Gutenberg Bible and a Shakespeare First Folio. From an impregnable safe."

East looked at Grey. Grey glared at Gow. "Hold on," East said. "Exactly who are you speaking for?"

Gow kept his focus on Franke. "Now, *if* the Van Gogh were to mysteriously find its way back to its rightful owners, *and if* you were willing to plumb your sources to help us locate the perpetrator of the Bain heist, we might be willing to let this Picasso matter slip. On technicalities."

Grey stepped up and grabbed Gow by the arm. "What the hell are you doing? *What* technicalities? Does your boss know about this?"

Gow made a show of plucking Grey's hand away. "He does, Detective. So does yours."

Marple winced. So this was the game. She absolutely despised snakes like Luka Franke. And now he was about to slither free.

CHAPTER 66

AN HOUR LATER, still furious about Franke, Marple was on her way to Westchester. She'd been ready to take a late-night train from Grand Central, but Poe insisted on lending her his precious Oldsmobile.

For Marple, the powerful sedan was a total waste of horsepower. The speedometer had barely touched 55 the whole way up the Hutchinson River Parkway. Now, on the narrow back roads of Bedford, she was barely crawling.

The homes in Westchester's pricey horse country were set far back behind rustic stone walls. The GPS only got Marple close to her destination. Now she inched forward in first gear, a few yards at a time, shining her headlights at mailboxes until she found the right address.

The long driveway curved through a stand of elms as it approached the massive country house. When Marple pulled to a stop in the gravel circle, the front door opened.

A white-haired man in a wheelchair rolled to the threshold, backlit by the warm glow from inside. Marple climbed out of the car and walked toward him. The man eyed the muscle car.

"Get any speeding citations?"

Marple smiled. "Belongs to a friend. I'm just happy I didn't strip the transmission."

Stepping up to the entryway, Marple bent down and gave the man a gentle hug.

"Thank you for seeing me so late."

"Any time, any reason—you know that," he said, turning his chair in a slow 180. "Come in, Margaret." Marple walked alongside as he wheeled himself into a large library off the main foyer.

"Sherry?" he asked.

"You know better, Your Honor. I'm driving."

"Sorry. Didn't mean to corrupt you. How about some tea, then? Chamomile, was it?"

"Excellent memory," Marple replied.

Her host pressed a button on a table. Seconds later, a middle-aged woman appeared through an arch at the back of the room. "Yes, Judge?"

"A cup of chamomile tea for Ms. Marple, please, Bea. Brandy for me."

Marple took a seat on the sofa. As she looked across at the frail man in the metal chair, she flashed to a memory of him standing tall in front of a cluster of press microphones, his deep voice cracking as he begged for the return of his only child.

Everybody in the audience knew that he'd lost his wife to cancer a year earlier. His daughter, just fifteen, was all the family he had left. The girl had disappeared on a school ski trip out west. When the case went cold, the anguished father had turned to a fledgling female private investigator who promised results—and delivered.

Marple glanced over at a framed photo of a dark-haired teenager on the bookshelf, frozen as a high school junior.

"How is she?" Marple asked.

"Medical school," the judge said proudly. "Thanks to you."

"Lydia has a 140 IQ," said Marple. "I'm pretty sure she got into med school on her own."

"Maybe so," he said. "But without you, she'd still be a sister wife to that maniac."

Bea came in carrying a tray with a cup of tea and a snifter of amber liquor. She placed it on a low coffee table. "Thanks, Bea," said the judge. Bea nodded and made her exit.

Marple lifted the teacup and took a sip. She closed her eyes dreamily, savoring the aroma and flavor. "Perfect," she said.

The judge swirled his brandy. "What can I do for you, Margaret? Carry permit? Green card? Restraining order?"

Marple smiled. Over the years, the judge had done so much for her. She put down her teacup and leaned forward.

"Well, Your Honor, since you asked..."

CHAPTER 67

HOLMES LOOKED UP as Marple walked back into the office. It was almost 1 a.m.

He was sitting with Poe in the common area. Helene Grey was at her makeshift desk, and the rest of the squad was scattered around the first floor, back from their earlier drug bust—which had apparently turned out to be a waste of time. Virginia was long gone.

Grey looked worn and frustrated. Holmes understood why. She'd been outranked by the FBI on the Charles kidnapping. A dirty backroom deal had let Luka Franke walk. And the subway murder case—the one she was supposed to be solving—was going nowhere.

Holmes watched as Marple handed Grey a neatly folded document.

"What's this?" Grey asked.

"Just read it," said Marple.

Grey unfolded the paper. She absorbed the contents at a glance, then shook the page at Marple. "How did you get this?"

"Never mind," said Marple. "All you need to know is that it will hold up in court."

Grey stared at Marple for a second. Then she grabbed her walkie-talkie out of its belt holster. Her voice blasted out from every other police walkie-talkie on the floor.

"Saddle up, everybody. We've got a search warrant."

The sleep-deprived task force roused itself for another mission. Detectives pulled blue NYPD windbreakers from bags and started checking their handguns. Police walkie-talkies squawked more. Within seconds, the whole squad was on the move.

Holmes felt a rush of excitement and then—out of nowhere—an inexplicable flood of dread. He looked across the room as Poe moved in to huddle with Marple and Grey. He started toward them, then stopped halfway.

His chest started to tighten. His hands started to tremble. His mouth went dry, and he felt a sheen of sweat on his forehead. He was suddenly terrified, unable to take another step. He knew what was happening, and he couldn't stop it.

He was in stage one of a full-blown panic attack.

As his vision began to blur, he steadied himself against a wall. Cops and detectives milled around him. Sounds went in and out. His breaths came in short gasps. He made his way through the maze of temporary desks toward the staircase that led to the apartment level. He couldn't let anybody see him like this.

He climbed the stairs slowly, clinging to the rail, then kept one hand on the wall as he moved along the upstairs hallway toward his apartment. The attack was getting worse. He felt like his heart and lungs were about to seize up and quit.

Just a few feet more...

He staggered into his bedroom and jerked his closet door open. He reached behind the row of suits and shirts and tapped the combination to his wall safe. The thick metal door popped open. He reached in and pulled out a small bag.

His emergency supply.

Not the best quality, but it would have to do.

He opened the bag and carefully poured a pinch of heroin onto the soft mound between his bent thumb and forefinger. He put one nostril to the powder and inhaled, hard and deep. He blinked and sat back on the floor of the closet. He felt his heart rate settling. He took a few deep breaths and let his senses stabilize.

Relief.

Holmes tucked the bag back into the safe and closed the door. He grabbed a handkerchief and dabbed the sweat off his forehead, then angled his face toward a mirror to check for residue on his nostrils.

Good to go.

He also grabbed his pistol for good measure.

When he walked back downstairs, the place was in the full throes of paramilitary prep. Two huge black SWAT trucks had pulled up to the building entrance. Sturdy men in tac gear were strutting through the office, passing out equipment, barking orders. The macho energy was palpable.

Poe looked up as Holmes approached. "Where have *you* been?" he asked.

"Loading my weapon," said Holmes. "When do we leave?"

A uniformed sergeant rushed up with an armload of ballistic vests and helmets.

Holmes grabbed a vest and lowered it over his shoulders. He looked across at Marple and Poe, already suited up. In their bulky gear and wobbly helmets, they looked like kids playing soldier. But this was no game.

A SWAT officer in head-to-toe tac gear stepped up and pointed toward the front door. "*You! You! You!* You're with me!"

Holmes checked his watch. If he'd timed the dose properly, he'd be in full flight by showtime.

CHAPTER 68

MARPLE STAYED TIGHT between her partners as they headed out the front door. The two massive SWAT trucks were idling by the curb. Their escort pointed toward the open rear doors of the second vehicle and gave them each a hard slap on the back.

"Go! Go! Go!"

They climbed onto the narrow metal step to the interior, then slid along the bench that ran the length of the right side. A row of SWAT officers sat on the opposite bench, adjusting their night-vision goggles and checking their automatic rifles. The air smelled of leather and oil and coffee breath. Marple turned toward Holmes. His head was leaned back against the side of the truck. He had a faraway stare, as if he were looking straight through the roof. Marple nudged him with her elbow.

"Brendan, you okay?"

"I'm fine," Holmes replied, his tone low and flat.

Goddamnit! Marple turned to Poe and whispered tersely into his ear. "He's high."

"Make room!" A loud voice from the truck's rear door. Marple looked over as a massive German shepherd leaped into the truck, followed by a handler gripping a thick leather leash. The doors slammed shut behind them. The engine growled as the truck rolled forward, almost knocking the handler off his feet.

"Down, Gunner!" he commanded.

The sturdy canine crouched by Poe's feet.

"Drug dog?" Poe asked nervously.

Marple held her breath. Who knew what Holmes was carrying.

"Cadaver," said the handler.

The truck rounded a turn and Marple felt her stomach heave. It was like being rolled in a barrel. She glanced again at Holmes. His body was loose, his eyes now fixed on the opposite wall. She grabbed his arm and dug her nails into his forearm through his shirt. She brought her lips up to his ear and spoke softly through clenched teeth.

"Don't blow this, Brendan," she said. "Just ... *don't!*"

No reaction.

Marple realized that her partner was already on his own separate planet.

CHAPTER 69

IT WAS A bumpy five-minute ride to the target. For Holmes, the time floated by. He felt safe. Warm. Happy. He stared at the men with guns and smiled. Wondered why they didn't smile back.

Suddenly, he felt the truck come to a jerking stop. Two seconds later, the rear doors burst open. One by one, the black-suited SWAT cops moved out and jumped down onto the street, rifles ready. Holmes could see the brick mansion on the corner, framed by the opening at the back of the truck; it reached his brain in the form of a beautiful painting.

As the SWAT team moved across the street, Holmes saw Helene Grey lean into the back of the truck. Her voice boomed in his brain. "Listen up! You three stay behind me the whole time. Got it? No stragglers."

"You hear that, Brendan?" Marple was in his ear.

He nodded and pulled himself up by holding on to a metal hand-grip. He felt like he could drift right out of the truck. And then fly over the house. And then . . .

"Brendan!" Poe shouted into his face. "Are you okay?"

Holmes blinked. Took a breath. Focused. Put his hand on his

partner's shoulder. "I'm fine, Auguste. Lead on." He felt Marple beside him, her arm wrapped tightly around his. He knew she would look after him.

Grey led the way to the side of a thick hedge edging the mansion property. Holmes looked up and down the street, still wet from the weekend rain. The puddles swirled with kaleidoscope colors. He heard Poe's voice again.

"What now?" his partner asked.

"We wait," Grey replied. "It's their show."

As Holmes watched, a small group of shadows emerged from the hedge on the opposite side of the property and moved up to the front door. One of the shadows held a long, thick metal object, stockier than a rifle. It looked like a log with handles.

The figure at the head of the right-hand column pounded on the door.

"NYPD! We have a warrant!"

The cop leaned back. Holmes could see his fingers in profile against the bricks, counting down the time.

Five...four...three...

"We're going in right behind them," said Grey. "Stay tight and keep out of their way."

BAM!

Holmes saw light pouring onto the porch from the place the door used to be. He heard footsteps pounding on the grass. It took him a few seconds to realize that he was alone by the hedge. Grey, Poe, and Marple were already moving across the lawn. Holmes ran to catch up, blinking beads of sweat out of his eyes. The pleasant swirls of color were gone now. He stared at the mansion. Even in his altered state, he knew Poe was right about this place. It radiated evil.

CHAPTER 70

MARPLE RAN TOWARD the porch behind Grey and Poe.

She looked back. *Where the hell is Brendan?*

There he was, coming out of the shadows. Marple reached back, grabbed his vest, and pulled him forward. "Keep up, Brendan! Keep it together!"

Marple stayed close behind Poe as they moved up the porch stairs. She heard the sounds of heavy boots and loud shouts from inside as the SWAT teams moved from room to room.

"Clear!"... "Clear!"... "Clear!"

As Marple stepped into the vestibule, she could hear loud footsteps and slamming doors from the floor above.

When she looked around, her two partners were off in different directions. Poe, wearing blue surgical gloves, was in the dining room to the left, nudging SWAT officers aside as he tapped his knuckles against the walls. Holmes was in the library just off the entryway, pulling books off shelves and running his gloved hands along the back panels, as if searching for some secret button. His helmet was resting upside down on a coffee table.

Suddenly, he turned to grab on to a large wing-backed chair, then slumped heavily into the seat. His face was pale, his eyes hollow.

No! thought Marple. *Not here. Not now.*

Holmes sat up abruptly. Then his head started to nod. The weight of the armored vest seemed to pull him forward. Suddenly, he was tipping, unstoppable, toward the floor.

"Brendan!"

Marple lunged toward him. Too late. Holmes landed hard. His head bounced from the impact. Out of the corner of her eye, Marple saw Grey spin and sprint across the room. In seconds, they were both kneeling next to Holmes, rolling him onto his back. Grey shook him by the shoulders. "Holmes! *Holmes!*"

His body was limp, his pupils as small as pinholes. There was a reddish bruise forming on his forehead.

Grey shouted toward the entryway. *"Medic!"*

"It's okay," Marple said firmly. "I've got it."

She reached into the cross-body bag she wore and pulled out a bottle of Narcan.

CHAPTER 71

"CAN YOU TELL me your name?"

"Brendan."

"Your *full* name."

"Holmes. Brendan Mark Holmes."

"Do you know where you are?"

"On a very expensive Persian carpet."

"Do you know what happened to you?"

Holmes was looking up at a woman in blue. His senses were mostly numb, but he could make out the tactical medic patch on her sleeve. Three other faces were leaning over him, coming slowly into focus. Poe. Marple. Grey.

"I appear to have overmedicated," said Holmes.

Holmes felt the medic detach the BP cuff from his arm. She was now talking to Grey. "He's oriented times four, Detective Lieutenant. We can run him in for observation, but he's probably fine."

"I'm not going anywhere," Holmes said firmly.

"Your call," said the medic, leaning into his face. She nodded toward Marple. "You should thank your friend here. She saved your life."

Holmes blinked. His senses were muted. Faces and figures were blurry. He watched as the medic stuffed the BP cuff back into her kit and headed off toward the foyer. Grey followed her. He was alone in the living room with Marple and Poe.

Marple leaned down and stared him in the face. He could see her features clearly now. Her jaw was set and her eyes were steely. She reached into his jacket and removed his pistol.

"Sorry, Margaret," Holmes whispered. "I owe you. Again."

"We'll talk about this later," said Marple, slipping the gun into her bag. "Unless I kill you first."

CHAPTER 72

AS MARPLE STALKED off toward the foyer, Poe helped Holmes to his feet.

"How long was I gone?" asked Holmes.

"Four minutes, thirty-two seconds," said Poe. "A new record."

As Holmes looked around, he could see that the search was winding down. The only energy seemed to be from the cadaver dog, who was sniffing his way around the dining room baseboards.

"Did they find anything?" asked Holmes. "Anything at all?"

Poe shook his head. "No drugs. No weapons. No bodies. No brothers."

"What about the basement?" Holmes asked.

"Wine cellar, just like the plans said."

"There's something here. I can *feel* it," said Holmes.

He was still a bit unsteady as he walked through a cluster of cops and into the enormous kitchen. It was a complete gourmet setup. Viking range. Pricey espresso machine. The refrigerator was the size of a self-contained pantry, with heavy brass latches. Holmes ran his hand over the wood-paneled front as Marple came in from the dining room.

She walked right past him.

When he looked across the room, Poe was locked in a tense discussion with Helene Grey on the far side of the enormous kitchen. He was sure they were talking about him. Marple was opening cupboards one at a time and poking through the contents.

Holmes walked across the room and slumped against the kitchen island. Maybe the best thing he could do now was stay out of the way. Shut up. Not make things worse.

The island was massive, with storage cabinets underneath and a thick slab of richly veined marble on top. A basket of oranges sat in the middle.

Holmes stared at the oranges, then realized that he couldn't smell them. Another scent was making its way into his chemosensory system. Far more powerful. He jumped back from the kitchen island like it was a hot stove.

"Over here!" he shouted.

Four huge SWAT guys moved across the kitchen like an NFL front line. They braced themselves against one side of the island and pushed. The basket tipped over. A dozen oranges bounced onto the floor and rolled in every direction.

The SWAT team kept shoving and grunting. Suddenly, there was a loud metallic *snap* from the base of the island, like a latch breaking. The whole unit swung aside to reveal the floor underneath.

"Holy shit," said one of the SWAT guys. The crowd in the kitchen leaned forward. Holmes moved in first. There in the floor, set flush with the footprint of the island, was a neat rectangular hatch.

Holmes went clammy. He glanced over at Poe, then at Grey, then at Marple. He put his hand over his mouth, stifling his gag reflex. The smell was coming from beneath the hatch.

"There are people down here!" Holmes shouted.

The dog was in the kitchen now, sitting on his haunches.

"Why isn't the dog alerting?" asked Poe.

"He's a cadaver dog," said Holmes. "Whoever's down there is still alive."

CHAPTER 73

HOLMES STOOD CLOSE as the SWAT team lifted the hatch cover—two inches of wood backed with another inch of solid steel. One of the biggest SWAT guys held it open while a squad of four stood around the opening, rifles aimed into the darkness underneath.

"There's a ladder!" one of the cops shouted, shining a flashlight into the hole.

Holmes lunged forward and swung his feet onto the third rung, knocking a gun barrel out of the way. The flashlight beams hit his face as he dropped into the hole, two steps at a time.

"Hey! Asshole! Stop!"

His feet touched ground. He stepped away from the ladder and heard the bang of boots following him down.

Holmes plunged ahead, hands against the walls, toward the horrible smell. He could feel the cops behind him. The beams from their flashlights shot past him into the tunnel ahead.

Holmes kept the lead, pacing the distance as he went. Ten yards. Now twenty.

He rounded a corner and stopped. He could see the end of the tunnel.

It ended at a huge metal door.

Holmes felt a hand grip his shoulder as one of the SWAT guys yanked him back and shoved him against the wall, face-first. He heard the rustle of gear and then a shout.

"Breach!"

There was a flash of sparks and a loud boom. Holmes felt the shock wave against his eardrums, and for a second, all he could hear was a loud hum.

When he looked back, the massive door was blown off its hinges. Through the haze of smoke, Holmes got a glimpse into the opening and the dark space beyond. As the hum in his head receded, he heard a wild mix of voices, male and female. Screaming. Sobbing. Wailing. The smell was now like a thick vapor. One of the cops pulled off his helmet and vomited into it. Another shouted into his shoulder mic.

"Medical! We need medical!"

Holmes pushed his way through to the opening as the cops waved their flashlight beams across the interior.

It was like staring into the pit of hell.

CHAPTER 74

IN THE NARROW shafts of light, Holmes could make out shapes below. Voices rose from the shadows, cracking and desperate.

"Help us! Please!"

One female voice rose above the others. "Get us out! Hurry! Before they come back."

Holmes heard footsteps behind him. A second later, he felt Marple and Poe over his shoulder. Helene Grey pushed through the SWAT guys and raked her flashlight across the space. "Jesus Christ," she muttered.

Holmes could make out a huddle of figures against a far wall, pulling against some kind of restraints.

"Don't be afraid!" Grey shouted into the pit. "We're here to help you!"

Holmes felt his repulsion being overwhelmed by rage. As he blinked, the horror came to him in quick, grisly snapshots.

He saw a large rectangular sunken space, a pit lined with thick metal walls. In the center was a cluster of men and women. Each prisoner had a metal band around one ankle. The bands were attached to cables looped through thick eyes in the wall.

There was a hole in the floor, rimmed with human waste. The prisoners were all dressed in identical blue PPI gowns, torn and soiled, with patches of raw skin showing through.

Holmes saw a cop moving along the wall, stepping through the filth to slice the cables with a bolt cutter. The freed prisoners surged forward, zombielike, moaning and weeping.

As Holmes reached the bottom step, a tall woman fell into his arms like a child. Her blond hair was matted, her expression feral and crazed.

In seconds, the whole crowd of prisoners pushed toward the door, almost engulfing the rescuers. "Stay back!" Grey shouted, hands raised. "Please! Stay back!"

Holmes turned to see Poe reaching down to pick up a young man too frail to stand. Then he saw Marple working her way into the dark shadows of the pit, tears streaming down her face.

"Zozi?" she called out. "Zozi Turner? Zozi and Eton Charles? Are you here? Can you hear me?"

There was no reply.

A woman's voice rose from the pack, weak and raspy.

"Save it," she said. "If they were ever here, they're dead."

CHAPTER 75

BACK ABOVE IN the kitchen, Poe watched as the wasted men and women made their way up the ladder from the tunnel. EMTs and paramedics reached down to help them to the top.

Poe walked over to the other side of the kitchen, where Grey was standing with Holmes and Marple. A young woman with huge eyes sat shivering on a stool. Grey had wrapped a blanket around her shoulders. The woman's knees were bruised and filthy. The metal cuff was still on her ankle, with purplish bruises all around it.

"I'm Detective Lieutenant Helene Grey. These people are private investigators—Mr. Holmes, Mr. Poe, and Ms. Marple."

The woman's eyes darted back and forth from one face to another. She looked dazed and disoriented.

"I'm Davina," the woman said. "Davina Kane."

Poe felt a jolt. He recognized the name: the missing hotel maid.

"Davina," Grey said gently. "How did you get here? Can you tell us what happened?"

The young woman closed her eyes and took a couple of quick breaths. Her answers came in short bursts.

"They took me," she said. "On the street. At night. I was on my way home from work..."

"The Clairmont Hotel," said Poe.

Davina nodded. "Part time. Housekeeping."

"*Who* took you?" asked Marple. "When? From where?"

"Two men. They asked for directions to a theater. I didn't know the name. I felt something sharp in my arm. That's all I remember."

"And when did you realize you were here?"

"The next morning, I think. I was"—she nodded toward the hatch—"down there. I screamed and yelled at first. But I think they put something in the water. I think we were all drugged. After a while, everybody just got weak and quiet. Numb. They fed us just enough to keep us alive."

Holmes leaned forward. He held up his cell phone with an image of the Sigliks. "Are these the men?"

Davina twisted away. "Oh, Jesus! *Yes!*"

"Enough!" said Grey, pushing the phone down. She touched Davina's arm gently. "And what did they do when they came? These two men."

Davina took another deep breath. She looked up at the ceiling, then back down to meet Grey's eyes. "They came down together. They looked us over. Poked us. Groped us. Like we were animals. Sometimes they brought down somebody new. Sometimes they took somebody away. Out the door and through the tunnel. The way you came in."

"Davina," asked Marple, "did any of the people who left with the men ever come back?"

Davina started sobbing softly. She wiped her nose on the blanket. "No," she said. "Never. Nobody came back."

A paramedic rolled a gurney up. "I need to take her now," he said.

"Right. Of course," said Grey. She stood up and rested her hand lightly on the young woman's bony shoulder. "Thank you, Davina. We'll find these men. I promise."

Poe looked at Grey as the gurney rolled away. This was darker than anything he had imagined.

"Hey! Detective!"

One of the SWAT cops was standing on the ladder, his upper body poking out of the hatch.

"What's up?" asked Grey.

"If you've got the belly for it, you need to follow me."

"Where?"

"There's another room."

CHAPTER 76

THE BRANCH OFF the main tunnel had been invisible in the dark. But now the whole underground was lit up by NYPD scene lights. Bright as day. The cop led the way to the hidden chamber, about ten yards off to the side.

As they approached the doorway, Poe could hear the low hum of powerful electric motors. The cop went in first. Grey followed. When she gave the all clear, Poe stepped over the steel threshold, with Holmes and Marple right behind him.

"Jesus," he muttered. The room was smaller than the space that had held the prisoners. Everything here was clean, precise, pristine. Unlike the steel lining of the pit, the walls and floor here were covered in gleaming white tile. Huge vents passed through the walls at the back of the room, and a powerful hum came from the outside.

"There's your heavy-duty air cleaning," said Grey.

"And that's the reason," said Poe, pointing at two large steel bins against the wall. They were about the size of oil drums, coated in plastic. Flexible orange ducts led from the tight-fitting bin lids to the wall vents.

Holmes sniffed. "Acid baths."

"Just big enough for a body," said Marple.

"Body *parts*," said Grey.

Poe looked around to take in the whole room. "This is the skeleton factory."

Two stainless-steel tables rested on pedestals in the center of the room. Openings at the base of each table were connected to drains in the floor. Rolling hospital carts alongside each table held an assortment of surgical instruments. Pliers. Clamps. Saws.

Holmes walked to the corner of the room and opened the door to a large stall shower. "They cleaned up down here, before transferring the bones to the subway tunnel."

"But why?" asked Grey.

"They were following a pattern," said Poe. "A protocol somebody else set."

"What's in there?" Marple asked, pointing to a row of metal cabinets against the left-hand wall.

Still wearing surgical gloves, Poe started working his way down the row, opening the doors as he went. The first cabinet held two sets of head-to-toe rubber suits on hooks. The next contained a neat stack of heavy-duty black plastic bags and respirator masks. The third cabinet had shelves with plastic containers marked "HCl" and labeled with a skull and crossbones.

The last cabinet was empty except for a metal pail at the bottom, covered with a blue surgical towel. Poe lifted the pail out and set it on the floor as the others gathered around. He reached in with a gloved hand and plucked the towel away.

At the bottom of the bucket was a pile of blood-encrusted teeth.

CHAPTER 77

FIVE MINUTES LATER, as ambulances and CSU vans crowded the street in front of the house, Holmes walked with Poe to the back, near the detached garage. He knew his partner was frustrated and disappointed in him. He could see it in Poe's eyes and hear it in his voice. He knew he had it coming.

"Brendan," said Poe, "this ridiculousness has to stop. You need to listen to me. I'm your closest friend. This. Has. To. Stop."

Holmes knew it was true. His OD had put the whole operation— and the firm's reputation—in jeopardy. "It will stop," he said. "I promise..."

He looked across the driveway at the open garage. The Sigliks' red Lamborghini sat in front of them in a large bay. There was an APB out for the brothers, but Holmes worried that they were already on a plane out of the country.

He watched as Poe walked slowly around the sleek sports car. The vehicle straddled a narrow channel in the floor, outlined in reflective yellow stripes.

"Unbelievable," said Poe. "These bastards have their own personal work pit."

"Maybe they don't trust Midas Muffler," said Holmes.

He leaned down from the other side, shining his small Fenix flashlight under the car and into the channel below. A set of metal stairs led down from the rear. Holmes could smell gasoline and motor oil.

But other things too. Isopropyl alcohol and benzyl acetate, with notes of sandalwood.

Aftershave.

Holmes took a breath to center himself. Was his brain playing tricks on him? He slid his slender frame under the car and dropped into the concrete trench. He passed his flashlight beam around the perimeter of the concrete walls, and then on the short metal staircase that led down from the floor level. Everything else about the place was precision fitted. Something wasn't right.

"Auguste!" he called up. "Get down here!"

Poe swung his legs over the edge. He supported himself with his forearms on the lip and then dropped in feet first.

"Look," said Holmes. He yanked on the left-side railing of the steps. A gap opened in the concrete wall behind the staircase. Poe grabbed the other rail. Together, they pulled straight back. The stairs moved toward them.

Holmes bent forward and shined his light into the exposed opening in the wall.

Poe poked his head halfway into the opening.

A gunshot almost blew it off.

CHAPTER 78

THE BULLET RICOCHETED off the concrete wall and pierced the gas tank of the Lamborghini. Gasoline sprayed down into the pit. Holmes flattened himself against the wall. Poe pulled out his Glock. The next second, he was crawling through the opening. Holmes followed close behind. His head was clear now, his heart pounding.

After a stretch of about twenty yards, the tunnel widened slightly and opened onto a dank circular chamber lined in rusted metal. A metal utility ladder led up to a round opening. The chamber vibrated with the sound of moving traffic.

"Storm drain," said Poe. "We're under a street."

Holmes led the way up the ladder and out of the hole. Cars honked and whizzed past, inches away. He stumbled forward. Poe yanked him onto a curb. Holmes shuddered. Maybe his reflexes were still a little off.

He looked up the street toward a somewhat busy intersection, even at this hour. The light turned red, bringing traffic on their side of the street to a slow halt. At the head of the line, a white Mercedes GT revved and inched forward impatiently.

Suddenly, Holmes saw two men approach the Mercedes from either side. One of them smashed the driver's window with the butt of a pistol. He prompted the driver out at gunpoint and shoved him to the pavement, then took his place in the driver's seat. The man on the right jumped in on the passenger side.

"It's *them*!" shouted Holmes.

The doors slammed shut and the car took off through the red light, barely missing an oncoming van.

Holmes looked to his left. They were just one block north of the police perimeter. He could see the portable white barriers and the blinking blue lights on the police SUVs.

He turned back just in time to see Poe disappear into the front lot of an auto body shop. When Holmes reached the entrance, a 1990s vintage Ford was pulling out.

"Get in!" shouted Poe. He reached across and pushed the passenger door open.

Holmes slid into the seat. The interior smelled like mold. He glanced at the steering column and saw a screwdriver jammed into the ignition slot.

"Couldn't find the key," said Poe.

He cranked the wheel and careened onto the street, just making it through the intersection on a yellow light. The chassis rattled and the engine whined.

"There!" shouted Holmes.

The Mercedes was a block ahead, inching through another red light, angling for an opening. As soon as the driver found room, he gunned the car through the gap.

"Dammit! Move!" Poe shouted. Holmes was jammed back against his seat as Poe floored the accelerator, following the Mercedes up the ramp onto the 278 Expressway. They were pushing 70 now, heading toward Sunnyside. Holmes glanced at the dashboard just as the oil pressure icon started blinking.

"Hold on!" Poe shouted. "This thing could seize up or blow."

The Mercedes swerved onto an exit ramp, barely missing the barrier. Poe slammed on the brakes. The Ford went into a skid. A pickup careened around to the left, clipping the rear bumper. Poe jammed his foot down on the accelerator. He fishtailed across the white stripes bordering the exit, then straightened out on the ramp.

"Left! Left!" shouted Holmes, leaning forward to keep the Mercedes's taillights in sight. Poe roared down the incline and yanked the wheel hard into the turn, tires squealing. They were just three cars behind.

The Mercedes made a sharp right onto a one-way street. Poe followed.

"Wrong way!" Holmes shouted.

"No choice!" Poe shouted back.

When they rounded the corner, a delivery truck was barreling toward them, horn blaring. Poe swung the Ford onto the sidewalk. Holmes ducked as the passing truck knocked the mirror off his side.

Poe gunned the Ford off the curb and accelerated down the narrow street. The sound of the engine echoed off the building walls. One block. Two blocks. Then a hard right onto another main drag. Holmes leaned forward onto the dashboard. He spotted the Mercedes's taillights a block ahead.

"On the right!" he shouted.

The Mercedes was sitting at an angle, having crashed halfway through a set of elaborate wrought-iron gates. The hood was crumpled, and the front car doors were hanging partway open. Poe pulled to a hard stop a few yards behind, then kicked his door open and jumped out, pistol raised. Steam was pouring from under the Ford's hood. As Holmes scrambled out of the passenger seat, he saw Poe sweeping the interior of the Mercedes.

"Empty!" Poe shouted. He looked to the right. "This way!"

Holmes sprinted down the sidewalk and followed his partner through the gates. He looked up and saw:

CALVARY CEMETERY.

CHAPTER 79

"THERE!"

Holmes pointed toward a pair of moving shadows about twenty yards ahead. He heard a loud pop as a shard of stone stung his cheek.

Poe ran forward and ducked behind a huge obelisk. Holmes ran up beside him and pressed his back against the thick pillar. He peeked around the corner, making a quick scan through the bleak forest of stone.

Nothing moving.

"Let's go!" said Poe. "Stay close!"

They moved in a crouch across the patches of green between the monuments.

Holmes saw a fleeting motion behind a massive headstone. A gunshot blasted the face off a statue two feet from his head.

"I don't suppose you've got a spare?" asked Holmes, nodding at Poe's gun.

"Where's yours?" asked Poe.

"You don't remember?" said Holmes. "It's back at the house. Marple disarmed me."

Poe stared ahead into the darkness. "Can't blame her."

He took off at a run, weaving between the marble markers and statues. Holmes followed. As they crossed a small meditation park, Holmes spotted the two shapes again, moving in front of a small mausoleum. Within seconds, the door was open. The figures slipped inside.

"That's it!" Holmes called out. "They're cornered."

It was a twenty-yard sprint to the mausoleum steps. Holmes and Poe pressed themselves against the vine-covered walls on either side of the door, which was hanging ajar. Poe raised his Glock and nudged the door open with his foot. He inched into the entryway, pistol first.

Holmes slipped in after him. The air inside was damp and musty. There were no sounds. Poe nodded. Holmes clicked on his flashlight and swept it around the small chamber. The walls and floor were made of thick stone. Metal-grilled vents near the roofline allowed slivers of ambient city light to pass through.

Toward the rear of the chamber, a massive marble crypt rested on a granite platform. Poe walked slowly around to the back, staying low. Holmes followed. The flashlight beam cut through the shadows. The space behind the crypt was empty.

Holmes paced the length of the back wall, pressing on stones, looking for an exit. He looked back at Poe and shook his head. The only way out was the way they came in. But that was impossible. Unless they'd been chasing spirits.

Holmes leaned back against the crypt. He could feel the cool stone through his clothes. Poe walked toward him—and stumbled. Holmes beamed his light at Poe's feet. The rectangular floor stones were neatly set. Except one.

Holmes felt a fresh pump of adrenaline. He squatted down next to the rogue stone, slightly loose and out of line with the others. He dug his fingers into the gap up to his second knuckle and leaned back for leverage. The stone started to shift, then tip. Holmes slid around to the narrow end of the stone and muscled it up until it was resting upright.

Underneath was a rusted metal frame outlining a rectangular opening, about eighteen inches wide. Holmes dropped flat onto the dank stone floor and shined his light into the space beneath.

"Don't tell me," said Poe, breathing hard.

"These two love tunnels," said Holmes.

He swung his feet over the opening, then lowered himself into the hole. It was a short drop to the solid dirt floor. He turned off his flashlight and felt Poe drop in next to him.

The space was dark and deathly silent.

A tomb beneath a tomb.

CHAPTER 80

HOLMES STARED AHEAD into the gloom and waited for his eyes to adjust. His nostrils filled with the smell of loam and clay. And then—again—a whisper of aftershave.

They passed under a grate that let in fragments of light, enough to see that the passage widened just ahead. Holmes could make out an indentation in the wall a few yards up. Poe spun and aimed his gun into the opening, then waved Holmes forward.

Holmes beamed the flashlight in the direction of the gun barrel.

They were staring into a small underground room with a crude wood floor. A half dozen unlit kerosene lamps sat on a card table. Two metal folding chairs were tucked underneath. A row of rusted storage bins lined one side of the room. An ancient chemical toilet was nestled in the opposite corner. The odor was caustic—formaldehyde and bleach. Holmes stepped across the threshold and got a quick waft of sweat and sandalwood. He blinked—and took a stunning blow to his right temple.

Holmes dropped onto the tunnel floor, sparks flashing in the periphery of his vision. Something wet and warm oozed down over his right eye. Through the blur, he could make out a pair of expensive dress shoes in front of him. Then he felt something cold and hard against his head.

"Get up." A man's voice. Low and calm. He felt a rough hand grip under his right armpit, lifting him to his feet and dragging him back into the room. Holmes tried to control his breathing and fought to stay conscious.

He heard the squeak of metal. He blinked and looked up. He could make out the lower half of a second man's body as he slammed one of the folding chairs down in the middle of the room. Then he saw Poe being pushed onto the seat. His left cheek was bruised. The man behind the chair put a gun to Poe's head.

Poe's gun.

Holmes felt his vision fade in and out. He saw Poe make a slow half turn and look up at the man behind him, the one with the well-groomed stubble. "Richard. Am I right?" said Poe. His speech was slightly slurred and his face looked contorted with pain.

"Shut the fuck up," the man replied.

Poe turned back and looked over at the man holding Holmes. "And that makes you *Nelson*." He leaned forward, smiling through a split lip. "I always thought your Instagram shots were better."

Richard gave Poe a hard slap on the back of his head.

Holmes felt warm breath in his ear. "Your friend is a wiseass," said Nelson.

"Just observant," said Holmes.

"Good," said Nelson. "Because he's about to watch you die."

Holmes felt himself being pushed forward, the gun pressing even harder against his skull. For a second, he met Poe's eyes. He knew he had to do something. He bent forward at the waist, coughing and spitting.

"I'm going to be *sick!*" he mumbled, drool spilling from his mouth.

"Not on me!" Nelson shoved Holmes roughly toward the chemical toilet. Holmes dropped to his knees and placed his hands on the corroded metal bowl. It was filled with foul blue liquid. The fumes burned his nostrils.

Nelson was right behind him, pressing his head down. "If you're gonna puke, *puke!*" he growled.

Holmes held his breath and slid one hand off the rim and into the blue liquid. He cupped his hand and whipped around, splashing the chemical into Nelson's face. Nelson twisted away, clawing at his eyes. *"Fuuckkk!"* His gun dropped and clattered on the floor.

Richard took a short step toward his brother. For a split second, the gun barrel slid off Poe's temple. Poe spun off the chair, grabbed it by the back, and brought it up hard under Richard's chin. Richard rocked backward. Poe dived for Nelson's loose gun and rolled hard to the side. Stunned and off-balance, Richard fired two wild shots. Bullets splintered the flooring next to Poe's head. Poe whipped his arm around and fired once. The top of Richard's right ear blew off in a bloody mist. He grabbed his head, dropping Poe's gun, and spun onto the floor, screaming.

Nelson lunged blindly at Holmes, driving him against the wall, hands around his throat. Holmes whipped his left hand around and stabbed two fingers into the side of Nelson's neck, compressing the junction of the carotid sinus. Nelson dropped like a sack of cement and hit the floor, unconscious.

Poe staggered to his feet, wincing as he scooped up his gun and pointed it across the room at the wailing, bleeding Richard Siglik. He glanced at Nelson's inert body, then at Holmes.

"Nice takedown," he said. "Who taught you that?"

Holmes was bent over with his hands on his knees, catching his breath. "I learned it from Margaret," he wheezed.

One more thing to thank her for.

CHAPTER 81

IN THE MIDDLE of New York Harbor, the early morning air was cool.

Helene Grey rested her arms on the starboard railing of the Staten Island Ferry as it chugged across the water. The Statue of Liberty glowed in the distance. The passenger count was sparse crossing out of Manhattan's Whitehall Terminal. A bunch of twentysomething clubbers heading home from the city. A few sanitation workers and housekeepers on their way to their jobs.

Grey had spent the last few hours booking the Siglik brothers and taking their statements, which amounted to total confessions. Case closed. Finally. She was bleary-eyed and exhausted. But this was an appointment she did not want to miss. Because she had another mystery to solve. Three of them, in fact.

"Nothing like a little sea air." A man's voice.

She hadn't even heard him approach. She smiled to herself. After all these years, he still had it.

"When the wind is just right," said Grey, "you can almost taste the landfill."

The man took a spot to her left at the rail. She glanced at him sideways. Still handsome. The goatee was new.

"When did you leave the company?" she asked.

"Six months ago."

"Enjoying retirement?"

"Retirement is for pansies."

Grey turned to face her companion. It had been fifteen years. But the old stirrings were still there. Faint but deep.

"What's up?" the man asked.

"Three people," she replied, handing him a folded slip of paper. He opened it, glanced at it, then tore it into pieces, letting the scraps flutter into the water.

"They're kidding with the names, right?"

"I'm not sure," said Grey. "They're PIs. Smart. Highly skilled. And no tracks at all. Like they appeared from Mars. And they're all totally dark on social."

"Nothing from facial recognition?"

"All that shows up are their driver's licenses."

"Fakes?"

"The best."

"DNA?"

"No matches. They're not in the database."

"I'll see what I can find."

Grey cleared her throat. "Tread lightly, please."

The man leaned in to look Helene in the eye. She turned away. But not fast enough.

He smiled. "Which one are you sleeping with?"

Grey stared out over the water.

"Sorry, Helene," he said. "That was inelegant."

"Good to see you again, Raymond," she said, gazing at Lady Liberty. When she turned back, he was gone.

CHAPTER 82

"OH, MY GOD! This is *true*?"

Virginia wheeled her office chair closer. She was clutching a copy of Nelson Siglik's confession. Her eyes were wide. Marple was sitting with her partners in the common area a few yards away, happy to have the office back to normal.

"What part?" Marple asked.

"*All* of it! This really happened?"

"It's a sworn statement," said Holmes. "And the evidence backs it up."

Even Marple was amazed at how quickly it had all happened. The Sigliks had not even requested a lawyer. They understood the evidence. They were both smart enough to know how hard it would be to fake insanity. And they refused to turn on each other. Brothers to the end.

In return for full confessions to multiple homicides and providing the identities of their victims, they asked for only one thing: to be assigned to the same prison and the same cellblock. Never separated for the entire length of their sentences, which would no doubt be the rest of their natural lives. It was the easiest deal the DA had ever made.

Marple listened as Virginia read aloud from Nelson's statement, which matched his brother's in every important detail.

"'Suspect states that he knew his father, Aldrich Siglik, to have committed multiple homicides of men and women and that his father frequently displayed bodies to him and his brother in the basement of the family funeral home and discussed with them techniques of dismemberment and...'" She stumbled over the next word. "...'excarnation'?"

"Flesh removal," said Poe.

Holmes leaned forward in his chair. "Daddy was desensitizing the boys. Grooming them. Training them to follow in the family business. The *real* family business."

Virginia went back to reading. "'Suspect states that at age eight, he and his brother witnessed the strangulation murder of their mother, Anna Siglik, by their father, Aldrich Siglik, at their Brooklyn address and were then made to assist in the dismemberment and disposal of her body...'"

"Like father, like sons," said Holmes.

Virginia looked up from the report. "So who was buried in the mausoleum? The mother? The father?"

"Nobody," said Poe. "The vault is vacant. Pristine. Never occupied. Aldrich Siglik built that place as his Alamo. A last-resort hide-out. When he died, he willed it to the boys."

"Did they kill him too?" asked Virginia.

"Heart attack," said Marple. "Lucky man."

The office phone rang. Virginia put down the pages and picked up the handset, shifting to her bright, professional voice. "Holmes, Marple, and Poe Investigations. This is Virginia."

Marple saw Virginia's posture stiffen as she listened to the caller.

"Yes, ma'am," she said. "Of course. She's right here."

Virginia covered the bottom of the handset as she handed it to Marple.

"Special Agent Brita Stans," she whispered. "About the Zozi Turner kidnapping. She sounds *really* pissed off."

CHAPTER 83

"MARGARET! THANK GOD!"

Addilyn Charles jumped up from her chair and hugged Marple like a long-lost sister. Holmes and Poe got polite nods. Helene Grey silently stood nearby. Brita Stans elbowed her way into the group and got right down to business.

"This way," she said. "We need to talk."

Marple looked around. The once-impeccable Charles apartment now had the familiar look of a law-enforcement occupation. Paper coffee cups and empty takeout containers everywhere. Laptops, two-way radios, and accessory cords were spread out on the tables. Men and women with shoulder holsters were all over.

Stans led the way to a seating area near the grand piano. Holmes, Marple, and Poe sat side by side on an elegant sofa. Addilyn and Grey settled on the piano bench. Stans stood with her legs apart, hands on her hips, like General Patton.

"We got another call," she said.

Marple looked at Grey. "Same as before?" she asked. "The woman?"

Grey nodded. "Same voice, same filter."

"They've changed the ransom demand," said Stans.

"What do they want now?" asked Holmes.

"They want cash *and* my jewelry," said Addilyn, her voice shaking. "My diamonds and pearls."

"And here's the capper," said Stans. "They want Addilyn to deliver the ransom personally."

"So why are we here?" asked Poe. "I thought you didn't want us involved."

"I don't," Stans said bluntly.

Addilyn turned to Marple. "I told Agent Stans I wouldn't do it unless you came along, Margaret." She was wringing her hands in her lap. "I'm afraid they're going to kidnap me too!"

"That's not going to happen," said Stans. "We'll be there, close by."

"We will too," said Poe.

"The hell you will," said Stans. "I don't need the three frigging musketeers. All I need is Marple."

"The handoff is tonight," said Grey. "Watchung Reservation in New Jersey."

"Oh, that's lovely," said Marple.

Stans turned toward her. "You know the place?"

"I'm a devoted birder, Agent Stans. I know every tree in the park."

CHAPTER 84

BY TWO THE next morning, the FBI unit was huddled in a wooded corner of the sprawling reserve, twelve miles west and a world apart from the busy streets of Newark. Stans and the other agents were in forest-pattern camo. Helene Grey had chosen commando black.

Marple had followed suit. She wore black leggings and a tight-fitting black top, her hair tucked neatly under a watch cap. Addilyn wore slacks and a light sweater. She paced anxiously behind the shelter of a stand of evergreens.

Marple reached into her purse and pulled out a silver flask.

"Sherry?" she asked.

Addilyn shook her head.

"How about some warm tea? I have a thermos in my backpack." She leaned in close. "Or maybe a Xanax?"

"No drugs," Brita Stans bluntly said. "She needs to be alert."

Stans straddled a nylon duffel bag containing the currency and jewelry. It was a bulging load. On the scale, the package had weighed in at a bit over sixty-five pounds. Which presented an obvious problem. Addilyn Charles, fully clothed, weighed only about a hundred pounds. No way she could carry it.

Marple watched as a young agent rolled up in the Bureau's solution: a golf cart commandeered from the nearby Watchung Valley Golf Club.

"Ever driven one of these, ma'am?" asked the agent.

"Of course," said Addilyn. "But not in the dark."

"You'll be fine," said Marple. "It's a gentle slope from here."

Stans tapped her watch. "Okay, Addilyn. It's time."

An agent hoisted the bag onto the back of the cart. Addilyn climbed into the driver's seat. Marple leaned in and gave her a tight hug. She could feel Addilyn trembling.

"I'll be right here when you get back," said Marple.

"Remember," said Stans, "pay attention to height, weight, build, skin color, accent. Anything that can help us with an ID."

"All right," said Addilyn. "I'll try."

"There's a tracker sewn into the lining of the bag," said Stans. "Wherever they go, we'll follow." She leaned in close. "And we'll find your family."

Addilyn pressed the accelerator and drove slowly down the grassy slope toward the designated pickup point. Marple ducked back into the bushes with Stans and the other agents to watch. The agents nearby were invisible, hidden among the trees and equipped with sniper rifles.

The white canopy of the cart caught the moonlight as it moved toward a rustic trail at the bottom of the hill. As Marple and the agents raised their binoculars, the cart made a slow turn onto a dirt path and disappeared behind the foliage.

"There's one thing I can't figure out," said Stans. "Why five million? Why not ten? Why not twenty? This family is *loaded*."

Marple had wondered the same thing. "Maybe the kidnappers live light," she said. "Or maybe they just prefer diamonds."

CHAPTER 85

STILL SHAKING, ADDILYN drove the cart slowly down the dark trail and stopped at the designated historical marker. She shut off the electric motor. The trail was bordered by tall trees. Their branches muted the moonlight. The soft rustle of leaves overhead was the only thing Addilyn could hear. Not counting the thump of her heartbeat in her ears.

She slid slowly off the seat and stood next to the cart, her hand wrapped tightly around one of the roof supports. She'd hoped the FBI would wire her for sound, maybe put a camera in a blouse button. Or even give her a gun. But the kidnappers had thought of all that. "No mics, no video, no weapons," the caller had said. "We'll know."

Addilyn waited a minute. Then two.

Suddenly, she heard movement in the bushes, a few yards off the path. Her mouth went dry. She felt her chest tighten. She peered through the foliage, searching for a human shape. Maybe the woman from the phone calls. A woman would be better than a man, she thought. Maybe they could talk. Negotiate. Come to an understanding. Anything to get her daughter and husband back home alive.

JAMES PATTERSON

"Hello?" Addilyn called out tentatively. "Who's there?"
No answer.
The rustling came closer.
A shape moved through the underbrush. Low and lumbering.
Not human.
In a flash, the shape burst out of the bushes. Addilyn covered her mouth to stifle a scream. It was a dog. An enormous mastiff with pale white fur. Even bigger than Zozi's black mastiff, Toby. Addilyn crawled back into the cart and slid to the other side, tucking her knees up against her chest, afraid she was about to be eaten alive.

The white dog circled the cart slowly, sniffing the air, its massive jowls shaking. On its back was a nylon harness with straps hanging down.

The huge beast moved closer. It placed both front paws on the side step of the cart, tipping it. Addilyn saw a folded piece of paper under the dog's leather collar. She reached forward with a trembling hand and plucked it out. She unfolded the paper and read the neatly typed note:

    Strap the bag onto the harness. When it's
    tight, say FIND.

Addilyn stared in disbelief. The kidnappers weren't coming. The dog was the courier.

She dropped the paper, then moved to the other side of the cart and slid out. She inched her way slowly to the back and took hold of the straps on the ransom bag. When she turned, the giant dog was right there beside her, drool dripping from its mouth.

Addilyn pulled with everything she had and slid the bag from the cart shelf onto the dog's back. The animal cocked his head and settled under the sudden weight. The bag was draped over its spine, threatening to tip off one side or the other. Addilyn held it in balance with one hand as she reached down to pull the harness straps up and over. She fastened the heavy plastic clasps and tightened the slack. The dog looked like a pack mule. God knows it was almost the size of one.

Addilyn gave the bag a gentle shake. She could hear the rattle of her jewelry as it settled on either side. She backed away slowly toward the front of the cart. The dog followed. Addilyn peered into the bushes, looked up and down the path. She saw nothing. The dog was panting under the load. It looked up at Addilyn expectantly, as if it were hoping for a biscuit.

Addilyn realized that the animal was waiting for the command.

"Find," she said softly.

The pale mastiff didn't move. It just pawed the dirt. Addilyn took a breath and cleared her throat. This time she shouted it:

"Find!"

Immediately, the dog turned and lumbered across the path. A second later, it disappeared into the underbrush. Addilyn fell back against the side of the golf cart, and felt the world go black.

CHAPTER 86

"A DOG?" SAID Holmes. "What kind?"

"A big white one," said Marple. "Big enough to carry a sixty-five-pound sack."

"How's Addilyn?" asked Poe.

"She passed out," said Marple. "Seems to be okay. They're taking her in for observation."

Marple was sitting in the back seat of Poe's GTO, which was parked in a scenic turnoff about a quarter mile from where the transfer had happened. As soon as Addilyn had been sent off to the hospital, Marple pretended to join the search for the dog. Instead, she made a beeline to join her partners. She knew for certain that Brita Stans didn't want Poe or Holmes anywhere near the operation. She also knew that Holmes had his own elaborate plan for tracking the ransom—and she wanted to be in on it.

Assuming it worked, of course.

Poe was tapping impatiently on the steering wheel while Holmes fiddled with an app on his cell phone. The app he'd coded that afternoon.

Marple adjusted her earbuds, listening in on the FBI frequency.

The snipers near the pickup site had sighted the huge courier dog as he disappeared into the woods. Now agents were scouring the underbrush for any trace of the animal—or the kidnappers.

Suddenly, the channel crackled with new information. Marple listened carefully, then pulled her earbuds out. "They found the bag with the tracker," she said. "But no ransom. The money and jewelry are gone."

"They switched bags," said Holmes with a satisfied expression. "Did I not tell you?" Marple leaned forward as his screen lit up with a detailed map of the Watchung Reservation. Their position was marked with a pulsing blue dot. Holmes tapped in a few more parameters.

Marple watched with amazement. Holmes drove her crazy, but she had to admit that he was a technical wizard—when he was clean. Earlier that day, he'd given her a tiny round device to attach to one of Addilyn's necklaces before it was packed in the ransom bag. It looked like just one more pearl in the string. Not even Stans had noticed. Now, with any luck, that tiny pearl was traveling with the rest of the ransom. Wherever it was.

Suddenly the screen lit up with another dot, this one green—and moving. "Got it!" said Holmes. The electronic pearl was close, and heading in their direction.

Marple leaned forward to look at the screen. Just then, a blur shot past on the road. She caught a black shape on a sleek motorcycle—with a large duffel bag lashed to the back.

The green dot moved in sync with the bike, until it zipped right off the screen.

"That's it!" yelled Holmes. "Go!"

"Hang on!" Poe yelled back. He started the Pontiac and cranked it into a tight 180 turn, then accelerated down the road. The bike's taillight was just a blink in the distance.

"Got him!" Holmes shouted. The moving green dot was back on

his screen. It was headed south on Summit Lane, leading out of the park and toward a residential area. As Poe gained on it, the rider whipped around a roundabout and headed onto a main road. Fast and agile.

"He's good," said Poe.

Two panel trucks blocked the lanes ahead. Poe swerved onto the median and gunned past them. He followed the bike down several residential streets again. He was just a few car lengths behind when it merged onto the Garden State Parkway, weaving through traffic and pulling away fast.

Marple glanced at the highway signs as they whipped past.

The chase was headed toward the Jersey Shore.

CHAPTER 87

"DAMMIT!"

Holmes flinched as Poe pounded the dashboard.

They'd lost the bike five minutes ago. The rider had made a wild turn off the highway, then aimed east toward Asbury Park. Somewhere on the backstreets of the seaside town, he'd simply evaporated into thin air. Now Poe was driving in a slow crawl up Ocean Avenue North, dodging sloppy-drunk college kids heading back from the clubs.

"It doesn't work as well in congested areas," said Holmes, tapping his phone.

Poe looked over at the empty screen. "You mean it works for *shit* in congested areas."

Holmes let out an exasperated sigh. Poe was right. They were searching blind.

"I think we should get out and split up," said Poe. "We can cover more territory that way." He swung the car into a parking spot and cut the engine. "Find the rider and he'll lead us to the kidnappers." All three climbed out and gathered around the trunk of the car. Holmes checked his app one more time.

"Nothing," he said. "If it starts working again, I'll text you."

"I won't hold my breath," said Poe. "Margaret, you check the hotels. I'll check the parking garages."

Marple nodded.

"I'll take the boardwalk," said Holmes.

"Good hunting," said Poe. "Keep in touch."

Holmes waited for his partners to head off in opposite directions. Then he patted the holster in the small of his back, the one holding his backup pistol—the one nobody else knew he was packing.

After his near-death experience at the Siglik residence, Marple had refused to give back his favorite gun. Poe had agreed with the ban. But Holmes wasn't about to walk around unarmed, especially on a case like this. His gun. His secret. He figured that what his partners didn't know couldn't hurt them.

He moved quickly toward the fabled wooden walkway along the beach. From a mural on the side of a building, a topless mermaid in a sailor's cap stared down at him. Holmes walked briskly, sweeping the crowd for a man in leather with a large bag. As if it would be that easy. He knew the rider could have gone to ground anywhere in the city. Or he could have delivered the bag and headed out of town. He might have ditched the bike and switched to a car. Or a boat.

He was worried for Zozi Turner and Eton Charles. With the ransom in hand, the kidnappers might kill the prisoners to cover their tracks. If Zozi and Eton weren't dead already.

Five minutes up the boardwalk, Holmes heard the sound of laughter from the beach. He looked down and saw a gaggle of teenage girls, shoes held high, playfully dodging incoming waves. His head started to spin. He closed his eyes. Then he started to sweat.

In his mind, the laughter became screams. For a second, he was back under the Siglik mansion, staring at gaunt faces and vats of acid. He felt dizzy and weak. The boardwalk lights went blurry. The fishy smell of the surf morphed into another kind of rot. The sickish odor of decaying flesh.

The laughter got louder. The screaming.

Not again. Not here!

Holmes squinted into the distance, down the boardwalk. He saw three young men huddled in the shadow of an abandoned building. He steadied himself and made a slow pass, checking the group in his peripheral vision. Haggard, pale faces. Money and small packets were changing hands.

The smell in his brain was getting worse. The smell of death. His breaths were coming hard and fast. Suddenly he flashed on a photo of Zozi Turner, smiling, in a pink bathing suit. The picture was lying in the sand as foamy waves washed over it, erasing it in an instant.

More screams in his head.

This was sharper and stronger than the panic attack in the office. There was only one way to stop it. Holmes reached into his pocket, felt for the wad of bills, and headed across the boardwalk.

Something told him that the strangers in the shadows might have just what he needed.

CHAPTER 88

POE MOVED SLOWLY through a silent parking garage three blocks from the ocean. Half of the overhead lights were broken. The rest cast ominous shadows.

As he crouched behind a row of parked cars, he spotted a black plastic weather cover draped over a motorcycle. He lifted it high enough to see underneath.

Dammit.

It was a heavy-duty Harley. Wrong make. Wrong color. Wrong everything.

"Hey, handsome. Got a minute?"

Poe froze, then turned around slowly. A young man was emerging from a dark stairwell that led down from the street. He had both hands in the pockets of his cheap nylon bomber jacket. Poe sized him up in a second. Skittish, reckless, and armed.

"If you need directions," said Poe, "I'm not from around here."

"That's a nice suit, man." The kid was an arm's length away. He was short and thickset, with pecs bulging under his T-shirt. "Armani?"

"Brioni," said Poe.

"Here on pleasure?"

Poe's eyes darted around the lot. Nobody else in sight. "I wish," said Poe. "All business."

The kid pulled out a four-inch knife and jerked his head toward a dark corner. "In that case," he said, "step into my office."

"Wait!" said Poe, raising both hands. "Don't hurt me. Here. I'll give you my wallet." He reached toward his back pocket and whipped out his 9mm Glock 45 pistol. Before the kid could blink, the barrel was pressed against his forehead.

"Fuck!" the kid muttered.

"I'm waiting," said Poe, pressing harder.

The knife dropped to the concrete. Poe kicked it through the opening of a storm drain. "What else have you got that can hurt me?"

"Nothing. I swear," said the kid. "You a cop?"

"Worse," said Poe. He turned the kid around and shoved him forward onto the hood of an SUV. He held the gun against the kid's back as he patted him down. "You local?"

"Seasonal," the kid said, his bravado gone.

"You want to live to next season?" asked Poe.

The kid nodded. Poe yanked him around.

"I'm looking for a bike. I followed it off the parkway about a half hour ago. Kawasaki. Neon-green trim. Big fat duffel bag tied across the back."

"Yeah," said the kid. No hesitation.

"Yeah *what*?"

"Yeah, I saw it. Ninja 650. Green trim, like you said. It's parked near where I crashed last night."

"Are you lying to me?" He raised the gun to eye level.

"No, I swear! I work in a body shop. I know bikes. And I noticed the rider."

"What about him?"

"Not him. Her. Female. Red hair."

CHAPTER 89

MARPLE GOT THE text from Poe as she was checking the lobby of the Empress Hotel. She shoved through the front door and started running toward the address on the screen. As she ran, she glanced down at her phone, looking for a response from Holmes.

Nothing. He was off the grid.

It took Marple only two minutes to reach her destination. She leaned against the wall of a darkened drugstore and looked across the intersection.

The location was a grim-looking motel with six ground-floor units and another six on top. The sign on the roof blinked BEACH MANOR. The pockmarked parking lot was mostly empty. Four sedans, two pickups, one U-Haul van.

And one motorcycle.

Marple saw a shadow huddled against a tall stockade fence that separated the motel units from a cluster of dumpsters. She crossed the street and walked past the motel office with a CLOSED sign in the front window. When she got to the edge of the fence, Poe reached out of the darkness and pulled her down.

Marple looked behind him. "Where's Brendan?"

"No clue," said Poe. "I haven't heard from him since we left the car."

Marple leaned forward and looked down the row of motel units. She ducked back. "Are we sure that's the right bike?"

Poe nodded. "Unit 6. First level. Far end."

"Maybe we should wait," said Marple. "I don't even have a gun."

"Why not?" asked Poe. He and Holmes were always telling Marple to keep a pistol in her purse.

"Brita Stans," said Marple. "She told me to come to the park unarmed."

"No matter," said Poe, racking the slide of his pistol. "We need to go in now."

Marple knew Poe was right. If the courier was in the room, there was a good chance the kidnappers were there too. And with the ransom in hand, they might decide that the hostages had outlived their usefulness.

"Okay," said Marple. "Let's move." She slid around the corner and pressed her back against the motel wall, ducking down as she passed the front window on each unit. She could feel Poe right behind her.

The curtain behind the window of unit 6 was pulled shut. No light from inside. Marple crossed quickly to the far side of the door. Poe took a position on the other side. Marple scanned the parking lot. No movement. She gauged the door. Weather-worn wood. Cheap hardware.

Marple pressed her ear against the top door panel. She heard the sing-song cadence of a fast-food jingle coming from a TV speaker. No other voices.

Poe pivoted to face the door squarely. He bent his right leg at the knee, then thrust his foot forward in a powerful kick. The frame splintered as the door swung open, snapping the feeble chain lock. Marple took a single step into the room. She heard a low growl. Poe swung his gun toward the sound.

A girl screamed. *"No! Don't shoot!"*

CHAPTER 90

MARPLE SWEPT HER hand up the inside wall and flicked on the ceiling light. On the floor between two rumpled beds, a teenager with a dark pixie haircut gripped the collar of a massive black dog.

"Toby! Down!" the girl shouted.

The dog settled back onto its haunches.

Marple recognized Zozi Turner in an instant, even with the short hair and the drugstore dye job. She recognized Eton Charles too. He was crouched next to Zozi on the floor, ten days of beard growth on his face and a bandage over his right ear. He grabbed Zozi and pulled her back against his chest.

"Who the hell are you?" he asked, his eyes flitting from Poe to Marple.

"It's okay," said Poe. "Relax. You're safe now."

Marple heard a rustle from the other side of the room. Poe swung around, gun ready.

A tall girl in black leather rose from behind the second bed with her hands raised. Pale skin. Bright red hair.

"Don't kill me!" the girl sobbed. "Please don't kill me!" Marple recognized her too—even without the Catholic school uniform. The redhead with something to hide.

"I have the money!" the girl said, her voice cracking. "It's right here!" She reached down and heaved the heavy satchel onto the bed. "I was just trying to help my friend!" She looked over at Zozi, then fell back against the wall and slid down to the floor, hands over her face.

Marple looked back toward the bed. Zozi had her arms wrapped tight around her stepfather. It wasn't just fear. Something else.

Dear God.

In an instant, Marple saw the whole thing clearly, and it made her stomach turn. "Zozi," she said. "We're private investigators. Your mother hired us to find you."

Zozi squeezed Eton's arm and looked up at Marple with tears coursing down her cheeks. "We're not going back," she said. "Not ever. We're in love."

Marple shifted her stare to Eton. What was he—three times Zozi's age?

"I know how it looks," he said. "You don't understand."

"I certainly do," said Marple. She couldn't disguise the disgust in her voice.

"He doesn't need to explain," Zozi said defiantly. "He hasn't done anything wrong. I want to be with him. It's my choice. My decision. My life."

Marple sat down on the edge of the bed. She had a lot of questions, but all she could think about at this moment was Addilyn Charles. Poor terrified, betrayed Addilyn.

Across the room, the redhead stood up slowly, still speaking through sobs. "What do we do now? What's going to happen?"

"Well, for starters," said Marple, "you're all going to jail."

CHAPTER 91

MARPLE STOOD WITH Poe near the hood of the patrol car. Eton and the two girls had already been loaded in. An Animal Control officer had just finished managing—barely—to fit Toby into the kennel space in his truck.

The brusque Asbury Park cop flipped her notebook shut. "Okay," she said, "we'll hold 'em at the station overnight. You can transport 'em back to the city in the morning."

Her partner, a baby-faced officer with a wisp of a moustache, was doing his best to fit the girl's medium-sized motorcycle helmet over his head. "Officer Grant will handle the bike. I'll log the bag and lock it up for you. Animal Control will babysit the dog."

"We appreciate it," said Marple.

"Quite a little soap opera," said the cop.

"Could have turned out worse," said Poe.

The cop just stared at him. "Really? Is that what you're gonna tell the wife?"

Marple walked back and looked in the open rear door of the car. The two girls were scrunched in the back seat with Eton in the middle. All three were cuffed behind their backs. The redhead looked dazed, her head pressed against the rear side window.

Zozi squirmed against the cuffs. "I don't understand," she said, her cheeks wet and red from crying. "I'm not a baby. I'm old enough to choose who I want to be with. How can that be against the law?"

"Zozi, be quiet," said Eton. "My lawyer will handle this."

Marple leaned in. "You're right, Zozi," she said. "We can't control who we fall in love with. But faking an abduction? Extorting money? That *is* illegal. You're definitely old enough to know that."

"Time to go," the cop said. She pushed the rear door shut and slid behind the wheel. Her partner swung his leg over the Kawasaki and fired it up. The patrol car pulled out first, with the young cop on the bike right behind and the Animal Control truck at the rear. Marple watched as they drove off down the street and disappeared around a corner.

"I'll call Helene," Poe said.

Marple nodded. As Poe reached for his phone, a loud pop sounded from the other side of the parking lot.

A gunshot.

CHAPTER 92

POE YANKED MARPLE to the ground and pulled out his pistol again. He swept the barrel around the parking lot, scanning the motel front and the sidewalk across the street. Nothing moving.

A low moan rose from behind a car at the edge of the lot. Poe crouched and moved forward. The hairs on the back of his neck prickled. As he came around the other side of the sedan, he froze. A figure lay crumpled on the pavement. Poe took one step toward the shape. A jolt went through him.

No!

"Brendan!" he shouted.

Holmes was lying on his back, blood oozing from under his head. A thick, dark puddle was forming near his shoulder. His eyes were open but his expression was slack.

Poe dropped to his knees. He whipped off his jacket and put it under his partner's neck. A second later, Marple was crouched down next to Holmes, her lips by his ear. "Brendan! What happened? Who did this??"

Holmes turned toward her, eyelids flickering. The white of his right eye was clouded with blood. "I bought drugs, Margaret... on

the boardwalk." His voice was weak and monotone. "Someone...
must have...followed me...My fault. I'm sorry."

Suddenly, a door opened on the second floor of the motel. A young
woman with a baby in her arms stepped out onto the balcony.

"Get back inside!" Poe shouted. *"Now!"* The young woman turned
back into the room and slammed the door behind her.

Poe pulled out his phone and pressed SOS.

The dispatcher picked up on the second ring. "Nine one one.
What's your emergency?"

Poe spoke slowly and clearly. "Beach Manor Motel. Male. Gunshot
wound to the head. Critical!"

Holmes shuddered. His chest started to heave. His head rolled
limply to the side, eyes closed now. His breaths were shallow and
unsteady. Poe rested a palm on his partner's chest and peeked under
the edge of the blood-soaked jacket to get a closer look at the damage.

The bullet had plowed a furrow along the scalp above the right
temple, exposing a strip of white bone. Poe dabbed blood away from
the gash and pulled a small flashlight out of his pocket. In the sharp
beam, he could see that the direction of the shot was front to back.
He looked closer.

He saw black stippling at the entry point.

Poe looked at Marple. "It's a contact wound," he said.

Marple dropped down and stretched out flat on the pavement.
She turned her head sideways and looked under the sedan next
to where Holmes was lying. She stretched her arm underneath,
reached behind the right rear tire—and pulled out a pistol by the
barrel. When she held it up, Poe could read the initials on the
grip: BH.

Marple sniffed the barrel and then slowly held it up to Poe's nose.
He nodded. Just fired.

Marple tucked the gun into her pocket as sirens echoed from a
few blocks away. Poe turned back toward Holmes and whispered in

his ear. He wasn't sure his partner could hear him, but he was going to say it anyway.

"Brendan, we know the truth. Nobody followed you from the boardwalk. The shooter was *you*."

Marple sat hugging her knees, tears in her eyes.

"Maybe you changed your mind at the last instant," said Poe. "If this is a cry for help, help is here. We won't let you go. Not this way. We love you too much for that."

When he looked up again, the parking lot was filled with flashing emergency lights.

CHAPTER 93

HELENE GREY WALKED out of the Overlook Medical Center, about two miles from the Watchung Reservation. It was five in the morning. She was exhausted and achy. Her unmarked sedan was still parked at an angle near the emergency entrance. Addilyn Charles was stable, but they were keeping her overnight. She was sedated and sleeping.

Grey looked at her watch. It would be an hour's drive from Jersey back to Manhattan. She figured she'd make a quick change at her apartment before heading back into the office. No time for rest.

The FBI team had finally found the huge white courier dog. No collar. No tags. They'd taken partial impressions of the motorcycle tire tracks at the edge of the park road, but that was it. Dead end.

As Grey slid into the car, her cell phone rang.

The ID said POE. She tapped Accept.

"Where the hell are you?" asked Grey.

Poe's voice was clipped. "Jersey Shore University Medical Center," he said. "Brendan shot himself."

"What?" said Grey. "How? *Where?*"

"At a motel in Asbury Park. We found Zozi Turner and Eton Charles."

"Wait. Slow down. The girl and the stepfather? They're *alive*?"

"They're fine," said Poe. "They're under arrest. The Asbury Park cops are holding them."

Grey's head was spinning. "Under arrest for *what*?"

"I have to go," said Poe.

"Auguste!"

The call ended.

Grey started her car and peeled out of the hospital parking lot, lights flashing, siren wailing.

For a second, she thought about speed-dialing Brita Stans. But she realized she had no idea what to tell her.

CHAPTER 94

GREY FLASHED HER badge as she dashed past the hospital nurses' station. Her adrenaline was pumping. She could see Marple and Poe sitting in plastic chairs outside a row of curtained treatment rooms. They both stood up as she got there.

"What happened?" asked Grey. "What's his condition?"

"They're working on him," said Poe. "Not sure how much damage he did."

"And the kidnapping?" she asked. "What the hell happened there?"

"Not a kidnapping," said Marple. "A relationship."

"Relationship?" said Grey.

"Zozi and the stepfather," said Marple.

Grey felt a little twist in her gut.

"They were on their way to Belize," said Marple.

"Hold on," said Grey, pressing her hands against her temples. "Start at the beginning."

"Not now," said Poe, nodding over her shoulder.

Grey turned as a tall woman in blue scrubs approached, her rubber-soled shoes squeaking on the tile floor. "I'm looking for Auguste Poe," she called out.

"Right here," said Poe, raising his hand.

"I'm Doctor Hamsha, the trauma surgeon. You're Mr. Holmes's healthcare agent?"

"I am," said Poe. "How is he?"

"The bullet creased the right parietal bone. No cranial penetration, fortunately. But he bled a lot. We've sedated him, and we're watching for signs of swelling or concussion. He's very lucky. Another inch to the left and half his brain would be gone."

"Is he stable?" asked Marple. "His heart? His lungs?"

"For now," said Hamsha. "We need to run more scans. Then we'll see how he does." The doctor took a step closer toward Poe and lowered her voice. But Grey could hear every word. "I need to tell you that your friend had some very nasty drugs in his system," Hamsha said. "Street grade. The worst. Frankly, I'm surprised he lived long enough to shoot himself."

"When can we see him?" asked Marple.

"Not for a while," said the doctor. She turned and headed back up the corridor, shoes squeaking.

As soon as the doctor was out of earshot, Grey turned to Marple and Poe. "We need to talk," she said.

"About what?" asked Poe. "You heard what she said."

"About Asbury Park," said Grey. "I need to know what happened down there."

Poe rubbed his eyes. "Like Margaret said, it wasn't a kidnapping. It was a bad romance. Case closed."

Grey bristled. It had been a long day and her nerves were fried. She wasn't about to settle for a brush-off like that. Not on a case this important. Especially not from Poe.

"That's enough!" she snapped. "You can't cut me out of the loop like this. And you sure as hell can't cut the FBI out of the loop. You guys were told to let them handle the Charles case, and instead you took off on your own, like vigilantes! I'm glad the girl and the stepdad are alive. That's better than the alternative. But this is not how law enforcement works!"

"It's not our fault if everybody else is two steps behind," said Poe. "We're very good at what we do."

"Really?" said Grey. "If you're really good at what you do, then why is your partner lying in the ICU with a gunshot wound to the head?"

Poe looked away.

Grey knew it was a low blow, but she wanted to make a point. She took a deep breath and spoke slowly and deliberately. "I want to hear about your whole night," she said. "Every single detail. I need to call Brita Stans, and when I do, I don't want to sound like a goddamn idiot."

Poe sat down heavily in one of the plastic chairs and looked up at Marple. "*You* explain," he said. "I'll keep watch."

"Perfect," said Grey, taking Marple firmly by the arm. "Girl talk."

CHAPTER 95

SITTING AT A small table in the hospital cafeteria, Marple unspooled it all for Grey. The hidden pearl transmitter. The chase through New Jersey. The scene in the motel room. As she talked, doctors and nurses shuffled past in white coats and wrinkled scrubs. At other tables, families and visitors huddled in conversation. When she was done, Marple set her cup of vending-machine tea aside. "We need to tell Addilyn," she said.

"Let her sleep," said Grey. "I'll talk to her in the morning."

Marple nodded. "I'll come with you."

"Hello, Mrs. Charles," said Grey, as if practicing a speech. *"The good news is, your husband and daughter are alive and well. The bad news is, they're a couple."*

Suddenly, a loud voice blasted from the hallway. "FBI! I'm looking for Detective Lieutenant Helene Grey!"

"Oh, shit," said Grey. "That didn't take long."

Marple saw Grey take a deep breath as Special Agent Brita Stans pushed through the doors and headed for their table. She was still shouting when she got there.

"Helene! I just talked to the Asbury Park station. What in the living *fuck* is going on?"

"Have a seat, Brita," Grey said calmly. "We'll explain everything."

Stans looked anything but calm. "Why are my kidnapping victims in holding? Where the hell are the kidnappers? Who's the goddamn redhead in leather?" She looked at Marple. "And why are you here?"

Marple's reply was low and even. "Because my partner was shot."

Stans yanked out a chair and sat down. "Which partner?"

"Holmes," said Marple. "He'll pull through. Thanks for asking."

"Who shot him?" asked Stans. "The kidnappers?"

"Self-inflicted," said Grey.

"Jesus!" said Stans. "What a clusterfuck." She leaned in toward Marple. "Look. I'm sorry about your partner. I am. This is a great hospital, and I'm sure they're doing everything they can. But I'm working a kidnapping case. Enlighten me."

Marple cleared her throat. Obviously, she was going to have to go through the whole story again. "Agent Stans," she said, "there was no abduction. The daughter and the stepdad ran away together. They were staying out of sight until they could put together new identities and get out of the country."

"They're romantically involved," said Grey.

Stans shook her head. "Oh, for the love of Christ . . ."

Marple went on. "The whole kidnapping scam was Zozi's idea. She kept Eton in the dark about that. She demanded five million dollars because that was the amount in her trust fund, which she was set to inherit at age twenty-one. She figured it was her money. Why wait until then to collect it?"

"So who's the redhead?" asked Stans. "And please don't tell me they're a threesome."

Marple shook her head. "School friend. Idolizes Zozi. Her name is Darla Ross. Zozi hooked her into making the ransom calls and arranging the pickup. Darla trained a rescue dog to make the pickup. Then she switched bags and carried the ransom to the motel. The dog was disposable. The jewelry was going to be Darla's cut."

"What about the shirt?" asked Stans. "The stepdad's blood."

"An accident," said Marple. "Eton sliced his ear with a pair of scissors while he was trimming his beard. Zozi decided to send the shirt to Addilyn as a way to make the kidnapping seem legit."

"Holy shit," said Stans. She leaned back in her chair, then sat up straight and looked at Grey. "Can we nail Daddy on statutory rape?"

Grey shook her head. "Zozi turned eighteen last month. Age of consent in New York. We can't prove a relationship before that date. Incest won't stick either. They're not blood relations. And he never adopted her."

"*Dammit!*" said Stans. "This is *sick!*"

"You can go after the girls for conspiracy and extortion," said Marple. "But Darla's still a minor. It would be a first offense for both her and Zozi. And the entire ransom was recovered. So they'll probably just get a slap on the wrist. Probation. Maybe a few months of community service. No serious time."

"And then," said Grey, "Zozi and her stepdad can do whatever they want."

Marple could see that Stans was angry, and grasping at straws. "We'll sue him for the cost of the investigation," she muttered. "Every goddamn penny."

"Go ahead," said Grey. "Eton Charles won't even blink. He'll just write a check."

"Right," added Marple. "Maybe he'll send it from the honeymoon."

CHAPTER 96

Three days later

VIRGINIA HELD ANNABEL in her arms as she looked out the window. She could see the flashing lights through the office window from a block away. They were almost here! She set the cat down on a brick windowsill and headed outside. She ran through her mental checklist for the homecoming, just to make sure she hadn't neglected anything.

A seven-thousand-dollar adjustable hospital bed had been installed in Holmes's bedroom. The prescribed medications were locked in the office safe. Most important, according to Poe's instructions, Virginia had removed every single weapon and sharp object from Holmes's apartment. Down to the very last pushpin.

Virginia hurried out through the front door just as the GTO rolled up to the curb, preceded by an NYPD patrol car, lights flashing. Helene Grey had arranged for the escort all the way from New Jersey. *Sweet touch,* thought Virginia.

As the patrol car drove away, she saw Poe emerge from the driver's side of the Pontiac and hurry around to the passenger side. When he opened the door, Holmes swung his legs out and stood up.

He had a white bandage around his head, extra thick on the right side, just above his ear. He looked good, Virginia thought. A little tired. But better than she'd expected for a man who'd been shot in the head just seventy-two hours ago.

Virginia hurried down the steps, nervous and excited. "Welcome back, Mr. Holmes!"

"Everything ready?" asked Poe, his hand on his partner's elbow.

"Just like you asked," said Virginia. "Oh. And I made matzo-ball soup."

Holmes gave her a little smile. "My electrolyte balance feels better already," he said.

As Poe escorted his partner up the steps, Virginia saw Marple folding the passenger seat forward from inside the car. She was shouting from the back seat. "Hold on, hold on!"

Suddenly a huge dog with pale fur jumped out of the back seat and onto the sidewalk. Marple maneuvered out too. "Be careful, Virginia! He's a *beast*!"

Virginia bent forward gently as the strange dog approached her, trailing a long leather leash. She kept her eyes lowered and her movements slow. The dog was a pale mastiff, the size of a miniature horse.

"He's beautiful!" said Virginia. "Who does he belong to?"

"Nobody," said Marple, closing the car door. "His previous owner has no more use for him."

The dog's giant head nudged against Virginia's chest as he explored her with urgent sniffs. She reached out and ran her hand gently along his back and sides, feeling the rise and fall of his massive chest under her fingers. The dog reared up and put both enormous paws onto Virginia's shoulders, then placed his muzzle in the crook of her neck and gave her a sloppy lick.

"What's his name?" she asked.

"Not a clue," said Marple. "Holmes calls him the Hound of the Baskervilles."

"Baskerville," said Virginia, giving the dog a kiss on the snout. "That suits him."

"Okay, then," said Marple. "I guess now he belongs to you."

CHAPTER 97

Two weeks later

MARPLE WAS EVEN more impressed by El Viaje than she had expected to be. The restaurant's spacious dining room extended out in the shape of a fan over the lower Hudson River, as if suspended in midair. The place was so new that musicians and movie people were still tripping over one another in the lounge every night. But the young chef did not seem the least bit awed. Dario Aquilar was a star in his own right, and he acted the part.

Marple had been a fan of the young Peruvian's first establishment—a tiny Brooklyn gastropub. Now he finally had the space to indulge his whims. He was vain, but his food justified it. Besides, Marple was used to ingenious people who were totally full of themselves. She lived with two of them.

Holmes, happily free of his bandages, was just finishing his appetizer—a colorful mix of persimmon tomatoes and martini cucumbers. "Insanely good," he mumbled between bites.

Marple smiled. Aside from a permanent crease in his scalp, her partner seemed back to normal. Whatever normal meant for

Brendan Holmes. At least his urine was clean. Marple was sure of that. She'd tested it herself that morning.

Poe and Grey sat next to each other on Marple's left. They were sharing a bowl of acorn squash puree with hickory nuts.

"Do they ever serve this in your break room?" asked Poe.

"Only when we run out of instant oatmeal," said Grey. She closed her eyes as she took another silky spoonful.

The dinner had been Marple's idea. Part celebration. Part peace offering. She knew that Helene hadn't totally forgiven the firm for catching the kidnapping case on the sly—or for solving it without her. Grey had taken a huge dose of shit from Police Commissioner Boolin, and she was now on Agent Brita Stans's permanent blacklist. This was a way to patch things up between Grey and the firm. Maybe. At least a start. Marple liked Helene. And she liked that Helene liked Poe. He hadn't looked this happy in a very long time.

Dinner and drinks were on the house tonight, thanks to a favor Marple had called in a few months back. Aquilar's sous chef had been stuck in immigration limbo until the proper documents mysteriously appeared in his attorney's mailbox. God bless America.

Marple sipped her sinfully expensive sherry, the one Luka Franke had recommended. The other three were drinking wine. The alcohol loosened the mood and heightened the anticipation. When the sampler of main courses arrived, there were actual gasps around the table.

"Outrageous," pronounced Holmes. And it was. Also decadent, sensuous, and mind-bending. When the squad of waiters departed, the table was filled with plates that looked like modern art. Cheese ravioli in pasta as clear as glass, foamy castles of strawberry and caviar, translucent bubbles of taro root, tinted cubes of beef gelatin topped with dark buttons of olive puree, and a delicately deconstructed lobster Bolognese. Forks were raised. Everybody took their first bites.

For several minutes, the table was silent, except for the clink of flatware and moans of pleasure. As the food disappeared, Marple tapped her glass.

"I'd like to propose a toast," she said. The others picked up their wineglasses. "To Brendan Holmes, a man who abhors the dull routine of existence. Welcome home."

Holmes bowed his head solemnly, then broke out in a warm smile for the whole table. "Thank you all," he said. "For making my existence *anything* but dull."

Marple turned to her left, glass still raised. "And to Detective Lieutenant Helene Grey, our sister in crime."

Grey nodded graciously. All four lifted their glasses toward the center of the table and tapped lightly. Marple took a quick sip and set her sherry down. She placed her palms flat on the table and leaned forward with a mischievous glint in her eye.

"Now," she said, "let's play a game."

CHAPTER 98

A GAME? THOUGHT Grey. *What is Marple up to?*

So far, Grey had limited herself to a single glass of Chardonnay. She didn't want to let her guard down. Inside, she was still angry about the kidnapping case, and she wasn't sure if she should trust any of them. Even the one whose hand was resting lightly on her thigh.

"The game is…" said Marple, inserting a dramatic pause, "Two Truths and a Lie."

Grey squirmed in her seat. Was this a joke? The last time she'd played this game was in her college sorority house, tipsy on cheap Chablis. The truths and lies that night had been mostly about celebrity crushes and multiple orgasms. It was an icebreaker—a getting-to-know-you game, with no real consequences. She wasn't sure how to play in company like this, or if she wanted to play at all. But Marple was already leaning in her direction, eyebrows raised.

"You first, Detective."

What the hell, thought Grey. Better to join in than to seem rude. It was just a game after all, and at least she was in control of her turn. She looked around the table as she considered her options, then settled on three choices. *Don't ever explain,* she reminded her-self. *Keep it short. Don't blink.*

"All right," she said. She took a deep breath and let it out before making her statements, as matter-of-factly as she could manage.

"I was the top marksman in my academy class. John Mayer once invited me to dinner. My father died in prison."

She picked up her glass and took a slow sip of wine. Marple drummed her fingers lightly. Poe glanced up at the ceiling, as if the answers might be revealed in the plasterwork. Holmes leaned forward.

"Did you accept?" he asked.

"Accept what?" asked Grey.

"Mr. Mayer's overture."

Grey felt herself blushing slightly. "No. I did not." That was true.

"And you're a deadly shot," Holmes said definitively.

Grey took another sip. She nodded. Also true.

"Which means," Poe said grandly, "that your father was never in prison."

Grey tipped her glass at him. "Three for three," she said. "How did you guess?"

"No guessing involved," said Holmes, leaning back. "Simple observation. Pupil dilation."

Grey felt a vibration in her pocket. She pulled out her phone and glanced down. Grey pushed back from the table. "Sorry," she said. "Business."

"Pity." Marple pouted. "We were just getting started."

CHAPTER 99

GREY TOOK THE call as she walked up the polished wood staircase to the mezzanine. "Raymond? What've you got?"

"A lot," said the voice on the other end. "And nothing."

"I'm listening," said Grey. She stopped at the center of a thick railing overlooking the dining room. As she glanced down, Poe lifted his glass toward her.

"Pay attention," said Raymond, his voice terse. "Don't take notes. None of this goes in writing. Is your phone clean?"

"Squeaky," said Grey.

"Okay," said Raymond. "Afghanistan. Eighteen years ago. Three deep-cover operatives went missing in Shorabak province. Two males, one female. No next of kin. Kidnapped, killed, defected—nobody knows. The official report was buried. Like it never happened."

"So they'd be in their late thirties, early forties now," said Grey, looking down at the three partners, chatting animatedly as waiters cleared the table.

"Right. Give or take," said Raymond. "But here's another nugget. I turned up something from Ukraine. Right after 9/11, three

Moldavian operatives escaped from a military prison near Bila Tserkva. Again, two men, one woman. Next day, intelligence found three bodies in the Dnieper River. They were cremated on the spot. My people think the bodies might have been decoys. Which means the real three could still be out there."

"With new names and identities," said Grey. "What about the business in Bushwick?"

"It's a straightforward limited partnership," said Raymond. "And they all pay their taxes."

"So they've got Social Security numbers," said Grey.

"They do," said Raymond. "The numbers are real. They belong to one Auguste James Poe, one Brendan Mark Holmes, and one Margaret Ann Marple."

"The names are legit?"

"Apparently. Or they found some way to hack the federal government."

"I wouldn't put it past them," said Grey. "What about genealogy?"

"We did a deep dive on Edgar Allan Poe, Arthur Conan Doyle, and Agatha Christie. Couldn't find any loose leaves in their family trees, but doesn't mean there aren't a few. Holmes and Poe aren't that unusual as surnames. And you can find a dozen Margaret Marples on Facebook."

"None with a PI license, I'm guessing."

"Correct. And by the way, the original Miss Marple was a *Jane*."

"Good to know," said Grey.

"Tell you what, Helene," said Raymond. "These guys are ghosts. Best I've ever seen. But if you want, I can keep digging."

Grey thought for a moment. "Forget it," she said. "All you'll find is more smoke."

"Watch yourself, Helene," said Raymond. Then he clicked off.

Grey got back to the table just as dessert arrived. Four waiters held out helium-filled balloons made from clear raspberry taffy.

A culinary magic trick. Holmes took his balloon by the stem and placed his lips against the clear membrane. When he sucked in, the balloon popped, leaving a ruffled tail of candy on his plate.

"Th-th-th-that's all folks!" said Holmes, his voice pinched by the helium to sound like a cartoon character. Grey simply poked her balloon with her fork and took a small bite of the exploded taffy, sweet and gooey. It reminded her of a state fair.

"I hope you were suitably enchanted tonight." A man's voice, with a rich Spanish accent.

Grey turned around. Chef Dario Aquilar, in crisp kitchen whites, was standing behind her chair.

"Nothing but surprises," Grey said with a smile.

"Fantastic," said Holmes.

"Totally original," said Poe.

"Dario," said Marple, "it was divine." Aquilar swept over to her, took her hand, and kissed it gently. "Thank you again, Margaret," he said. "I will forever owe you."

As they walked to the waiting limo, also comped by the restaurant, Grey felt Poe's fingers graze her hand. Almost imperceptibly. Even so, it sent a shiver through her. She leaned in until her lips barely brushed his ear.

"Take me to bed," she whispered. "Whoever you are."

CHAPTER 100

THE NEXT MORNING, as usual, Helene Grey was the first one in the office at One Police Plaza. The night with Poe had been terrific, enough to make her nagging questions recede for a while. The coffee in bed had been wonderful too. But now Grey felt the need for a cup from the office pot. Precinct blend. Diesel strength. A couple of sips cleared the remaining cobwebs.

As her colleagues filtered in, exchanging mumbled greetings and corny jokes, Grey ruffled through the paperwork that had accumulated on her desk over the last twelve hours. Crime stats. New regulations. Personnel announcements. The usual crap. She glanced quickly through the pile and tossed most of it into the wastebasket.

At the bottom of the stack was a white envelope, crisp and elegant. No markings. No address. Just her name and title, handwritten. Grey shook the envelope and held it up to her desk lamp to make sure it wasn't stuffed with some kind of suspicious powder. But all she could see and feel inside was paper. She sliced the end of the envelope with her penknife and pulled out a neat packet. It was a stack of financial spreadsheets, dense with account numbers, dates, and transfers. But it was the name at the top of the forms that caught her attention.

Bain Enterprises.

Grey sat up straight in her chair, now fully awake. She flipped slowly through the documents, page by page. She'd taken only one forensic accounting seminar at Quantico, but she knew enough to understand that what she was looking at was pure dynamite. Evidence of extensive corruption, tax evasion, and illegal campaign contributions. She wondered how it had landed on her desk instead of in the Financial Crimes unit. Routing mistake? Wherever it came from, she knew it was enough evidence for a spectacular, career-boosting takedown.

A gift from the gods.

CHAPTER 101

AFTER THE LONG previous evening of celebration and chat at the restaurant, Marple was taking some recovery time in the second-floor library, searching the shelves for something soothing. As usual, she found herself in the mystery section and, in particular, in the world of English villages and country gardens.

When it came to Agatha Christie, it was hard for Marple to find a work she didn't already know by heart. That morning, something pulled her to a volume titled *Miss Marple's Final Cases*. She thumbed through the contents to a story called "The Case of the Perfect Maid." She recalled starting it years earlier, but she'd never actually finished it.

Book in hand, Marple walked out of the library and closed the door. As she walked back down the hall toward her apartment, she looked over the balcony and sensed a commotion below. She placed the book on a hall table and walked downstairs to investigate.

As she reached the first floor, Marple saw Holmes on his knees in a corner, with the top half of his body stretched behind the shredding machine. Poe and Virginia were crouched behind him. Virginia's new dog, Baskerville, hung close to her side. The two were now inseparable.

"Did somebody lose a contact lens?" asked Marple.

No response from Holmes or Poe. They were both too focused on the task at hand. Virginia stood up and gently pulled Marple aside. She spoke in a whisper. "Remember how I told you about the night when I...?" She pointed toward the back of the room. "When I felt the..."

Marple nodded. "The night you smelled the bread." The two women exchanged a meaningful look. Marple had told Virginia about the building's history as a bakery and the fate of young Mary McShane. Only later did Marple realize that Virginia's experience had occurred on the anniversary of Mary's murder.

"This morning," said Virginia now, "I dropped a page behind the shredder. When I reached underneath to get it, I cut myself." She held up her right index finger, tightly wrapped in gauze. "I feel like this building is trying to tell me something."

"Can you see anything?" asked Poe, crouched on the floor beside Holmes.

"Something's stuck between the bricks," Holmes called out from behind the shredder. Marple heard a sharp grunt, then, "Got it!"

She watched as Holmes slid back and stood up, a small headlamp strapped around his forehead. He held a sturdy set of pliers in his hand. Gripped tightly in the jaws was a serrated eight-inch blade, oxidized along its entire length.

Poe leaned in close. "Bread knife," he said.

"Well preserved," said Holmes, turning the blade from side to side. "Hidden from light for decades." He pulled out his magnifying glass and held it a few inches from the relic. "Edge blackened and pitted," he mumbled.

Marple grabbed Virginia by the arm as Holmes walked over and waved the blade slowly in front of them.

"This is not just oxidation," he pronounced. "It's blood rust."

Marple felt her heart pounding. She realized exactly what she was looking at.

"Put that in a bag," she said softly. "It's the murder weapon."

CHAPTER 102

"SNOOOOOOZE-VILLE! YOU'RE BORING the living *shit* out of me."

Huntley Bain leaned back in his chair at the head of his teak conference table and mimed an elaborate yawn. Naomi Gild, his director of overseas operations, stood frozen at the other end of the table, her finger hovering over the space bar of her laptop. The slide on the screen showed a chart of quarterly returns from one of Bain's Turkish cable services. Slide two of a ninety-slide deck.

"Speed it up," barked Bain. "I've got a flight to Saint Lucia."

The other twelve executives around the table squirmed and coughed awkwardly into clenched fists. Naomi felt the sweat seeping through her blouse. Suddenly, the heavy doors burst open. It sounded like a gunshot.

"FBI! Hands on the table! Nobody move!"

Two men in boxy suits took positions in front of the screen. Naomi closed her laptop lid and stood with her hands folded in front of her skirt.

A third agent came through the door and walked straight to the head of the table. A sturdy-looking woman with a no-nonsense attitude. Naomi saw Bain push his chair back toward the door to his private office. The female agent stopped him with a firm hand on his shoulder and spun him back around.

"Mr. Bain, I'm Special Agent Brita Stans, and you're under arrest for wire fraud, tax evasion, bribery and corruption, and violation of New York State campaign finance laws. We have a warrant to search the premises. Stand up, please."

Bain rose slowly out of his chair with a bitter scowl. Stans produced a set of handcuffs from under her jacket. "Face the wall."

The agent clapped the cuffs onto his wrists, then started marching him toward the door. Bain twisted against the cuffs and glared at the two executives sitting next to Naomi. They were both staring intently into their coffee cups. "You're my *lawyers!*" Bain shouted. "*Do* something!" Neither man looked up.

One of the agents at the front of the room grabbed Bain's other arm. "Let's leave your lawyers out of this, Mr. Bain," Stans said. "For all we know, they're co-conspirators."

As soon as her boss was escorted out of the conference room, Naomi slipped through the door into the main space. All across the vast office floor, she could see more agents pulling files and hard drives out of cubicles while employees stood against the walls, texting furiously. Her heart was pounding, but mostly with relief. She definitely wouldn't have to finish her presentation.

Looking across to the nearby lobby, Naomi saw a woman in a dark business suit standing in front of the elevator bank. She was attractive and fit, her blond hair neatly smoothed and tied behind her head. As the agents escorted Bain over, the woman stepped forward and flashed a badge in front of his face.

"Mr. Bain," she said, "I'm Detective Lieutenant Helene Grey, NYPD. I need to advise you of your rights."

CHAPTER 103

THE EXPRESS RIDE down from the top floor of the Bain Building took thirty seconds—long enough for Grey to make sure that her suit was straight and her gun properly holstered. Bain and Agent Stans stood to her left. Behind her were two NYPD uniforms and a pair of detectives from the Financial Crimes Task Force. They would officially share the collar.

When the doors opened, Stans held on to Bain and nodded at Grey. "You first, Detective Lieutenant."

Grey nodded back. She took a breath and stepped out into a storm of camera flashes. The sleek marble lobby of Bain's headquarters was packed with reporters, all clamoring for a quote. Somebody had obviously alerted the media to the time and place of the high-profile perp walk. The sound echoed against the lobby's glass windows and marble walls. Insane. *What a circus!*

Shelbi Scott of Channel 4 was already doing a live stand-up report, using the procession as a backdrop. "The biggest financial takedown since Madoff," Grey heard her saying. Other reporters crowded frantically along the barriers and thrust mics and mobile phones in Bain's direction.

"Will you take the mayor down with you, Mr. Bain?"

"Will you declare Chapter 11?"

"Mr. Bain, is it true that you're still profiting from porn?"

"Are you hoping for a prison with tennis courts?"

Grey heard a second commotion from overhead. She looked up. On the mezzanine level above the lobby, hundreds of Bain employees were crammed along the railing. Some were applauding.

As she led the way through the media mob, Grey kept her eyes straight ahead and her expression neutral. She maintained her poker face when she spotted Holmes, Marple, and Poe leaning against a column near the revolving doors to the street.

You're welcome, Poe mouthed as their eyes met.

Grey pretended not to notice.

CHAPTER 104

POE AND HIS partners watched from the elegant plaza in front of the skyscraper as a five-car caravan escorted billionaire Huntley Bain off for processing.

"One domino down," said Marple.

"If the mayor is smart," said Holmes, "he's packing already."

In the hours since juicy details from the spreadsheets had been mysteriously leaked to a financial blogger, the press had already traced the dots from Bain's accounts to the campaign coffers of Mayor Felix Rollins. The maximum allowable contribution was fifty-one hundred dollars within a four-year election cycle, the blogger pointed out. Bain was going to have trouble explaining many multiples of that amount, no matter how elaborately the donations had been disguised.

New Yorkers had already drawn the connection between the mayor's visits to Bain's Caribbean villa and the quick approvals for his projects all over New York. But now there was hard evidence of actual bribery. A classic quid pro quo. The relationship between Bain and Rollins didn't just look cozy. It looked criminal.

"Think Boolin might get caught in the undertow?" asked Poe.

"Don't count on it," said Marple. "He's a pretty strong swimmer."

Poe knew that Police Commissioner Boolin was not a fan of their firm, starting from the day they'd cornered him in his driveway about the Sloane Stone case, and especially not since they'd upstaged him at the press conference. The fact that they'd recently collared the Siglik brothers and solved another high-profile crime spree didn't make them any more popular at One Police Plaza. Boolin was not the type to share credit gracefully. Not with the state police. Not with the FBI. And definitely not with a team of smart-ass PIs.

The plaza was crowded with media vehicles, makeshift camera platforms, and portable light rigs. Poe led the way across the plaza through a maze of TV cables and equipment boxes. He'd left his shiny Pontiac Trans Am parked between a News12 van and a CNN satellite truck.

Poe was driving the '77 Pontiac everywhere while his other vehicles were being detailed by an expert in Hoboken. As he and his partners came around the back of a van, Poe saw two muscular camera techs admiring the Pontiac's rakish front end.

"This *yours*?" asked the larger of the techs, looking Poe and his partners up and down. He wore a Dish Network T-shirt that stretched over his bulbous belly.

"Why?" said Poe. "Don't I look the type?"

"Sweet little chariot," said the second tech. He leaned over the hood until his grizzly-man beard brushed the gleaming black finish. "What's the horsepower—180?"

"For insurance purposes, 185," said Poe. "Between us, 220."

"Awesome," said the bearded tech, adding a low whistle.

Poe slipped behind the wheel and fired up the engine as Marple climbed into the back seat.

"Four hundred cc displacement!" Holmes called out as he took his place in front. The techs stepped aside as Poe pulled slowly out of the tight space. Holmes leaned out his window. "Three hundred twenty-five foot-pounds of torque at twenty-four hundred rpm."

Poe smiled. He was glad to see that a bullet to the head hadn't affected his partner's penchant for esoteric trivia, no matter the topic. Holmes's mind, as his namesake would say, rebelled at stagnation.

CHAPTER 105

IN MIDDAY TRAFFIC, the drive from the west side of the city across the Manhattan Bridge to Bushwick took almost an hour. Marple was stiff and achy from riding in the back seat. By the time Poe pulled up to the curb in front of their building, she was more than ready for a stretch.

"Release me!" she groaned.

Holmes stepped out, folded the passenger seat forward, then offered his hand to help Marple pry herself out.

Poe exited from the driver's side. "Built for speed, Margaret, not for comfort."

"All in all," said Marple, "I'd rather ride a bike."

As she reached the front steps of their building, Marple heard a roar from the street, followed by a pair of loud screeches. She turned a split second before her partners did. Two black Suburbans jumped the curb and stopped abruptly halfway across the sidewalk. The rear doors on the lead vehicle burst open. A man and a woman in full tactical gear and face masks jumped out, pistols raised. No badges. No markings.

"Stop right there!" the male shouted.

"Turn around and put your arms out to your sides!" the woman called out.

"What the hell is this?" Holmes whispered to his partners.

"Luka Franke's revenge?" asked Poe.

Marple lifted her arms as the two masked figures approached. She wouldn't put anything past the foiled art thief. But this didn't feel like his style. Too in-your-face. The female in black had her hands on Marple now, running her gloves over her body. Quick but thorough. "Clean!" the female shouted, yanking Marple's phone out of her pocket and her purse out of her hands.

"Gun!" her companion shouted, pulling the Glock from inside Poe's jacket. The female pointed her pistol at Holmes. "What about you?"

"Yes," Holmes said crisply. "I'm armed. Belt holster, behind my back."

The man reached in and plucked out a pistol. The woman patted Poe's pockets and took his phone, then did the same with Holmes. Marple considered making a move, but she could see that the operatives were too well trained. And the last thing she wanted was for Holmes to get reinjured in a street fight. A second later, the option disappeared. The female in black whipped out a zip tie and fastened Marple's wrists behind her back. The man did the same to Poe and Holmes.

"Let's go," said the female.

She shoved Marple across the sidewalk and into the back seat of the rear vehicle. Holmes and Poe got pressed in right alongside her on the bench seat. A solid metal divider separated the back seat from the front. Marple heard heavy door locks snap shut and then the slamming of the two front doors in quick succession.

The SUV lurched off the curb and made a hard U-turn. Through the side window, Marple saw the other vehicle take the lead. In seconds, both cars were zooming through the streets of Brooklyn.

Poe kicked his foot against the partition.

"Who are you? Who sent you? What do you want?"

A small speaker set into the partition crackled. Then the woman's voice came through loud and clear. "Sit still and shut up."

In tense situations with no immediate solution, Marple found that it helped to occupy herself with a practical mental project. As the two-car motorcade sped along the city streets, she started running through the firm's possible enemies, starting with the letter *A*.

CHAPTER 106

FROM HIS FIRST moment in the car, Holmes had been trying to cut through his zip tie with the metal seat-belt bracket, but he couldn't find the right angle. He eased up on his efforts to check the geography passing by his side window.

"We're taking the Williamsburg Bridge," he whispered to his partners. He hadn't expected to be heading back to Manhattan. His prediction would have been someplace remote—the wilds of Jamaica Bay or maybe the Connecticut woods. Wherever they were headed, the kidnappers hadn't bothered to blindfold them or put hoods over their heads. *Not encouraging,* thought Holmes. He knew it predicted a one-way trip.

As soon as the cars crossed the bridge, they turned south toward downtown Manhattan. A few minutes later, they were in a neighborhood that Holmes knew well. The cars passed Chinatown, then the Metropolitan Correctional Center. A few maneuvers later, they were heading down a side street behind One Police Plaza. The cars stopped in front of an industrial-sized garage door, wide enough to admit a tank. The door went up. The cars drove through, then stopped.

"The Joint Operations Center," whispered Poe.

Holmes nodded. "We've been kidnapped by cops."

The door on his side opened. The man in black grabbed him by the arm and pulled him out. Poe got dragged out next, then Marple. Holmes looked around. They were in an underground compound with thick pillars and a concrete floor. Along the far wall, paramilitary police vehicles were lined up like rental cars.

"Move!" The man and woman were behind them now, prodding them forward toward an elevator door behind a concrete barricade. The door opened. Holmes and his partners were herded in. Suddenly, he felt the zip tie being snipped. He turned around.

The elevator door was closing. Poe and Marple were both rubbing their wrists.

They were alone in the elevator car.

Free. But clearly *not* free.

The elevator door opened. They stepped out into a huge bare room. Holmes's olfactory membranes registered the scents of new construction—drywall mud, fresh paint, carpet, concrete. They were on an office floor without windows. Or offices.

Holmes heard a door shut behind them. Then a man's voice.

"Tell me, assholes," he said. "How does it feel to be ambushed outside your home in broad daylight?"

CHAPTER 107

MARPLE TURNED. POLICE Commissioner Boolin had entered the room from a stairwell near the elevator. Three young men in business suits flanked him, along with Helene Grey, grim faced. She looked as if this were the last place on earth she wanted to be. The door opened again. Boolin waved in the new arrival.

"I think you three know Mayor Rollins."

The mayor stepped up beside Boolin and looked from Poe to Holmes to Marple.

"We met once before," Rollins said bluntly. "I'm hoping this will be the last time."

Holmes glanced around the bare space. "Interesting look," he said. "Did somebody cut the furniture budget?" He stared directly at the mayor. "Or maybe the funds were...diverted?"

"Holmes," Grey said softly. "Stop talking." She looked deadly serious.

"Know what's nice about raw space?" said Boolin. "No cameras."

Marple felt a chill. She pushed through it. "Are you threatening us, Commissioner?"

"I didn't say anything of the sort." He pointed at the men behind him. "And these fine attorneys will back me up. What I want to know..." He glanced over at Rollins. "What *we* want to know... is where you got the documents concerning Huntley Bain's finances."

"Well, as I'm sure you can imagine," said Marple, "our methods are proprietary."

"Bullshit!" said Boolin.

Marple took a step forward. "As private investigators," she said, "we are prohibited from impersonating law enforcement officers or company employees as a ruse to obtain financial records. We did neither of those things. As you know, surveillance is permitted under our license, as is the examination of discarded trash."

"You didn't get this shit by dumpster diving," said Rollins. "We want to know how you did it. You have no right to withhold that information."

"Actually, we do," said Marple. "As these attorneys can tell you, documents obtained by private investigators in anticipation of litigation are covered by work-product privilege." Marple looked intently at one of the young lawyers, who lowered his eyes nervously toward the floor. "Do I have that right, Counselor? I'm citing *Costabile versus County of Westchester.*"

"So you were hired by an attorney?" asked Rollins.

"A judge, actually, with an active law license," said Marple, "someone who prefers to keep his interest in this case anonymous for the moment."

"Let's see how that argument holds up once we revoke *your* licenses," said Rollins.

"On what grounds?" asked Marple. "According to section 79 of the General Business Law as it applies to revocations or suspensions, there are only five possible justifications. You'll need to be quite specific."

Boolin turned to his lawyers. All three were now scrolling urgently on their phones.

Marple picked up again. "Also, according to paragraph 1, subsection 5, Mr. Mayor, you are required to give us notice in writing of any intention to revoke or suspend, and allow us fifteen days to prepare our rebuttal."

Marple could see Rollins's lips curling in fury. "By then," she said, "I expect we'll be dealing with your successor. Unless, of course, you think Huntley Bain would rather spend ten years in Wallkill than flip on you."

Rollins turned on the commissioner, cold steel in his voice. "Tell me something, Boolin. How does Nancy Drew here know more about this crap than you do?"

"I'll fix this," Boolin said gruffly.

"You've fixed enough," Rollins said curtly. "You're fired."

Marple looked at Grey. "In that case, Detective Grey, my partners and I decline to make a citizen's arrest of the former commissioner for false imprisonment. Let's just call it a misunderstanding."

"As long as we get our guns back," said Poe.

"And my purse," said Marple.

"And a ride home," added Holmes.

Boolin took a step forward, hands clenched into fists. For a second, Marple thought he might actually take a swing at somebody. Even her.

"Don't make it worse, Boolin," Rollins called out. "You could lose your pension."

The mayor led the way out of the room, kicking the door open with his foot. Boolin turned on his heel and followed, trailed by the attorneys. The slamming door echoed through the empty space. Marple let out a long breath.

"Margaret," said Holmes, "that was remarkable."

Poe put his arm around her shoulders. "My hero."

Helene Grey stepped forward and looked Marple in the eye. "How in God's name were you prepared for all that?"

Marple looked right back, her voice even and calm. "I watch a lot of television. I have a photographic memory. I was first in my law school class." She lifted her eyebrows and flashed an enigmatic smile. "Two truths and a lie."

CHAPTER 108

"NICHOLAS! LOOK OVER there! Did you see the heron?"

Macy Dale and her eight-year-old son were kayaking the quiet waters of the Croton River. They were about a quarter mile upstream from the rental site on the banks of the Hudson, about forty miles north of Manhattan. The air on the river was cool and refreshing, well worth the trip from the city.

Nicholas sat in the front seat of the cockpit, paddling energetically, while Macy handled steering from the rear. They'd set out from New York at 6 a.m. to beat the crowds. It had worked. So far, they hadn't seen anybody else on the water.

That didn't mean they were alone. The river and its banks were brimming with life. The blue-grey heron was wading in the shallows, turning its long neck to groom its feathers. They'd also seen red-tailed hawks, Canada geese, and a pair of ospreys.

As they steered around the edge of a small midstream island, Nicholas pointed excitedly toward the bank. "Look, Mom! Wild turkeys!" Sure enough. Macy steered the red kayak toward the gathering of huge black-feathered birds at the edge of the island. They were perched on a dead log half submerged at the shoreline.

"They're so *ugly*!" Nicholas called back. He splashed water toward the flock with his paddle, but the birds weren't bothered. They were too busy poking and pecking at their breakfast.

"Nicholas, stop!" said Macy. "Leave them alone."

As they glided past, Nicholas got distracted by the ripple of a turtle making its way toward the opposite shore. Just then, Macy got a whiff of something horrible.

She glanced back at the turkeys and got a sick tingle in her belly. At second look, they weren't wild turkeys. They were turkey *vultures*, with skeletal reddish heads emerging from cloaks of black feathers. She angled her paddle in the water to slow the kayak. Now she could see that the birds were crowding over a shape just below the surface. She splashed her paddle in the water. The birds moved off into the reeds.

Nicholas called back. "Why are we going so slow?"

Macy quickly angled the kayak away from the island. "Nicky! Don't turn around! Don't look!"

She glanced back just long enough to see the mottled body bobbing just below the surface. The figure was tall and vaguely female, with filthy blond hair waving like a cloud around the head. A denim-clad leg was angled partly out of the water, and a Western-style boot was hooked on a low branch. On the side of the boot was a large tooled pattern in red.

The unmistakable shape of Texas.

CHAPTER 109

THIRTY-SIX HOURS LATER.

"I still cannot *believe* you didn't tell me," Helene Grey said.

It was the third time that evening she'd said it. Otherwise, she hadn't spoken much at all. Marple could tell that the detective was still pretty angry. When Grey told her about the discovery of the young Texas model's body in the river, Marple had finally come clean about the mystery cowboy on Hart Island, and the white pickup with the Lone Star decal.

"What was I supposed to tell you?" said Marple. "That I was on a secret mission to follow up on an obscure tip about a buried body that might possibly be Zozi Turner? We'd already been kicked off the case. Remember? When I saw the guy following me, I thought there might be a connection. But then we found Zozi alive and well, and I thought maybe I'd been imagining things."

"A guy jumps off a ferry to get away from you, and you think that's normal?"

"You're right," said Marple. "Consciousness of guilt. I should have said something. I need to work on my sharing."

Marple prided herself on diligence, and it truly bothered her that she might have let something so significant get away from her—especially on another case that turned out to involve an innocent girl. She was determined to see this through now, no matter where it led. No matter how dangerous.

She and Grey were currently sitting in Grey's unmarked sedan, staking out a run-down SRO hotel in the South Jamaica section of Queens. From their angle across the street, Grey and Marple could see the entrance of the hotel clearly. The residents coming and going looked ragged and strung out, living in the margins.

"There used to be fleabag joints like this all over the city," said Grey. "They were good for a few spicy calls every shift." She sounded a bit wistful. "Now they're all boutique hotels."

"Gentrification," said Marple. "The city's gone to hell."

She saw a slight smile from Grey. First one all day.

Grey had a printout of the deceased model on the console between them. The picture showed the girl posing playfully in a bright blue cotton sundress, her blond hair curled around her shoulders and her face radiant. The name printed on the border of the picture was "Lucy Lynn Ferry." Stuck alongside it was a high-school graduation photo of a good-looking boy with dark eyes. The name under his picture was "Carson Lee Parker."

After the body had been ID'd, Marple went with Grey to interview the head of the modeling agency, Betsy Bronte. She told them that she'd gotten a text from Lucy at least three weeks ago, saying that she'd gone back to Texas. Couldn't handle New York, the message said. No question that the text had come from Lucy's phone. Grey checked. It had pinged off a cell tower in Westchester.

Bronte said it wasn't unusual for young models to flake out and run back home. The pressure was too intense for some of them. Especially the ones from small towns. But a few days ago, Lucy's parents had called Bronte from Texas, looking for their daughter. They hadn't heard from her. And they hadn't seen her ex-boyfriend,

Carson, around either. They thought they might have run away somewhere together. Maybe eloped.

"You think this guy killed her," said Marple.

Grey tapped the steering wheel.

"He and Lucy were high school sweethearts," she said. "Maybe he took it hard when she left. He's got a minor-league rap sheet back home. Shoplifting. Auto theft. Small-time stuff."

"Violence?" asked Marple.

"Nothing that shows up," said Grey. "But I've seen it come out of nowhere. So have you."

"What about the truck?" asked Marple.

"E-ZPass shows it coming back into Manhattan from Westchester the same day Bronte got Lucy's good-bye text."

"That's right before I saw the cowboy on Hart Island."

"Correct," said Grey. "And why would he go to a graveyard unless he was looking for somebody he knows is dead? He was probably worried that the body had turned up."

"Or maybe he felt guilty," said Marple. "Or just wanted to say good-bye."

"He probably ditched the truck after he realized you'd spotted him," said Grey. "We're checking the chop shops and scrap yards. At this point, it could be anywhere."

Marple looked through the windshield just as a young man passed in front of the car, heading across the street toward the hotel entrance. New baseball cap. Same faded denim outfit. Same long-legged lope. Earlier, the guy at the front desk had given Grey a positive ID on Carson Parker. But under a different name. The cowboy would probably be back, the kid had said. He'd paid for his room a few days in advance. All cash.

"That's him," said Marple, slipping low in the seat. "That's our cowboy."

CHAPTER 110

GREY PICKED UP her walkie-talkie and called for backup. She waited for the cowboy to walk through the entrance before she opened her car door. Marple exited from the passenger side.

"I should really lock you in the car," said Grey.

"You know I'd escape," said Marple.

"Stay behind me, okay?"

"Yes, ma'am."

By the time they crossed the street, the backup car had pulled up. Grey leaned into the front window. The two uniformed cops were babies, both of them. Grey tapped the driver on the shoulder. "You take the back exits," she said. She pointed at his partner. "You cover the fire escapes on the north side. Suspect is male, five ten or eleven. Slender build. Denim outfit. Mets cap. Could be armed. Watch your backs."

The cop behind the wheel nodded. "Copy."

As the young cops exited the car to take their positions, Marple followed Grey through the doors and into the hotel lobby. The whole place reeked of mold. The tile floor was littered with fast-food wrappers and cigarette butts.

Marple looked to the right. A cardboard OUT OF ORDER sign was attached to the elevator door with masking tape. A huge man was slumped on a battered office chair with his massive bald head hanging down between his knees. Drunk, stoned, deranged, or maybe all of the above, thought Marple.

Grey slipped past him toward the stairwell. Marple followed. When they pushed through the heavy metal fire door onto the first-floor landing, the odor of stale urine hit Marple like a slap. She saw a broken syringe in one corner, a used condom in another.

"I'd hate to see the breakfast bar," she said.

Grey pulled her pistol out and leaned forward to look up through the gap in the staircase. "Clear," she whispered. She led the way up, pausing on each landing to gauge the next flight. Marple stayed close behind.

When they reached the fifth floor, Grey leaned against the landing door and looked through the small center pane. She waved Marple into the corner as she tugged hard on the corroded door handle. The door wouldn't budge.

Marple heard footsteps on the landing below. Grey put a finger to her lips, raised her pistol, and took a step back down just as a man rounded the corner on his way up. His bulk almost filled the landing.

He was pointing a .45.

Marple recognized him in a flash. The sleeping guy from the lobby.

Wide awake now.

CHAPTER 111

"HOLD YOUR PIECE by the barrel and hand it over," he said.

"Police officer," said Grey. She opened her jacket to flash her badge.

"Ex-Army," said the guy, pointing the gun at Marple's head. "I win."

"Okay," said Grey. "Stay calm." She clicked on her safety and stretched her arm out. The vet grabbed the gun and stuffed it into the waistband of his pants. He moved up the steps until he was just one step below where Marple was standing.

"This is a very bad neighborhood for ladies," he said. With his free hand, he reached up and touched Marple's arm.

"Hey," said Grey, "you don't want to do that."

The man smiled with yellow teeth. "Oh, but I do. In this place, I do whatever I want."

In a flash, Marple grabbed his wrist and brought it down hard against her knee. The .45 clattered to the floor. Marple grabbed the railing for leverage and thrust her foot into the man's gut, knocking him back down the steps and onto the lower landing. Helene grabbed for her ankle holster and pulled out a small backup gun. She moved quickly down to the crumpled figure in the stairwell.

Marple reached into his waistband and retrieved Grey's primary weapon.

"What's your name?" asked Grey.

"Leon," he replied through a groan.

"You live here, Leon?" Grey asked, leaning into his face.

"Maintenance," he mumbled. "I do maintenance."

"That's perfect, Leon. You're our guy. We'd like the deluxe tour. Starting with floor number five." She hooked her fingers around his collar and yanked it. "Let's go."

Leon looked up at the two guns pointed at his face. He struggled to his feet and moved slowly up the stairs to the landing above. He stopped in front of the bulky fire door and gave it a solid kick below the bottom hinge. He pulled back on the handle with a muscular jerk. The door creaked open.

Grey moved through the door, gun first. She pulled Leon through after her. Marple followed.

"Five C," she whispered to Leon. "Which way?"

Leon pointed toward two doors down on the other side of the hallway.

"Does he know you?"

"Who?" asked Leon.

"The guy in 5C. Does he know who you are?"

"He's seen me around," said Leon.

Grey shoved him forward, gun at his back. "Knock. Tell him you need to fix something in his room."

"Like what?"

"Make it up, Leon. Sound believable. You're already down for assaulting a police officer. Do good here and maybe we can work something out."

Leon walked up to the door and knocked with authority.

"Yeah? Who is it?" A muffled male voice from inside. Texas twang. Marple glanced at Grey.

"It's Leon. I need to look at your radiator."

"Dude," came the reply, "it's 90 degrees out."

Grey pressed the barrel tighter against Leon's back.

"Just gotta check the valve," said Leon. "C'mon. I just need a minute."

Marple stood back behind Grey. She heard a shuffle of feet from inside. The door opened a crack, chain across the gap. Grey pushed Leon's face into the opening. Marple heard the chain slip. The door opened about two inches. Just for a second. Then it slammed shut again.

Grey looked at Leon, then nodded toward the door. "Do it!"

Leon stepped back to the opposite wall and then ran forward, ramming his thick shoulder against the door, about a foot above the knob. The door flew open and Leon crashed through, careening off a wooden dresser before landing hard on the floor. The cowboy was on the window ledge, with one leg out.

"Police!" Grey shouted. "Show me your hands!"

The cowboy froze, then slowly raised his arms. He turned until he was sitting on the windowsill, facing in. He lowered his eyes. His posture was slumped. He looked defeated, resigned—maybe relieved.

"Carson Lee Parker?" asked Grey.

The cowboy nodded. "You found her," he said softly.

"Yes," said Grey. "We did." She pulled her walkie-talkie from her pocket. "Ten twenty-six. Room five Charlie."

"*Copy that,*" came the staticky reply. Grey tugged the young man toward the bed and turned to Marple. "Cover him."

Marple pointed Grey's gun at the kid's heaving chest as Grey holstered her backup gun and pulled out her cuffs. She took the kid by the shoulders and turned him around.

"Give me your hands," she said.

"She was so beautiful," said Carson.

"Yes, she was," said Grey.

"I couldn't just let her go. I *loved* her. All I wanted to do was bring her home. That's all I wanted. To bring her home to Texas. That's where she belonged."

Grey cuffed him and sat him down on the saggy mattress. He was shaking his head as tears spilled down his angular face. "But she wouldn't leave. She wouldn't come back with me. I didn't mean to..."

Leon started to push himself up from the corner. "No, Leon," Grey said firmly. "I'll tell you when." He slumped back down again.

Marple took a step closer to the crumpled suspect on the bed. He didn't look like a desperado, just a very sad kid. In a way, she actually felt sorry for him. She heard the clatter of the two cops racing up the staircase.

Grey grabbed the cowboy under the arm and pulled him up. He looked up at Marple and squinted slightly, as if he were trying to place the face.

"Don't worry, Carson," she said quietly. "I'll make sure Lucy gets home."

CHAPTER 112

IT WAS ALMOST eleven in the evening when Grey pulled up in front of Holmes, Marple & Poe Investigations. Marple was slumped back in the passenger seat. She let out a breathy sigh as the car rolled to a stop. It had been a long, depressing night.

For a solid hour, she and Grey had sat across from Carson Parker as he wrote out his confession on a legal pad. Every single detail. The longest essay he'd ever written.

He had been slow and meticulous, describing the awkward reunion with Lucy in Manhattan, the drive out of the city in his truck, the argument in the park, the struggle, the fatal blow. He only broke down once—when he got to the part about sinking Lucy's body in the river.

Since it happened, he'd gone to every cemetery in the city, watching for burials, wondering if somebody had found her. Grey had asked Parker if there was anybody he wanted to call. There wasn't. Not even a lawyer.

"Thanks for the ride," said Marple, reaching for the car door handle. She stopped and turned toward Grey. "Can I interest you in a nightcap?" She knew she still had some fence-mending to do.

"What the hell, Margaret," said Grey. "You know I'm on duty." She looked at her watch, then smiled. "I'm off in exactly fifteen seconds."

They walked together up to the building's main entrance. Marple leaned in toward the new iris-recognition scanner. She heard the lock release and pushed the door open. Then she stopped. The entire downstairs office was dark. Not even a security light.

"Wait," said Marple. "Something's wrong."

Grey pulled out her pistol.

There was a squeaking sound coming from the center of the room. A slow, regular rhythm. Marple and Grey advanced slowly toward the noise. The light from the street outlined a figure in dark clothing rocking in a high-backed office chair.

Suddenly, a floor lamp clicked on.

Marple blinked. It was Luka Franke. There was a bottle on the small table beside him. He was swirling a snifter.

"Hands up!" shouted Grey.

"Don't worry, Detective," said Franke. "I'm unarmed. Margaret can tell you that I never go in heavy. Why would I risk the weapons charge?"

Grey lowered her pistol but held it ready.

Franke lifted the snifter toward Marple. "I brought you a fresh bottle of the Matusalem," he said. "Hope you don't mind that I started without you."

"Is that to convince me it's not poisoned?"

"Your security is excellent, by the way," Franke went on. "A worthy challenge. Not nearly as sophisticated as the alarms on Huntley Bain's vault, obviously. But first class all the way."

"I hope you're here with a lead on the Shakespeare and the Gutenberg," said Grey. "If I'm not mistaken, that was why the DA let you off the hook."

"As a matter of fact, Detective, I believe I can guide you to an arrest right now."

"I'm listening," said Grey.

Franke set the snifter down on the table. "As it turns out, your thieves work right here in this building." He leaned forward in the chair. "The theft of Huntley Bain's property was orchestrated and supervised by Holmes, Marple, and Poe."

Marple turned as the front lock clicked. Suddenly, Holmes and Poe burst in, guns raised. They took a few steps into the room, then pulled up short.

"What's going on?" asked Holmes.

"We got an alarm alert," said Poe.

"That was me," said Franke. A satisfied grin crossed his face. "And now we have all three conspirators." He looked at Grey. "I have extra cuffs if you need them."

"I'd need a lot more proof than your word," said Grey. "You're not exactly a reliable witness."

"I can provide all the details," said Franke. "Starting with their associates in Stockholm. The world's best safe designers are also the world's best safe crackers. And they're on the payroll of Holmes, Marple, and Poe Investigations."

Poe pocketed his pistol and shrugged. "I believe the individuals you're referring to are currently residing in the Maldives," he said.

"You told them to run!" said Franke.

"Swedes crave the sun," said Marple.

"Especially sunny countries with non-extradition policies," added Holmes.

"Unlike Iceland," said Marple, looking directly at Franke. "Where I believe you own some property. Stolen property."

Franke's lips curled into a bitter sneer. He stood up slowly.

Grey took a step forward. "I *could* arrest you for breaking and entering," she said. "From what I can see, Mr. Franke, you're still a person of interest in this case. In *many* cases. Maybe it's best that this one stays open."

Marple smiled. She liked Helene before. She liked her even more now.

"We won't press charges," said Marple. "On account of the free sherry."

Franke walked slowly toward the door. He stopped and turned toward Grey. "So you're part of this little vaudeville troupe now?"

"Until we meet again, Mr. Franke," Grey replied.

"Don't be mad, Luka," said Marple. "Some mysteries were never meant to be solved."

CHAPTER 113

THE NEXT MORNING, Virginia was standing in the middle of the office, facing a bare brick wall. Pouring rain rippled down the panes of the windows. She felt as if the dampness were passing right through the walls and into her body. Baskerville sat at her side, whimpering softly.

The row of filing cabinets at the back of the room had been moved aside. Holmes was standing up against the wall, examining the exposed bricks with his magnifying glass, scraping at the mortar with a small metal pick. Marple and Poe stood off to the side, watching him work.

"These bricks have been exposed to high heat for long periods," said Holmes. "This is where the baking ovens stood. Right against this wall."

He pulled a metal office ruler from a desk and walked to where Virginia was standing. "Is this where you saw it? The shape?"

"It was a little closer to the back," said Virginia.

"Show me," said Holmes.

Virginia took a few steps forward. She stopped, then inched to the right. Suddenly, she felt the blood draining from her face. "Here," she said softly. "Right here."

She sensed Holmes behind her. She felt the cold edge of the ruler against her skin as he drew it gently across the side of her neck. Her knees gave out. She started to collapse. Poe jumped in to catch her.

"Brendan, stop it!" said Marple. Virginia's head was spinning as Poe set her down on the sofa. Marple then sat beside her. Holmes prowled the space in front of them like an actor on stage.

"He sliced her throat here," he stated, planting his feet in the spot Virginia had indicated. "Then he walked to the wall." Holmes held the ruler at his side and moved to the corner. He knelt down on the floor and continued. "He jammed the knife blade between two bricks and snapped off the handle, leaving the blade buried, and coated with Mary McShane's blood." Holmes stood up. "And then he just...walked out. Just in time to open his business for the day. The Siglik Family Funeral Home."

"Wait," said Virginia, sitting up. "*Siglik*. Like the two brothers?"

"Their grandfather," said Marple. "It all started with him."

"How do you know that?" asked Virginia. "How can you know that from so little?"

"To a great mind," said Holmes, "nothing is little."

"The first few murders were in 1954," said Marple. "All young people without family connections. All within ten blocks of the Siglik funeral home. Mary was the first. After her, he figured out how to dispose of the bodies."

Virginia turned as Poe walked over with a file folder. He opened it and handed her a yellowed piece of paper. "This is where it started," he said. "This story is why we're in this building."

Virginia took the fragile scrap of paper in her hands. DEATH IN A BAKERY, the headline read. She took a deep breath. The newsprint felt warm in her hands. As she ran her fingers down the column, her hand trembled. She looked up. "If Mary didn't end up in the subway tunnel like the others," she asked, "then where's she buried?"

Virginia felt Marple's hand on hers.

"I think I can figure that out," said Marple, "within a yard or two."

CHAPTER 114

VIRGINIA WAS SHIVERING in the damp morning air. The ground on Hart Island was still wet from the hard rain the day before, which made the dig a little easier. Yellow police tape outlined the area around the interment site. Four uniformed cops had staked out the perimeter. A friend of Marple's had signed the exhumation order the night before. A judge from Bedford. Now a man named Stephen was directing the dig.

The backhoe had already excavated the first three feet of soil. Stephen and his crew were digging through the next yard of packed dirt with picks and shovels. They worked slowly, respectfully, inch by inch. From the date of death and Stephen's detailed maps of the site, Marple had narrowed down Mary's resting place to this small patch of earth.

Virginia stood with Marple on the right side of the hole. Holmes, Poe, and Grey stood a few yards away on the left. The only sounds came from metal slicing into earth. Virginia was thinking that otherwise, it felt a little like church.

She wished she could have brought Baskerville along for moral support, but rules were rules. No pets in the graveyard. She felt safe with Marple, though. It was like being with an older sister.

When they reached six feet down, two of the diggers climbed out of the pit, leaving Stephen alone below. "Hand me the small blade," he called up. One of the other workers grabbed a garden spade out of a tool bag. Everybody else leaned forward, peeking down into the rectangular opening in the ground.

"There," Stephen said, running the edge of the spade over a patch of dark earth. He was leaning forward over the vague outline of a coffin. Only scraps of wood and rusted nails remained. Stephen explored gently with his fingertips and tapped his blade lightly into the dirt, from side to side. He stopped. His tool was tapping against something hard. Virginia gasped. She stepped back from the edge, flushed and light-headed.

"Virginia? Are you okay?" Poe called out. "I can walk you back to the ferry."

Virginia shook her head. "No," she said, "I want to be here." She felt Marple's hand on her shoulder.

Holmes was on his knees now, reaching into the pit with gloved hands. The gravedigger passed him what looked like a long greyish stick. Holmes held it gently in both hands and settled back on his heels to examine it.

"Definitely female," said Holmes. "Late teens, early twenties. Interred for approximately sixty to a hundred years." He lifted the bone to the light and gently brushed away a few small deposits of dirt. "I'll have to do more tests to confirm."

Virginia sensed a cold wave washing through her, from front to back. It lasted for only a second. When it passed, she felt warm and calm.

"No need, Mr. Holmes," she said softly. "It's her."

CHAPTER 115

One week later

A WARM BREEZE was blowing through Calvary Cemetery as the small funeral party entered the former Siglik family vault. Marple led the procession. The granite edifice was no longer a crime scene. The yellow tape and fingerprint dust were long gone. And, in fact, the building no longer belonged to the Siglik family at all.

Until a week ago, the mausoleum had been confiscated property, taken by the city as part of the sentencing agreement with the brothers. It had been sold to a shell corporation in the Maldives in a multimillion-dollar cash deal, with the condition that the funds be distributed among the families of the Siglik victims. No one would ever know that the actual purchasers were three PIs from Bushwick.

At the center of the mausoleum, the marble top had been removed from the vacant crypt, and an elegant mahogany casket was suspended by a mechanical arm over the opening.

Helene Grey stood with Poe at the foot of the crypt. Marple stood with Holmes on the opposite side. All in their somber Sunday best. Virginia had not worn a dress since her high school graduation. Marple had loaned her a spare from her closet.

There was no priest or minister in attendance. The partners had wanted to keep it private. No ceremony had been planned. For a few moments, the group stood in awkward silence.

Finally, Holmes nudged Marple. "You should say something, Margaret."

Marple looked up to see everybody staring in her direction. She knew Holmes was right. Nobody was closer to this case—to this young woman—than she was. Except maybe Virginia.

Marple clasped her hands over her chest, closed her eyes, and quickly searched her memory. She recalled a prayer from another funeral service, for another young woman who had died too soon. She thought at the time how beautiful the prayer was. And now it came back to her, word for word. She cleared her throat and spoke it.

"Come in haste to assist her, you saints of God. Come in haste to meet her, you angels of the Lord. Enfold in your arms this soul, and take your burden heavenwards to the sight of the Most High."

In the silence that followed, Marple looked across at Poe. She could see tears brimming in his eyes. She knew he remembered the prayer too. Then she saw Grey reach down and wrap her hand around his.

As Holmes pressed the lever to lower the coffin into the marble vault, Virginia stepped forward and placed a bouquet of green blossoms on top. She spoke softly but clearly.

"Rest in peace, Mary McShane."

CHAPTER 116

"ARE YOU *SURE*?" asked Holmes. "I can take a town car." He was standing next to Poe on the outskirts of the cemetery. Poe handed him the keys to the Trans Am.

"Nonsense," said Poe. "Take it. Just watch out for speed traps." He tapped the hood of the Pontiac. "This thing is a trooper magnet."

Marple stepped up. "How long?" she asked.

"As long as it takes," said Holmes.

"Can we send up the bat signal if we need you?" asked Grey.

"You can try," said Holmes. "But I won't respond. Hanging up the suit for a while."

Virginia stepped forward and wrapped Holmes up in a hug. "I'll miss you, Mr. Holmes. You've taught me a lot."

"You've taught me a few things too," said Holmes. "And it is better to learn wisdom late than never to learn it at all."

Virginia leaned back with a smile of recognition. "*The Sign of the Four.* Sir Arthur Conan Doyle, 1890."

"Well done," said Holmes.

"I've been studying," said Virginia.

"I can see that," said Holmes. "I may just have to will you my portion of the library."

With that, he slipped behind the wheel of the car, turned the ignition, and drove away.

Five hours later, Holmes rounded the corner on a tree-lined road and turned into a gravel driveway. He was on the east side of Cayuga Lake, five miles north of Ithaca, at the entrance to an isolated estate. There was no sign, just two fieldstone pillars with a heavy metal gate between them. The gate opened as he approached.

He drove up the long, curving lane to a large brick building with Norman-style turrets. He pulled the Pontiac around the circle at the top of the driveway and parked near the main entrance. Then he pulled a leather bag from the back seat and walked inside. The entryway was just as he remembered it, natural stone and heavy oak. It looked like a millionaire's hunting lodge.

The scents were the same too. A mixture of aged wood and tea tree oil. The receptionist behind the desk looked up. "Can I help you? Visitor or physician?"

"Neither," said Holmes. "I'm checking myself in."

The woman clicked her keypad and checked her computer screen.

"Don't bother," said Holmes. "I'm not on your list. I came on my own."

"Were you referred to us?" the woman asked, her brow creasing slightly.

"I've been here before," said Holmes. "I came to visit my mother."

The woman dipped back toward her keyboard with a hopeful expression. "Is she a client?"

"My mother died twenty-five years ago," Holmes said softly. "I'm here for myself."

The receptionist leaned forward and spoke in a calm, even tone. "Sir. I'm sorry. Lake View is not a walk-in facility. We need to make advance arrangements, clear your insurance coverage, scan your medical files, consult with—"

"Stop," said Holmes. He set his bag on the desk. "This contains enough cash to pay your fee for as long as I need to be here. Two thousand a day. Am I right?"

The receptionist stared back at him for a few moments. This was obviously not her normal intake. But she had been trained to be as accommodating as possible, at least until the medical staff could be summoned.

"All right, sir," she said, easing back in her chair. "Let's start again. Can I have your name?"

"My name is Brendan Holmes. I'm a heroin addict. And I need help."

CHAPTER 117

MARPLE LOWERED THE windows on the white Ford F-150 pickup. To her surprise, she had discovered that she loved driving a truck. Especially one that was all hers.

After a three-state search, Carson Lee Parker's vehicle had finally been located in a Rockland County junkyard, just hours from being dismantled for parts. It had been released by NYPD forensics just a week ago. Parker had no use for the truck where he was headed. Marple had paid a fair price for it at the police auction.

The pickup was boxy and big, and it had plenty of power. Marple lowered the visor against the setting sun as the speedometer climbed to 75.

Over the past four days, on her drive through ten states, Marple had been hanging her arm out the side as she listened to a succession of country stations. She'd even gotten a bit of a trucker's tan.

Now she was on a Texas two-lane heading straight west on a line between Tulia and Dimmitt. The scenery was a mix of desert and low brush, interrupted by the occasional slow-moving stream. For miles on end, the white Ford was the only vehicle on the road.

As she closed in on her destination, her mood turned somber. She clicked off the radio and rode in silence.

Marple glanced at the GPS map on her phone. It showed a slim yellow line jogging to the south. As Marple made the turn off the main highway, her rear tires kicked up a cloud of yellow dust. After a mile on the dirt road, she saw a battered mailbox with the name FERRY on the side.

She drove down a rutted lane toward a well-kept Texas double-wide with a little barn out back. On the right, a small herd of horses ambled in a paddock. As she stopped the truck and turned off the engine, the door to the trailer home opened. A middle-aged man emerged, followed by a woman who looked slightly younger. Their clothes were simple—fresh jeans and button-down shirts. Their faces were creased from the sun.

Margaret opened her door and stepped down onto the coarse dry grass. She took a deep breath. Then she reached into the space behind the front seat and picked up a rectangular stone urn.

"You must be Margaret," called the woman from the steps. She was slender and pale, and almost as tall as her husband.

"I am," said Marple. "It's nice to finally see you both in person." She closed the truck door gently. "I wish it weren't for this reason."

She held the urn close to her chest as she walked up the short pathway toward the couple on the front steps. She tried to imagine what they must be feeling. Tried to put herself in their place.

"I'm Arnold Ferry," the man said. "This is my wife, Lynn."

"You're so kind for making such a long trip," said Lynn. "You didn't have to do this alone."

"I didn't mind the drive," said Marple, her hands wrapped tightly around the urn. "And I never felt alone."

She extended her arms and held the urn out. Lynn Ferry took the container in both hands, then cradled it in her arms, weeping softly.

Arnold touched the surface gently, then wrapped his muscular arm around his wife. He looked at Marple.

"Thank you," he said, his voice cracking.

"I'm so sorry for your loss," said Marple. "I'm glad your daughter's home."

CHAPTER 118

AFTER DINNER, MARPLE helped Lucy's mother bring the plates to the sink. Arnold was already out on the front porch, staring across the yard. The tip of his cigarette glowed orange in the darkness.

The meal had been simple but delicious. Baked chicken, creamed corn, homemade apple pie. All during dinner, the Ferrys had wanted—*needed*—to talk about their daughter. About how she'd always been the tallest girl in her class, about how excited she'd been when her picture first appeared in a local catalog, about how much she loved horses, and country music, and books.

Marple mostly just listened. After all, she only knew Lucy Lynn Ferry from her pictures and a coroner's report. And from her killer's confession.

After the dishes had been scraped and loaded into the dishwasher, Lynn dried her hands on a towel and touched Marple's arm. "Would you like to see her room?"

Marple smiled. "Love to."

Lynn led the way down the hall past the small master bedroom to the far end of the trailer home. She pushed open the door and flicked on the light, then stepped aside.

The room was tiny, with a neatly made single bed and a small pine dresser. A bulletin board on the wall held a cluster of school pictures and horse-show ribbons. Running along the far wall was a low white bookcase. The top shelf was stacked high with fashion magazines. The bottom shelf was crammed full of stuffed animals. On the center shelf was a row of books. Marple bent forward to look closer. She took a quick breath.

The shelf was filled with Agatha Christie volumes. All of them. In chronological order.

"Lucy loved mystery stories," said Lynn.

Marple ran her fingers gently over the worn spines. "So I see. She had excellent taste."

"It's funny," said Lynn. "When you told us your name on the phone, we thought what a strange coincidence it was—I mean, that you were the one to help solve her case. You. A real Miss Marple."

Marple looked up and smiled. "Something brought Lucy and me together," she said softly. "I'm sure of it."

"I'm sorry," said Lynn, her eyes suddenly filling with tears again. "It hurts too much to be in here..." She took a step back into the hallway. "You stay as long as you like." Her footsteps receded as she walked back toward the kitchen.

Marple sat down on the bed and slid one of the books off the shelf. A collection of short stories. She imagined Lucy sitting under the covers at night, devouring the tales, just as she had herself as a young girl—before death and deception became part of her actual life.

She picked up a pen from the night table and opened the book to the blank inside cover. She thought for a moment. Then, in flowing script, she wrote:

To the late, beautiful Lucy, from a fellow fan—

Whoever I am.

ABOUT THE AUTHORS

JAMES PATTERSON is one of the best-known and biggest-selling writers of all time. Among his creations are some of the world's most popular series, including Alex Cross, the Women's Murder Club, Michael Bennett and the Private novels. He has written many other number one bestsellers including collaborations with President Bill Clinton and Dolly Parton, stand-alone thrillers and non-fiction. James has donated millions in grants to independent bookshops and has been the most borrowed adult author in UK libraries for the past fourteen years in a row. He lives in Florida with his family.

BRIAN SITTS is an award-winning advertising creative director and television writer. He has collaborated with James Patterson on books for adults and children. He and his wife, Jody, live in Peekskill, New York.

Also By James Patterson

ALEX CROSS NOVELS

Along Came a Spider • Kiss the Girls • Jack and Jill • Cat and Mouse • Pop Goes the Weasel • Roses are Red • Violets are Blue • Four Blind Mice • The Big Bad Wolf • London Bridges • Mary, Mary • Cross • Double Cross • Cross Country • Alex Cross's Trial (*with Richard DiLallo*) • I, Alex Cross • Cross Fire • Kill Alex Cross • Merry Christmas, Alex Cross • Alex Cross, Run • Cross My Heart • Hope to Die • Cross Justice • Cross the Line • The People vs. Alex Cross • Target: Alex Cross • Criss Cross • Deadly Cross • Fear No Evil • Triple Cross • Alex Cross Must Die

THE WOMEN'S MURDER CLUB SERIES

1st to Die (*with Andrew Gross*) • 2nd Chance (*with Andrew Gross*) • 3rd Degree (*with Andrew Gross*) • 4th of July (*with Maxine Paetro*) • The 5th Horseman (*with Maxine Paetro*) • The 6th Target (*with Maxine Paetro*) • 7th Heaven (*with Maxine Paetro*) • 8th Confession (*with Maxine Paetro*) • 9th Judgement (*with Maxine Paetro*) • 10th Anniversary (*with Maxine Paetro*) • 11th Hour (*with Maxine Paetro*) • 12th of Never (*with Maxine Paetro*) • Unlucky 13 (*with Maxine Paetro*) • 14th Deadly Sin (*with Maxine Paetro*) • 15th Affair (*with Maxine Paetro*) • 16th Seduction (*with Maxine Paetro*) • 17th Suspect (*with Maxine Paetro*) • 18th Abduction (*with Maxine Paetro*) • 19th Christmas (*with Maxine Paetro*) • 20th Victim (*with Maxine Paetro*) • 21st Birthday (*with Maxine Paetro*) • 22 Seconds (*with Maxine Paetro*) • 23rd Midnight (*with Maxine Paetro*)

DETECTIVE MICHAEL BENNETT SERIES

Step on a Crack (*with Michael Ledwidge*) • Run for Your Life (*with Michael Ledwidge*) • Worst Case (*with Michael Ledwidge*) • Tick Tock (*with Michael Ledwidge*) • I, Michael Bennett (*with Michael Ledwidge*) • Gone (*with Michael Ledwidge*) • Burn (*with Michael Ledwidge*) • Alert (*with Michael Ledwidge*) • Bullseye (*with Michael Ledwidge*) • Haunted (*with James O. Born*) • Ambush (*with James O. Born*) • Blindside (*with James O. Born*) • The Russian (*with James O. Born*) • Shattered (*with James O. Born*) • Obsessed (*with James O. Born*)

PRIVATE NOVELS

Private (*with Maxine Paetro*) • Private London (*with Mark Pearson*) • Private Games (*with Mark Sullivan*) • Private: No. 1 Suspect (*with Maxine Paetro*) • Private Berlin (*with Mark Sullivan*) • Private Down Under (*with Michael White*) • Private L.A. (*with Mark Sullivan*) • Private India (*with Ashwin Sanghi*) • Private Vegas (*with Maxine Paetro*) • Private Sydney (*with Kathryn Fox*) • Private Paris (*with Mark Sullivan*) • The Games (*with Mark Sullivan*) • Private Delhi (*with Ashwin Sanghi*) • Private Princess (*with Rees*

Jones) • Private Moscow (*with Adam Hamdy*) • Private Rogue (*with Adam Hamdy*) • Private Beijing (*with Adam Hamdy*) • Private Rome (*with Adam Hamdy*)

NYPD RED SERIES

NYPD Red (*with Marshall Karp*) • NYPD Red 2 (*with Marshall Karp*) • NYPD Red 3 (*with Marshall Karp*) • NYPD Red 4 (*with Marshall Karp*) • NYPD Red 5 (*with Marshall Karp*) • NYPD Red 6 (*with Marshall Karp*)

DETECTIVE HARRIET BLUE SERIES

Never Never (*with Candice Fox*) • Fifty Fifty (*with Candice Fox*) • Liar Liar (*with Candice Fox*) • Hush Hush (*with Candice Fox*)

INSTINCT SERIES

Instinct (*with Howard Roughan, previously published as* Murder Games) • Killer Instinct (*with Howard Roughan*) • Steal (*with Howard Roughan*)

THE BLACK BOOK SERIES

The Black Book (*with David Ellis*) • The Red Book (*with David Ellis*) • Escape (*with David Ellis*)

STAND-ALONE THRILLERS

The Thomas Berryman Number • Hide and Seek • Black Market • The Midnight Club • Sail (*with Howard Roughan*) • Swimsuit (*with Maxine Paetro*) • Don't Blink (*with Howard Roughan*) • Postcard Killers (*with Liza Marklund*) • Toys (*with Neil McMahon*) • Now You See Her (*with Michael Ledwidge*) • Kill Me If You Can (*with Marshall Karp*) • Guilty Wives (*with David Ellis*) • Zoo (*with Michael Ledwidge*) • Second Honeymoon (*with Howard Roughan*) • Mistress (*with David Ellis*) • Invisible (*with David Ellis*) • Truth or Die (*with Howard Roughan*) • Murder House (*with David Ellis*) • The Store (*with Richard DiLallo*) • Texas Ranger (*with Andrew Bourelle*) • The President is Missing (*with Bill Clinton*) • Revenge (*with Andrew Holmes*) • Juror No. 3 (*with Nancy Allen*) • The First Lady (*with Brendan DuBois*) • The Chef (*with Max DiLallo*) • Out of Sight (*with Brendan DuBois*) • Unsolved (*with David Ellis*) • The Inn (*with Candice Fox*) • Lost (*with James O. Born*) • Texas Outlaw (*with Andrew Bourelle*) • The Summer House (*with Brendan DuBois*) • 1st Case (*with Chris Tebbetts*) • Cajun Justice (*with Tucker Axum*)• The Midwife Murders (*with Richard DiLallo*) • The Coast-to-Coast Murders (*with J.D. Barker*) • Three Women Disappear (*with Shan Serafin*) • The President's Daughter (*with Bill Clinton*) • The Shadow (*with Brian Sitts*) • The Noise (*with J.D. Barker*) • 2 Sisters Detective Agency (*with Candice Fox*) • Jailhouse Lawyer (*with Nancy Allen*) • The Horsewoman (*with Mike Lupica*) • Run Rose Run (with Dolly Parton) • Death of the Black Widow (with J.D. Barker) • The Ninth Month (with Richard DiLallo) • The Girl in the Castle (with Emily Raymond) • Blowback (with Brendan DuBois) • The Twelve Topsy-Turvy, Very Messy Days of Christmas (with Tad Safran) • The Perfect Assassin (with Brian Sitts) • House of Wolves (with Mike Lupica) • Countdown (with Brendan DuBois) • Cross Down (with Brendan DuBois) • Circle of Death (with Brian Sitts) • 12 Months to Live (with Mike Lupica) • Lion & Lamb (with Duane Swierczynski)

NON-FICTION

Torn Apart (with Hal and Cory Friedman) • The Murder of King Tut (with Martin Dugard) • All-American Murder (with Alex Abramovich and Mike Harvkey) • The Kennedy Curse (with Cynthia Fagen) • The Last Days of John Lennon (with Casey Sherman and Dave Wedge) • Walk in My Combat Boots (with Matt Eversmann and Chris Mooney) • ER Nurses (with Matt Eversmann) • James Patterson by James Patterson: The Stories of My Life • Diana, William and Harry (with Chris Mooney) • American Cops (with Matt Eversmann) • What Really Happens in Vegas (with Mark Seal)

MURDER IS FOREVER TRUE CRIME

Murder, Interrupted (with Alex Abramovich and Christopher Charles) • Home Sweet Murder (with Andrew Bourelle and Scott Slaven) • Murder Beyond the Grave (with Andrew Bourelle and Christopher Charles) • Murder Thy Neighbour (with Andrew Bourelle and Max DiLallo) • Murder of Innocence (with Max DiLallo and Andrew Bourelle) • Till Murder Do Us Part (with Andrew Bourelle and Max DiLallo)

COLLECTIONS

Triple Threat (with Max DiLallo and Andrew Bourelle) • Kill or Be Killed (with Maxine Paetro, Rees Jones, Shan Serafin and Emily Raymond) • The Moores are Missing (with Loren D. Estleman, Sam Hawken and Ed Chatterton) • The Family Lawyer (with Robert Rotstein, Christopher Charles and Rachel Howzell Hall) • Murder in Paradise (with Doug Allyn, Connor Hyde and Duane Swierczynski) • The House Next Door (with Susan DiLallo, Max DiLallo and Brendan DuBois) • 13-Minute Murder (with Shan Serafin, Christopher Farnsworth and Scott Slaven) • The River Murders (with James O. Born) • The Palm Beach Murders (with James O. Born, Duane Swierczynski and Tim Arnold) • Paris Detective • 3 Days to Live • 23 ½ Lies (with Maxine Paetro)

For more information about James Patterson's novels, visit www.penguin.co.uk.